KU-404-738

Alan M. Dershowitz is a renowned trial attorney, who has represented celebrity clients such as O. J. Simpson, Leona Helmsley, Claus von Bulow and Mia Farrow. Half of his cases involve poor defendants who he represents without a fee. He is a Professor of Law at Harvard University and the author of numerous non-fiction books, including the US number one bestseller *Chutzpah* and *Reversal of Fortune*, about the Claus von Bulow case, which was made into an Academy Award-winning film.

JUST REVENGE

For fifty years, Max Menuchen has kept the secret of his past; the sole survivor when his entire family was gunned down by the Nazi Marcelus Prandus, Max has made a new life in America. When chance brings Max face to face with Marcelus Prandus, the desire for revenge becomes an obsession. It is not enough simply to kill the old man, who enjoys the love of children and a grandson; Marcelus must witness the deaths of everyone close to him. But can it ever be just to kill the innocent to avenge the guilty? Max's solution is both monstrous and inspired, and the trial that follows will captivate the world.

ALAN M. DERSHOWITZ

JUST REVENGE

Complete and Unabridged

ULVERSCROFT
Leicester

First published in Great Britain in 1999 by
Headline Book Publishing
London

First Large Print Edition
published 2001
by arrangement with
Headline Book Publishing
a division of Hodder Headline Group
London

The moral right of the author has been asserted

All characters in this publication are fictitious
and any resemblance to real persons, living or dead,
is purely coincidental.

British Library CIP Data

Dershowitz, Alan M. (Alan Morton)
Just revenge.—Large print ed.—
Ulverscroft large print series: mystery
1. Revenge—Fiction
2. Holocaust survivors—Fiction
3. Large type books
4. Suspense fiction
I. Title
813.5'4 [F]

ISBN 0–7089–4345–4

Published by
F. A. Thorpe (Publishing)
Anstey, Leicestershire
Set by Words & Graphics Ltd.
Anstey, Leicestershire
Printed and bound in Great Britain by
T. J. International Ltd., Padstow, Cornwall

This book is printed on acid-free paper

Dedicated to the members of my family who were murdered by the Nazis and their collaborators. My great-grandfather, Avraham Mordecai Ringel — after whom I am named — had four sons. My maternal grandfather, Naftuli, came to America before the war. His brother, Yakov tried desperately to follow him, but was excluded by the Jewish quota and was killed, along with all his children and grandchildren, except for one son who immigrated to Palestine. Another brother, Anshel, was murdered, along with his four daughters. Another brother, Nussen, fled the Nazis and made it to Siberia, where he survived the war, though two of his grandchildren were killed and four died of starvation and disease. May the Ringel family and their millions of fellow victims never be forgotten.

Acknowledgments

Many family members and friends read drafts of this book. My daughter, Ella, and my wife, Carolyn, were involved in every aspect of my writing and editing. My sons, Elon and Jamin, provided the kind of loving criticism on which I have come to rely. My brother, Nathan, my sister-in-law, Marilyn, my nephew, Adam, my niece, Rana, my mother, Claire, my mother-in-law, Dutch, my father-in-law, Mortie, my brother-in-law, Marvin, and my sister-in-law, Julie all contributed their unique insights. My valued friends Michael and Jackie Halbreich, Sandy McNabb, Sue Levcoff, Alan Rothsfeld, Alex MacDonald, Ken and Gerry Sweder, Bob Nozick, Steve Gould, Rick Patterson, Alan Stone, and Mark Wolf exaggerated the book's virtues, while minimizing its faults and prodding me gently toward improvements. My oldest friends — Murray and Malkie Altman, Bernie and Judy Beck, Zolly and Katie Eisenstadt, Carl and Joan Meshenberg, Hal and Sandy Miller-Jacobs, Josh and Rochelle Weisberger, Barry and Barbara Zimmerman — gave it to me straight, as they always do. I learn so much from their wisdom. My usual thanks to Maura Kelley, who typed the manuscript at all hours of the night, and to John Orsini who always found the answers.

Special thanks to Frances Jalet-Miller and Jessica Papin for their brilliant editorial help and to Larry Kirshbaum for his tough love approach. My agent, Helen Rees, guided me through the process with her usual encouragement.

Finally, my eternal gratitude to the many survivors and children of survivors from whom I learned so much about the horror of the Holocaust. My cousin Israel Ringel provided me with information about our family. My hope is that I have written a book that may lead a few people to better understand and empathize with the victims of the worst crime ever perpetrated by one group of human beings on another — a crime whose perpetrators too often went unpunished and were even rewarded.

If you wrong us, shall we not revenge?
Merchant of Venice
Act III, Scene I

Prologue

Massachusetts: May 1999

The old man shifted his shaking right leg from the brake pedal to the accelerator as he aimed his 1989 Volvo directly at the spot where the eight-year-old child would soon cross the street. In less than a minute the smiling blond-haired boy, on his way to a second-grade assembly at the Sancta Maria Elementary School, would be a bloody heap of shattered bones. Within the hour his family would receive the dreaded news that their child and grandchild had been struck down.

The old man behind the wheel — the man who was about to murder an innocent child — did not appear capable of such violence. During his nearly forty years in America, he had never broken a law, never knowingly hurt anyone. Now his long-festering need for revenge would be satisfied. Finally, his moment was at hand. He had just learned something so terrible, so unforgivable, that he was willing to break any law or commandment, to incur any punishment, in order to secure his just revenge.

As the old man watched the portly crossing guard wave the youngster across the street, he slowly pressed his foot down on the gas pedal. The towheaded boy skipped toward the center of the street, holding a baseball glove and a ball. The old man gunned the accelerator. As the car lurched toward the terrified eight-year-old, the old man's mind exploded with the images that had brought him to the point where he could murder a child.

Part One

The Ringel Family

1

Cambridge, Massachusetts
Seven Months Earlier: October 1998

'It's great having you home from school,'
Abe Ringel said, hugging his twenty-two-
year-old daughter, Emma. 'But you do look
tired.'

'You've gotten a few more gray hairs
yourself,' the petite law student observed
as she stroked her father's unruly coif.
Abe was quickly approaching the midcentury
mark and was sensitive about the darkening
beneath his eyes and the lightening above his
forehead. He had always appeared youthful,
even through his early forties, but the past
few years had begun to take their toll on his
rugged good looks.

He held his daughter for an extra moment
as he whispered, 'I've really missed you,
sweetie.'

'C'mon. It's only been a month, and Yale
is only two and a half hours away from
Harvard by car — though it's light years
ahead in the way it teaches law.' Emma
couldn't resist the gibe at one of Harvard

Law School's most famous and loyal local alumni.

'No way I'm getting into an argument with a first-year law student — especially a Yalie. You kids argue in your sleep.' Abe smiled. 'Tell me all about your classes. Did you get to the case about the shipwrecked sailors who ate the cabin boy? That was the first case we studied in criminal law. I'll never forget it,' Abe mused nostalgically.

'We don't study that stuff at Yale, Daddy,' Emma retorted. 'It's Jurassic. When's the last time a sailor ate a cabin boy?'

'That's not the point, Emma. It's the principle of the case.'

'Yeah, yeah. We learn all that in legal history. We're even reading about one of *your* ancient cases. Boring!'

'Really? Which one?'

'No, Daddy, not really. God, you're so not with it. It was a joke. But we did study the Dred Scott decision about slavery.'

'And you think I represented the slave owner?'

'You would have, wouldn't you?'

'Only if he were charged with a crime,' Abe replied, smiling. 'Just kidding. I remember our deal. C'mon, let's stop talking about law school. Tell me about you. Did you meet any nice boys?'

6

'I don't meet boys. I meet men,' Emma teased, arching her back in a provocative pose.

'Enough,' Abe groaned, turning away.

'And, yes,' Emma continued, ignoring her father's discomfort, 'the class is full of nice men — and nice women, too.'

'So, so. Tell me everything.'

'No way. I'm over the age of consent, and the law says I don't have to tell you anything.'

As Emma said these words, Abe's wife, Rendi, jogged in, puffing and sweating. 'Is your dad being nosy again?'

'What else is new?' Emma said, smiling as she got up to hug Rendi. 'Whee, you stink. It must have been a good workout. I've missed you. Now *you* I want to tell about my sex — whoops, my social life. 'Cause I know you won't tell my dad.'

'I'd go to jail first. Like Susan McDougal. We can gossip later. I've missed you, Emma. I love your new do.'

'Daddy didn't even notice.'

'So what else is new? Your father wouldn't notice if I shaved my head,' Rendi said, playing with the auburn hair that cascaded to her shoulders and framed the bronze complexion and striking features of her face. A Sephardic Jew who was raised on a kibbutz in Israel and who had spent several years in the Mossad, Rendi was a tower of strength, both physical and psychological.

'Maybe I'll shave my head. We'll see if Daddy notices. He didn't notice my nose-ring,' Emma said, turning her face away from Abe.

'I'm not falling for that,' Abe said, sneaking a peek at Emma's profile.

Abe and Rendi had gotten married shortly after the second Joe Campbell trial. The Campbell case had changed everything in Abe's life. He had successfully defended the star basketball player from rape charges, despite his growing suspicion that Campbell had been guilty of raping Jennifer Dowling. Then Campbell had tried to rape Emma on her eighteenth birthday and nearly killed her. It took Emma the better part of a year to forgive her father and to begin to put her life back together. Although there were still tensions in the father-daughter relationship, the crisis had drawn Abe closer to Rendi, who had been his longtime lover and investigator and who was helping Emma work through her feelings toward her father. The marriage had changed very little in Abe's and Rendi's lives, except that they now lived together in Abe's large, modern Cambridge house. They still fought like children about nearly every legal issue on which they worked. But they loved each other passionately, and they both loved Emma.

Emma sometimes sounded more like a teenager than a twenty-two-year-old law student when she teased her father. Like a clock whose hands stopped at the moment of an explosion, their relationship had somehow gotten stuck at the time of her near death experience. Emma had never directly confronted her conflicting feelings about her father's role in the Campbell horror. In the meantime, she had maintained a psychological distance from her father through her adolescent teasing.

'What brings you home so soon in the school term?' asked Abe's wife.

'So soon?' Abe thundered. 'It's been a month.'

'No, really, is everything okay?'

'It's great. I love Yale. The teachers are so cool, especially the women. They're the best. My crim law prof was a Supreme Court law clerk for Justice Breyer. And then she worked as a rape prosecutor. I told her about my case.'

'Why did you have to tell her that?' Abe asked with a look of concern.

'I didn't *have* to tell her. I wanted to,' Emma said assertively, turning her head

9

to face her father. 'She announced at the beginning of the first class that if anyone had any life experiences that were relevant to the class, we should drop her a note. One guy in the class had been a cop for five years. A woman had been in jail for a month after she refused to testify against her boyfriend in a marijuana case. And I nearly got raped. It's nothing to be ashamed of, Daddy.'

'I know that, but it brings back some very bad memories, and it's nobody's business.'

'It's my business, and I'm dealing with it the best I know how — by talking about it. What else can I do? I'd love to cut off his — '

'Enough, Emma. You don't have to get graphic. I get the picture, and I don't like it. Taking revenge wouldn't make you feel any better.'

'How do you know?' Emma said, suddenly getting testy. 'You get guilty criminals off scot-free for a living! I should think you would want to cut it off for me, as my father.'

'Believe me,' Abe said emphatically, 'I know how strong the passion for revenge can be. I see it in the faces of the victims — and in the hate mail I get from them. It destroys them if they don't let go of it. You don't want to end up like one of those bitter people you see on TV all the time, screaming for the execution of the creep who murdered their daughter.'

'You don't know how it feels to be violated and not get even. Cutting up Joe Campbell would do me a lot of good.'

'Forget about it. It's illegal, and I don't want to have to defend my own daughter.'

'It's only a fantasy,' Emma said with a weary smile. 'I'm not the acting-on-it type. I'm the talking-about-it type. That's why I told my professor about our deal.'

'What exactly did you tell her?'

'I told her how you had represented Campbell and that you had gotten him off, even though you knew he did it.'

'*Suspected!* I didn't know. I *suspected.* Remember, he denied it.'

'Yeah. I understand the drill. I just don't agree with it. You knew he was guilty. And you still got him off. And then . . . '

'I know what happened then,' Abe said despondently, hanging his head. 'You don't have to remind me. I still have nightmares.'

'So do I,' Emma shot back, her voice rising both in pitch and volume. 'That's why I *have* to talk about it — and do something about it.'

'What do you mean, do something?' Abe asked in a worried voice.

Emma rolled her eyes. 'No. Nothing stupid. I'm doing a paper for my crim class. My project is to demonstrate that good lawyers shouldn't represent bad people.'

'But the system — '

'It was the system that made you get that bastard off. Don't you see how *not right* the system is?'

'Can we argue about this some other time? I just want to talk about you, not the system.'

'We are talking about me. I was telling you what I told Professor Stith. It's important to me.'

'I'm sorry. Please go on. I want to hear.'

'I said that as a result of my case you had decided never to defend somebody who you knew was guilty.'

'I hope you made it clear that I haven't changed my principles. I still believe — '

'I know what you believe. I told her I had to be satisfied with small victories when I deal with the Attila the Hun of the defense bar.'

'I'm not *that* out of touch. Most defense lawyers — '

'I don't care about most defense lawyers,' Emma said, doing her best imitation of Abe in his lecture mode. 'I only care about you. You're my special mission. By the time

12

I graduate from law school, I'm gonna convert you.'

'You've already converted me, sweetie. You don't have to rub it in.'

'I haven't converted you completely — yet. So far, all I got you to do is compromise your principles.'

'Isn't it enough that you've made a hypocrite of me?'

'It's a start. Some dead white guy once said that hypocrisy is the homage that vice pays to virtue.'

'I'm glad you're still quoting dead white males, sweetie.'

'Almost everyone we study in law school is a DWM. I appreciate your hypocrisy. I won't be completely satisfied until I convince you that the principle of representing guilty people is wrong. I know you agreed to the deal because of what happened to me, and it is a bit patronizing.'

'Give me a break here. After all, the root of 'patronize' is father. I'm entitled.'

The scars left by the Campbell situation had caused Abe to reevaluate the kinds of cases he took. He was still a zealous — some would say ferocious — defense lawyer for his clients, but now he was more selective about which clients he chose to represent. 'I hope you also told Professor Stith that I never

13

turn down a capital case — regardless of the defendant's guilt,' Abe added.

'Death is different,' said Emma, quoting the exact words her father had said to her many times. 'When the state wants to kill someone, it shouldn't be easy.'

Beyond the occasional death penalty case, there was nearly always a family feud about which cases Abe should take. Before he would agree to take on a paying case, Abe would try to assure himself on the defendant's innocence. It was not always easy. He remembered how convinced he had been of Joe Campbell's innocence when he took that case. But now Abe was more conscious of his old affliction — 'defense lawyer's blind spot.' He was no longer as susceptible to DLBS. Now he could see the evidence more clearly, and when it pointed to guilt, he would refer the case to his former associate, Justin Aldrich, or to other defense lawyers.

'I've paid my dues — and more — to the notion that it is better for ten guilty to go free than for one innocent to be wrongly convicted. I've represented too many of the 'ten guilty' defendants,' Abe acknowledged to Emma and Rendi. 'Now I've earned the right to defend some of the innocent ones.'

'I would never prosecute anyone I believed

was innocent, so why shouldn't the same rule apply to defense lawyers?' Emma insisted.

'Because the innocent shouldn't be prosecuted. The guilty *must* be defended,' Abe responded.

'But not by you, Dad.'

'Look, you've convinced me. A good lawyer knows how to sit down when she's won. Don't argue anymore, or you'll talk me out of it.'

'I'm getting great ammo from my profs.'

'What can you expect from a bunch of former prosecutors?'

'Low blow. There are also a few recovering defense lawyers.'

'Low blow yourself. Being a defense lawyer is not an illness.'

'Well, at least it's not contagious. That I can promise you.'

'Boy, you're good — and fast. But let's get back to you. How's your roommate . . . what's her name?'

'You know what her name is. You just don't like it. Angela Davis Bernstein. A genuine revolutionary.'

'She'll end up working for Cravath, Swaine and Moore — like the rest of them.'

'No way! Sue them, maybe. But work for them — never. And neither will I. I applied for an internship for the summer with Linda

15

Fairstein, the chief sex crimes prosecutor in New York.'

'After what you went through?' asked Abe, shocked.

'I'm a different person,' Emma continued. 'I learn from my mistakes.'

'It wasn't your fault,' Rendi insisted.

'Going out with that creep was my fault. What he tried to do to me wasn't. And anyway, nobody would dare try to rape a rape prosecutor.'

'Don't even joke about that,' Abe said.

'That's the way I deal with the pain, Daddy. And anyway, I'm serious. We'd cut his — '

'Enough already with your fantasies of surgery. Maybe you should have gone to medical school. My daughter the doctor. It certainly would have made Grandma Ringel happy.'

'I can't stand blood.'

'By the way, I know Linda Fairstein's husband. Good guy. A defense lawyer.'

'I bet he represents only innocent defendants.'

'As I do, sweetie. When I can find one. They're not so easy to find. My business has gone down quite a bit since I agreed to your deal.'

'It doesn't show. What's that?' Emma

16

asked, pointing to a new painting on the crowded living room wall.

'It's a Soutine.'

'It's ugly.'

'Life's ugly. He painted it as he saw it.'

'I like it, but I wouldn't want it in my bedroom.'

'I haven't offered. What do you have hanging in your bedroom?'

'Some Keith Haring posters, your old Ben Shahn litho of Martin Luther King, and a Beatles poster.'

'Talk about Jurassic. You're back in the seventies.'

'I love the seventies.'

'You were an infant in the seventies. What do you know about them?'

'Mom used to talk about them. She said the sixties really happened in the seventies. Then it all ended in the eighties.'

Emma averted her face, trying to hide her tears. Her mother, Hannah, had died in an automobile accident in 1987, and nothing had ever been the same since. Rendi was a wonderful stepmother — even more, a friend — but no one could ever replace Hannah. Abe saw the tears and put his arm around Emma's small shoulders. He took out his handkerchief and wiped away the tears as they fell.

'It all ended in the eighties,' he repeated. 'And then there was a new beginning in the nineties.'

Emma paused for a moment, then shrugged her way out from beneath Abe's arm. 'Daddy, I've invited a friend for Shabbat dinner tomorrow night. I hope it's cool. He's a graduate student from Amsterdam, studying human rights.'

'That's great. Max is coming, too.'

'Perfect. Jacob will love Max. They're both so European. Can't wait for you to meet him. But don't make a fuss. I'll die if you scare him away.'

'I'll be on my best behavior.'

'You've got to do better than that,' Emma said, pinching Abe's cheek.

2

The Next Night

'He's drop-dead gorgeous,' Rendi exclaimed. 'Where did you find him?'

'He found me in the library.'

'Well, that's no surprise. You're drop-dead gorgeous, too. Is he fun?'

'In a European kind of way. You know, not funny like Dad, who jokes about everything.'

'Tell me something I don't know!'

'Not that I don't love Dad's sense of humor. He uses jokes to avoid serious issues. I guess I do, too — with Dad. Jacob is different. He really loves serious discussions — about everything.'

'Even emotions?'

'Even emotions.'

'Well, that certainly is different from your dad. Are you sure he's really a man?'

'*That* I'm sure of. But he's a very unusual man. We talk about everything — all through the night.'

'And the sex?' Rendi asked, lowering her voice and arching her eyebrows.

'Very sensual. Very European. Very sophisticated.'

'Sounds like you can teach me something.'

'Let's not go there. Even you and I have to have some limits,' Emma said, laughing.

'Are you in love with Jacob?'

'I don't know.'

'You don't have to confront the 'L' word,' Rendi said.

'It's great for what it is.'

'A one-semester stand?'

'Maybe more. Maybe not. It's perfect for now.'

'Unless Abe screws it up. Do you trust Jacob down there with Ward Cleaver?'

'Thank God Max is with them. He'll keep Daddy under control.'

Max Menuchen had been introduced to the Ringel family by Abe's mentor, Haskell Levine. Haskell, who had died shortly after the Campbell case several years earlier, had been Boston's greatest lawyer and Abe's teacher at Harvard Law School. He had immigrated to Boston from Lithuania just before the outbreak of World War II and had become part of the Ringel family.

Though neither Abe nor Rendi was particularly religious, they always stayed home on Friday night for a traditional Sabbath dinner. Usually there were guests,

20

and Haskell had been a regular. His spirit still permeated the discussions.

Since Haskell's death, Max Menuchen had become the Ringel family's connection to their Jewish roots in the old country. Although Abe's grandparents had emigrated from southeastern Poland, Hannah's parents had come from a small town in Lithuania, not far from Vilna. Emma had felt a spiritual connection to her mother through Haskell and now through Max. They spoke with the same slight European accent, the same warm politeness, and the same love of tradition. Their enigmatic smiles were similar, reflecting experiences too painful to bring to the surface. They even dressed similarly, in old-fashioned conservative suits, neatly pressed white shirts and dark ties.

Despite their obvious similarities, Max was very different from Haskell. When Emma was younger, she had once described Max as having three hands and Haskell only one. 'Max always says 'on the one hand' and then 'on the other hand' and then 'yet on the other hand'. Haskell, the advocate, was more single handed.'

Max was a frequent guest at the Ringel Friday night dinners, especially when Emma was in town. Emma loved Max. Hannah had been a wonderful storyteller, and Emma was always reminded of her mother when Max told his Bible stories. Max was a professor of Bible at the Harvard Divinity School. Emma always looked forward to Max's latest twist on the old stories she had studied in Sunday school. There was never just one interpretation, always a second and third way of looking at the simplest of stories. She also loved Max's serene approach to life. She wished that her father could be more like his two older friends and mentors, and she even selected boyfriends who were more like Haskell and Max than like her own father.

Jacob Bruner, the graduate student with whom Emma was currently involved, was a human rights lawyer whose ambition was to become a judge at The Hague. He was studying at Yale for the year.

Emma and Rendi joined them in the living room, surprised to see Max and Jacob in animated conversation, with the usually voluble Abe sitting quietly listening to the two Europeans.

'Abe Ringel silenced! Details at eleven!' Emma exclaimed.

'We must have missed a great conversation,' Rendi chimed in. 'Fill us in.'

'Only if you fill us in on what you two gals were gossiping about in the bedroom,' Abe replied.

'Still with the 'gals', Daddy. Won't you ever learn?'

'I'm entitled to call my own daughter and wife 'gals' if I want to.'

'Not in front of company,' Max said in a tone of reproval. 'We don't want this young man to think you're — what's that word Emma always uses?'

'Jurassic, Uncle Max.'

'Yes, Jurassic. I love that word. It's elegant. Don't you think, Jacob?'

'Emma sometimes thinks I'm Jurassic, too, just because I'm almost thirty.'

'Better watch out. Soon she won't be able to trust you,' Rendi quipped.

'What do you mean?'

'Didn't Emma tell you that in America, you can't trust anybody over thirty?' Rendi mocked.

'That's a joke, right?' Jacob asked with an embarrassed smile.

'It's a joke,' Emma said reassuringly as she took Jacob's hand and led him to the dining room table, which was beautifully set with candles, a challah, and gefilte fish.

Even before they sat down, Abe began humming the traditional melody of 'Shalom Aleichem,' the greeting of the Sabbath. Rendi and Emma joined in. Jacob tried to pick up the melody. Max sat silently. Rendi and Emma then lit the candles, covering their eyes with their hands. Abe recited the blessing over the wine and invited Jacob to make the blessing over the challah.

As soon as the rituals ended, the conversation began.

'Tell us about your family,' Abe said to Jacob, glancing at Emma to see if he had said the wrong thing.

'My father escaped from Poland to Amsterdam in 1939. He knew Anna Frank's family. He also went into hiding and made it through the war and remained in Holland, where he met my mother, who had also survived.'

'What do your parents do?' Rendi asked.

'My father is a jeweler. My mother teaches high school math.'

'Tell us about the Jewish community in Amsterdam,' Max said.

'Mostly survivors like my parents. A few American expatriates, some Israelis in the diamond business. And now a lot of Russians and Ukrainians.'

'Any Lithuanians?' Max wondered.

'Not many. There were very few survivors from the Baltic countries. Is that where your family is from?'

'Yes,' Max said peremptorily.

'Did they survive?'

'No.'

'None of them?' Jacob probed.

'I am the only one.'

'I'm sorry,' said Jacob.

Max nodded. There was a brief silence, then the conversation moved on.

Abe knew that Max was his family's sole survivor, but even he — who had been Max's friend for years — did not know any more than that. He had once asked Haskell Levine about Max's family, but Haskell had promised Max that he would never discuss his family's tragedy with anyone.

The Shabbat dinner ended with one of Max's Bible stories.

'I've been thinking,' Max began, as he always did when he talked about the Bible. 'Would our biblical tradition approve of my dear friend Abe defending some of the terrible people he defends?'

'Not fair. Did Emma put you up to this?' Abe interrupted. Emma and Max both smiled as Abe continued to protest. 'Why don't you talk about the Garden of Eden or something abstract like that? Stop picking on me.'

'All right, I'm your guest,' Max replied with his characteristically enigmatic smile. 'If you insist, we will talk about the Garden of Eden. Does anyone remember what God's first prohibition was?'

Emma raised her hand as if in class.

'No need for such formality, go ahead,' said Max.

'Not to eat from the tree of knowledge.'

'Correct. Now what did God tell Adam would happen if he ate of that tree, Jacob?'

'I think God said he would die.'

'Right. Now he did eat of the tree. But he did not die. So why didn't God carry out his threatened punishment?'

'I know,' Abe said.

'Then tell us.'

'Because Adam didn't have a defense lawyer, and you can't carry out a death sentence without the defendant having a lawyer.'

'See,' Max said, smiling. 'I knew we would get back to my original question. Thank you, Abe.'

'You tricked me.'

'Just like the serpent tricked Eve,' Max said.

'Wait,' Emma said. 'Dad is wrong. There was a defense lawyer. Why do you think God created serpents?' She laughed as she high-fived Rendi.

'Very funny. First I was a dinosaur, now I'm a serpent. Nice way to talk about the man who's paying your law school tuition.'

'From money you earned defending people lower than serpents. I bet you would have defended the serpent — and got him off, too.'

Max cleared his throat. Emma and Abe understood this to mean that the old man wanted to try to give a serious answer to his original question.

'On the one hand, Abraham asked God to spare the sinners of Sodom if there were ten righteous among them.'

'See,' Abe interjected quickly, 'Abraham — my namesake — was the first defense lawyer, and he argued on behalf of the guilty.'

'On the other hand,' Max said, 'Abraham lost. There were no righteous people in Sodom.'

'Sounds like your client list,' Emma interjected.

'Yet on the other hand,' Max said in a tone of finality, 'the rabbis praised Abraham for his advocacy on behalf of the guilty and condemned Noah for not arguing with God when he told Noah that he was going to destroy the world. So the answer is yes, our tradition approves of what *our* Abraham does for a living.'

'But on the fourth hand,' Emma complained.

'There are never more than three hands,'

Abe said, making a 'V' for victory.

The conversation continued long into the night, until Max finally excused himself. After Abe and Rendi saw Max to the door, Abe whispered to his wife, 'Let's go upstairs. I don't want to know what the sleeping arrangements are for Jacob.'

'You know,' Rendi twitted Abe, leading him to their bedroom with a coy smile.

3

Half a Year Later: April 1999

'What should I ask Daddy for this year?'
Emma asked Rendi as they rummaged
through the basement for the box containing
the religious items used at the Passover seder.
As the youngest participant at their seder,
Emma, by tradition, would 'find' a special
matzah hidden by the 'leader' and demand
something in return for it.

'Don't you think your father has given you
enough, Emma? Tuition, a car . . . '

'Of course he has, but he loves giving me
things. Sometimes I wish he could give more
of himself.' Emma sighed. 'Let's at least not
deny him the pleasure of giving me stuff. I
think I'm going to ask for a new computer.'

'Your father gets a rash when the word
computer is even mentioned.'

'Only when he actually touches one. He
calls me to do computer searches for him.
He claims they're only for innocent clients.
I wonder.'

'Then I guess you should have an up-
to-date one,' said Rendi. 'What time are

29

you expecting Jacob?'

'Late. He's taking the train. I made Daddy invite Max. He hasn't been to a seder in more than fifty years. Doesn't like them for some reason. But Dad talked him into this one. Jacob loves talking to Max. I think Max is the real reason Jacob decided to come to our house for Passover rather than fly back to Amsterdam.'

'I suspect you also had something to do with his decision.'

'I sure hope so,' Emma said, wiggling her bottom and laughing.

Emma and Rendi spent the rest of the day preparing the seder meal.

At six o'clock sharp Max rang the bell. Abe went to the door.

'Max, you look terrible. Is anything wrong?'

'No, I'm fine.' He managed an apologetic smile. 'The seder makes me nervous.'

'Don't worry. It's just an informal meal with us. A few blessings, songs, and discussions. Nothing heavy. Why are you nervous?'

'I don't know. It's been so long.'

'Relax. You'll love it. You can help Emma find my matzah. In the meantime, Rendi and Emma need your sage advice about setting the seder plate. You're the only one around who studied this ritual stuff as a child.'

Max went into the kitchen, where Rendi was trying to teach a reluctant Emma how to make matzah balls.

A few minutes later Jacob arrived.

'Let's begin,' Abe said, leading his guests to the table.

Although the seder went smoothly, with spirited songs, lively conversation, and occasional prayers, it was clear that Max was uncomfortable. During dinner he excused himself three times to use the bathroom. He was sweating profusely and fidgeting. Most surprising, he was utterly uncommunicative. It was not the Max of the Shabbat dinners. There were no Bible stories, no philosophical questions. Just nervous silence. Something was wrong. But Abe knew enough not to probe, especially in front of company.

After the traditional meal of chicken soup, lamb, honeyed carrots, and plenty of wine and matzah, it was time for the ancient ritual of welcoming the prophet Elijah.

'Okay, Emma,' Abe said brightly, 'it's time for our special guest.'

Emma rose and began to move toward the front door.

Suddenly Max started screaming, 'No! No!' Bolting out of his seat, he blocked her path. The old man's hands were shaking as he grabbed her roughly by the shoulders. 'Do not open that door, Emma,' he said sternly. 'Do not even go near it.'

'Why not?' Emma asked incredulously as she pulled away from Max and continued toward the door.

'They will kill you. Stay away from the door!' Max shrieked, chasing after her with the speed and energy of a much younger man. As the frightened Emma dodged his grasp, Max turned to Abe with a frantic look in his eyes. 'Stop her,' he pleaded. 'Don't let her near the door.'

'Max, what's wrong?' Abe asked.

'They vill take her avay.' Max was nearly sobbing now. His European accent was becoming thicker as he continued.

'Ve vill never see our Sarah Chava again. Please, Grandpa Mordechai, please stop her,' Max persisted.

Abe placed his hands on Max's shoulders and shook him firmly.

'What are you saying, Max? There's no one named Sarah Chava here. That's Emma. And there's no Grandpa Mordechai. Look at me, Max. I'm Abe, your friend. Why are you so upset? What's wrong? There's nobody outside.'

'Yes, there is!' Max screamed. 'They are here. They are vaiting for us. Don't you understand? They vill kill us. Prandus and his men. Don't open the door. Run away. I can't save you.'

'Please, Max, calm down. You're frightening us,' Rendi pleaded.

Wild-eyed, Max turned to Emma and, pointing to Abe and Rendi, shouted, 'They can't protect you. Run avay, hide. Don't let them take you.'

Finally, in desperation, Rendi strode to the front door and flung it wide open.

'See, no one is out there.'

Suddenly, Max dropped to the floor like a marionette whose strings were cut. He lay there, panting, as Emma picked up the phone.

'No, don't call anyone. I am fine,' Max insisted in his normal voice as he sat up and stared at the empty doorway. Then he began to whimper. His hysteria quickly turned to embarrassment as he realized where he was and what he had done.

'I'm truly sorry, Abe, Rendi, Emma, Jacob,' he said, standing slowly and straightening his tie. 'I'm all right now. I'll just go home so you can complete the seder.'

Abe looked directly into Max's eyes. 'You're not going anywhere. We can't just pretend this didn't happen. There's something inside of you that you have to

33

get out. You've been keeping it locked up for years, and it finally burst open. You've got to tell us. Max, we're family. There are no secrets here.'

'I cannot.'

'Please,' Rendi implored. 'Please tell us. We want to help you, but we can't if you keep it to yourself.'

'I appreciate your concern, but I have been able to deal with my past only by keeping it to myself. Please, respect my privacy. Respect my decision.'

'No,' Emma said firmly, putting an arm around Max's shoulder and guiding him to a chair. 'You really frightened me. You owe it to me — to us — to tell us what you were so afraid of. We love you. And when you're in pain, we're in pain. Please, Uncle Max.'

Max was silent for what seemed like an eternity, with tears rolling down his face. He looked at Emma and saw her tears. Rendi was crying, too, as was Jacob. Then Max looked at Abe — the hard-nosed criminal defense lawyer who had seen it all. He saw Abe dabbing his eyes with a handkerchief.

'All right,' Max said quietly. 'You are entitled to know why I reacted as I did. I was worried about how I would feel even before I arrived at your house. Many times I picked up the phone to cancel. I knew that would upset you, so I came. When I saw you preparing for the seder, I knew it would be difficult. It was so much like the preparation of my family's last Passover seder — the one I dream about every night. I thought about my sister, Sarah Chava, and my grandfather Reb Mordechai. That is why I shouted their names.' Max paused as if to reconsider his decision. Then, with a look of apprehension trumped by determination, he continued. 'I will tell you about Sarah Chava, Reb Mordechai, and the rest of my family.'

Part Two

Max's Story

4

Memories of Vilna, Lithuania:
April 1942

Rendi poured Max a cup of tea as the old man thought about where to start his story. He took a sip, looked at the Passover table, and then began.

'As I watched you prepare for the seder, I saw my grandfather Reb Mordechai, the day before our last Passover. He was in the attic of our house, looking for the special box containing the religious items we used for the seder.

'We must have looked strange,' Max said with a warm smile as he remembered the scene. 'A portly old man with a flowing white beard and a fur hat, crawling around a dark attic, while his eighteen-year-old grandson, wearing a black suit and yarmulke, with curly sidelocks and the beginning of a never shaved beard, held a flickering candle.

'I remember as if it were yesterday, Grandpa finding the Pesach box and opening it, the way the flame of the candle reflected off the large silver chalice.

'The chalice had been in my grandmother Blima's family since 1492, when the Jews of Spain — where my grandmother's family had originated — had been forced to convert to Christianity. Grandma's family had pretended to convert, but secretly continued to practice their Judaism until they were able to immigrate to Lithuania. The Christians called them 'Marranos' — a derogatory term derived from the Spanish word for swine. During this time, a silversmith had created a beautiful chalice, which from the outside appeared to be Christian. The secret compartments contained all the religious implements needed to practice Judaism, including tiny candlesticks and even a miniature Torah scroll.

'Every year when Grandpa would unpack the chalice, he would ask me, 'Max, doesn't it make you proud to be descended from a family that could make something like this?' He would remind me how my ancestors risked their lives, and how if the Inquisition had discovered their hidden treasures, everyone would have been killed.

'Then Grandpa would promise that if I continued our tradition, he would leave the chalice to me, not to my father.

'You cannot know how much it hurt me to

hear my grandpa and my papa argue about religion.'

Max was reciting half-century-old discussions as if they had just taken place. He closed his eyes as he recalled the conversations. Occasionally he spoke directly to Abe and the other guests, explaining parts of the dialogue that he thought might be unclear.

'It was not as if my father, David, were an atheist,' Max said to Emma. 'Far from it. He was a moderately religious Jew who believed that a Jew could live a full secular life. He was against anachronistic rituals designed to keep Jews from interacting with gentiles. My father was an instructor of ancient history at the University of Vilna. He had many Christian friends, colleagues, and students. Some of them he would bring home. But Grandpa Mordechai did not want his grandchildren to become comfortable around non-Jews. 'Remember Chava,' he would always say — a reference to the character in Shalom Aleichem's short story about the daughter of Tevya the milkman who married a Christian boy. The Chava reference was meant especially for my younger sister, who was named Sarah Chava after two of her great-grandmothers.

'Sarah Chava was sixteen years old, though she looked younger,' Max said, looking off into the distance. 'Olive in complexion, she was a true beauty who was already the envy of every Jewish mother in the neighborhood. She had the most glorious smile. The most expressive eyes. When she spoke, her entire face lit up with joy. Sarah Chava had everything a prospective husband could want: a good family background, wealth, beauty, and intelligence. She was destined to marry the son of one of the great rabbis of the Vilna yeshiva.'

As Max described his sister, pain was etched in his expressive face. He closed his eyes as if to conjure up her image in his mind's eye. Then, after a brief pause, he was back to his story.

'The issue of associating with non-Jews had become moot since Christians were no longer allowed to socialize with Jews. My father had been fired by the university and was now teaching private classes to Jewish students who had been expelled from the schools. I remember watching in awe as my father taught the classes at home. I had never seen my father at work. The students treated him like a god as he stood in the dining room discussing issues I barely understood.

'Although my father lived a secular life — he dressed in modern clothing, was clean-shaven, read books in several languages — he did not try to make me or my sister follow in his ways. We had both chosen to follow more in our grandfather's footsteps, in my case forsaking a secular education for a rabbinic one.

'Emma, I know you will find this difficult to understand,' Max said, pausing to gauge his young friend's reaction. 'But I agreed to an arranged marriage when I was even younger than you.'

'How old were you?'

'I was seventeen, and my wife was fifteen. In those days, it was quite normal.'

'At fifteen I didn't even like boys.'

'Nobody asked Leah, or me, whether we were ready or whether we liked each other. I was very fortunate. Leah was a wonderful girl.'

'Pretty?'

'Lovely, and when she was pregnant, she was radiant.'

'How old was she when she became pregnant?'

'Leah gave birth to Efraim nine months after our wedding, and she was already pregnant with our second child at the time of the seder. She told me that she wanted to have six children,' Max said, lowering his head.

'Grandpa Mordechai loved Efraim because

he was the first great-grandchild and he represented the next generation of Menuchens. Grandpa's great passion was family.

'For Grandpa Mordechai, *yichus* was everything. *Yichus* was the family heritage traced as far back as possible, with as many great rabbis as the family could claim. *Yichus* was important to everyone in Vilna, and there was even an official *yachsin* — a tracer of family trees who 'certified' the bona fides of the claims made by families concerning their rabbinical lineage. Even in times of crisis, a family's *yichus* determined their social standing, and there were few families with better *yichus* than the Menuchens.

'Grandpa Mordechai's seventieth birthday fell on the day of Efraim's circumcision, and I will never forget his prayer that his children, grandchildren, and great-grandchildren should all reach the magical age of three score and ten, as he had been privileged to do. I hugged Grandpa Mordechai and said I wanted him to live forever. Grandma Blima, ever cautious, immediately went, 'Poo poo,' and waved her hand.'

'What was that all about?' Rendi interrupted.

'She was chasing away the evil spirits. She was worried that we might bring on a *k'nayna hura* — an evil eye.'

'Grandma Ringel always used to say

44

k'nayna hura,' Emma said, smiling at her father.

'The evil eye was all around Vilna in those terrible days,' Max continued. 'Several Jewish leaders, primarily political activists, had been taken away. Mr Bloom, the Zionist leader from around the corner, had been arrested. There were occasional shootings. An epidemic of influenza had taken some lives. And there were dreadful rumors. But death had not touched our family directly.

'Jews were not allowed out of their neighborhoods. For me, it was wonderful. We lived in a spacious old wooden house, whose boards creaked as if haunted by the spirits of the Menuchen rabbis who had inhabited it and held court in its vast library for many generations.'

'How long had the house been in your family?'

'Since the sixteenth century. It was really a compound, consisting of the large house shared by my father and mother, who lived upstairs with Sarah Chava. Leah and I lived downstairs with our baby. Grandpa Mordechai and Grandma Blima lived in the converted carriage house in the back. The extended family lived in the neighborhood and often visited 'the house', as the Menuchen compound was always called. Now more than ever, it served as a community center, synagogue, school, and meeting hall. For me, it was paradise, because everyone I loved was under one roof for much of the day.

'As the time for the Passover seder approached, the house bustled with preparations. Grandma Blima presided over the food preparation, assigning each woman and girl a task. She showed 'Surila' — that was what she called Sarah Chava — how to split open each raisin in order to get the most flavor in the stuffed cabbage. It was an old family recipe, and Grandma Blima showed her how to roll this cabbage so that it kept the meat and raisins from falling out. Grandma claimed that the secret was picking large cabbage leaves and then tucking them properly. And Grandma teased Sarah Chava by telling her sternly that no man would marry her if the meat and raisins fell out of her stuffed cabbage.'

Rendi laughed. Emma joined in the laughter as her stepmother gave her hand a squeeze.

Max paused once again for a sip of tea. Turning to Emma, he said, 'It must be hard for you to understand a girl like Sarah Chava, because you are becoming a professional woman. But in those days, girls like you were raised to become wives and mothers. We called them *baleboostehs*. It means those who care for the master of the house.'

A smile crossed Emma's face, as if she were trying to suppress a laugh.

'What is it, Emma? Did I say something funny?'

'No, it's just that the word *baleboosteh* sounds like 'ball busters,' which is what my generation of young women is accused of being.'

'That's not funny,' Abe chided.

'It's fine,' Max said, pinching Emma's cheek. 'As long as Jacob over there doesn't mind.' Jacob blushed and shook his head as Max continued his story.

'My grandfather and grandmother were known for their grand seders, to which they always invited the extended family.

'Our seder was a combination of prayerful spirituality, intellectual debate, and childish fun. A lot more prayers than yours, Abe. And more people. But the rest was not so different. My grandmother had been taught by her mother an old Sephardic trick for 'parting the Red Sea,' in commemoration of the biblical story. By carefully adding pepper, red dye, and liquid soap to a large dish of water, she could create the illusion of the water parting. The children loved it. I wish I remembered how to do it. I would teach it to you for your children,' Max said to Emma with a broad smile.

'After each prayer was recited, Grandpa would turn to the assembled guests and ask, 'Nu, does anyone have an interesting interpretation?' A flurry of responses would follow. About halfway through the seder, just prior to the meal, Grandpa asked about the ten plagues. 'Why was Egypt punished?' Grandpa asked. 'After all, it was God who hardened the heart of Pharaoh. If Pharaoh had no free will, how could he have done otherwise than refuse to free the Israelites?'

'Sarah Chava was the first to attempt to answer. I remember her saying that if God was both omnipotent and omniscient, then Grandpa's question had no real meaning, because what God did to Pharaoh was no different from what he does to everyone. Then she made the mistake of comparing Pharaoh to Hitler.

' 'Do not utter that name in this house,' Reb Mordechai announced sternly. 'That monster is not invited to our seder.'

'Sarah Chava apologized and tried to refocus the discussion by asking Grandpa whether Jews believe in heaven and hell.

'My father insisted there was no mention

48

of an afterlife in the Torah, but Grandpa said it was in the Talmud.

'The argument became contentious. Everyone around the table worried that it might escalate into a scene.

'My father gave me a gentle kick under the table, signaling me to suggest a compromise. I remember exactly what I said. 'Is it not true that one's descendants are their life after death? As long as a person has living descendants, part of him remains alive through them.' Reb Mordechai told me I was right and complimented me on my interpretation because it reinforced his commitment to the importance of *yichus*.

'The seder continued without incident until after the meal. The women had prepared a feast of gefilte fish, stuffed cabbage, chicken soup, roast chicken, honeyed carrots, and matzah kugel. As every dish was brought out, Grandma Blima proudly announced who had assisted in its preparation. The helper stood and made a polite curtsy, as the rest of the family applauded. The meal was accompanied by songs and spirited conversation.

'The highlight of the seder — in addition to stuffed cabbage — was always the arrival of the prophet Elijah, who never missed a Menuchen seder. No one could actually see him, of course, but Grandpa Mordechai could 'prove' he had been there. The tradition was to prepare a special chalice for Elijah, with each male contributing some wine from his own cup. We always used the ancient Marrano chalice, which contained a large wine cup. Grandpa Mordechai would show the children that Elijah's chalice was full, but then, at the appointed time for Elijah's appearance, the children would go to the door and open it for the invisible prophet. When the children returned, Grandpa Mordechai would show them that some of the wine was being consumed before their very eyes. 'See, Elijah is drinking it,' he would say with a smile. The younger children believed, while the older ones knew there must be a trick. At their Bar Mitzvah, Grandpa Mordechai would always confide the family secret. Several hundred years earlier, one of Grandma Blima's ancestors had fashioned a small valve in Elijah's chalice that permitted the wine to drain into the stem. Grandma Blima's ancestors had a sense of humor about their holy traditions.'

For a moment Max smiled as he recalled the happiness of his family seder. Then, suddenly, his entire body went rigid.

'This year it was different. Grandpa Mordechai showed the children the full chalice and told Sarah Chava to greet Elijah. As my sister opened the large wooden door, she jumped back. '*Gottenyu!*' she screamed. 'My God!' Someone was actually at the door. It was not Elijah. The man at the door politely introduced himself as Captain Marcelus Prandus of the Lithuanian Auxiliary Militia. I will never forget how he looked. Captain Prandus was a strikingly handsome man, tall, with neatly trimmed blond hair and deep blue eyes. He was accompanied by a group of black-shirted Lithuanian militiamen, wearing swastika armbands and carrying German machine guns.'

5

Cambridge
The Same Night

'I need to stop for a few minutes. I'm sorry. This is difficult for me,' Max said as he wiped the perspiration from his brow.

'Take your time. Do it at your own pace. We've got nowhere to go,' Abe said gently, holding Rendi's hand.

Everyone was anxious to hear what Prandus and his men had done, but they all sensed a need in Max to take a break and bring the discussion back to the present.

'Your family sounds so much like ours,' Emma said with a smile. 'Constant friction among the generations, a father who thinks he knows everything. Even the issues — is there a heaven or hell? We argued about that when I was ten.'

'Yes, all that is true,' Max interrupted. 'Like me, you love your father dearly — and you respect him.'

'But in my generation, the parent and the child have to earn each other's love and respect, mutually,' Emma said pointedly.

'In our generation, it was required that we show love and respect, even if we did not always feel them,' Max said, a gentle smile crossing his face.

'Now I know why I always liked your generation,' Abe quipped.

'I now understand why you shouted out the name Prandus. I still don't know why you called me by your sister's name.'

'I called you Sarah Chava because you remind me so much of my little sister. When I saw you going toward the door, I flashed back to Sarah Chava going to the door, and I became frightened for you — for her. You are a few years older than she was, but she was small like you and smart. And also beautiful. You would have loved her.'

'I know I would have,' Emma said.

As Max gathered his thoughts, Rendi poured him another cup of tea. 'It's impossible for people like us to imagine what you are describing — ghettos, shootings, Hitler — it's all so alien to our experiences,' she observed.

'As it was to ours,' Max replied, his voice bitter. 'We had nothing to compare it with. We had read about occasional pogroms. But this . . . it was so different, so unprecedented. No one was prepared for what was to come. It happened so quickly. One moment we

were together as a family, and then . . . '
Max could not go on. He buried his head
in his hands, trying to muffle the sobs he
could no longer control.

Abe reached across the table to Max's
arm. 'You don't have to go on if you
don't want to,' he said softly. 'I think we
all understand now.'

Abruptly Max sat up. 'Understand? You
cannot begin to understand.'

Abe was instantly contrite. 'I'm sorry, I
didn't mean that.'

'I'm not angry with you. It is important to
me that you do know something of what it
was like, though it is impossible for anyone
who wasn't there really to understand.'

6

The Ponary Woods
Memories of Vilna, Lithuania:
April 1942

Max took a deep breath and continued where he had left off.

'Marcelus Prandus ordered us to walk quickly to the large open truck parked in front of our house. We had to huddle together to fit into it for the half-hour drive to Ponary Woods. We were in a state of shock. Children were crying. The smell of urine was everywhere. It was terrible. We were all so frightened. The adults remained silent, clutching each other and the children.

'When the truck stopped in a glen in the Ponary Woods, I saw eight other trucks, each loaded with families. Although the family groups were kept apart, I recognized several of the people. They were all Jewish — from prominent families — everyone was dressed in their holiday finery. Men were wearing white *kittels*, the robelike vestments that are worn for seders — and burials.

'I later learned that the Nazis often selected

Jewish holidays for their roundups, or *aktions*, as they called them. They knew that families would be together on these holidays, and it was rare for anyone to try to escape when the entire family was taken away together. Also, on the holidays, Jews used their best silver, which was taken as booty by the police. Marcelus Prandus had personally confiscated the Marrano chalice while his men were leading the family into the trucks. He told us it was to become part of a museum being planned by the Nazis to document the customs of the Jewish race.

'The family groups were standing around, huddled together against the chill of the spring night. It was hazy, and the lights from the trucks created an eerie glow. I was holding my son, Efraim, with one hand and gently rubbing my pregnant wife's stomach with the other. I was scared. Everyone was scared. No one dared to speak above a whisper. The Lithuanians were businesslike and polite. They, too, seemed to be waiting for some signal. It was a long time in coming.

'Finally, after more than an hour, Prandus announced, 'It is time to dig.' The Lithuanians retrieved six old shovels from the truck. I was given one, as was my father and four of the other men. 'Papa, I've never used a

56

shovel before. I'm scared,' I whispered to my father.

' 'Just watch me. I'll show you how to hold it,' my father whispered back.

'The Lithuanians led us to a small hill and ordered us to start digging a ditch at its base. The earth was cold and hard at the surface, but it grew softer as the men dug deeper. I had difficulty with the shovel. Twice it fell out of my hand. Both times I quickly picked it up and continued digging. Then my shovel hit a rock, denting it. My father exchanged shovels with me.

'After a while, Prandus came to inspect the project. He seemed dissatisfied with the progress of the hole, but he declared it acceptable. The shovels were gathered up, and the men were taken back to the larger group. Again, there was waiting, whispering, shivering. Nobody mentioned death, although I now find it hard to believe that nobody was thinking about it. Why else the digging? Why else the entire trip? But it seemed inconceivable at the time. Prandus was so polite, so matter-of-fact. Could any of us have actually believed that nine family groups had been taken from their Passover seders to dig holes and then go home? Nothing was too absurd to believe in those terrible days.'

Max paused and turned to Abe, as if

seeking his approval. 'For years, I have tortured myself for my failure to recognize the obvious. Had I known, could I have done something? Could I have shouted warnings so that some could have escaped? But who? I would never have abandoned my pregnant wife and child. Nor my elderly grandparents. Maybe my father? Or my mother? My sister? A cousin? An uncle? A child? Escape was unlikely. There were more than a dozen armed militiamen. They had a truck, while our family was on foot. But escape for one or two was possible, if unlikely. At least they could have tried.'

Max began to shake. He put down his cup to avoid spilling the tea.

'You did everything you could,' Abe said in a gentle voice. 'Don't blame yourself.'

'I do not blame myself. I just wonder whether it could have been different.' Max paused for a moment. Then, putting two fingers around his chin and nodding his head, he said, 'I think I now understand my outburst. Tonight, I did what I did not do then — warn my sister. I'm so sorry to have inflicted that upon you.'

'It's not an infliction,' Abe said. 'It's an education.'

'Then I must complete the education,' Max said, and he resumed telling his story.

58

'We stood silently, huddled together, until finally Marcelus Prandus spoke. 'I have selected your family to be first,' he said as if he were talking about some special privilege. 'You have a right to know what awaits you. It will be over for you in a matter of minutes.' Then he took out a written statement and read from it. It went something like this:

' 'The Fuhrer has determined that the Jewish problem can be solved in only one manner. The seed of Abraham must be destroyed forever. It is not a question of individual guilt or innocence. It is not your fault that you are Jews, but the fault lies within your genes, within your seed.' As Prandus read, he directed his words as much to his fellow Lithuanians, some of whom were teenagers, as to his intended victims. 'What we are about to do is for the good of all humankind. You are about to fulfil the destiny assigned to you by the Third Reich. You may regard yourselves as soldiers dying on behalf of the Fatherland.' Prandus uttered these words without any semblance of apology or regret.

'Now there was no mistaking Prandus's intentions. Still, there was no panic, no shrieking, and no attempts to run.

'Prandus led Grandpa Mordechai to the

pit that the men had dug.

' 'This man is the patriarch of the Menuchen family. Who are his children?'

'No one responded.

'Prandus pulled a typed list from his pocket and looked at it. 'There is no reason to make it more difficult or painful than it has to be,' he said almost apologetically. Perhaps because he thought he could protect his family, my father stepped forward and said, 'I am Reb Mordechai's only son.'

'Prandus looked down at the list and said, 'There is another son, named Moshe. He, too, must step forward.'

'No one moved. Prandus pointed his rifle at Grandma Blima and said, 'Unless Moshe Menuchen identifies himself immediately, I will shoot his mother.'

'Moshe stepped forward.

'Still pointing the gun at Blima, Prandus called for grandsons.

'I joined my father near the pit, along with Moshe and his two sons.

' 'And now the great-grandson.'

'With that command, my family began to scream, 'No, no!'

'Desperately, I appealed to Prandus. 'He's a baby. He doesn't even know he is a Jew. Please spare him. Take him. You can't hurt a baby.'

' 'You don't understand,' Prandus replied evenly, meeting my gaze with steel-blue eyes that I will never forget. 'The children are the most important. All previous attempts to end the existence of a race have failed because of an unwillingness to kill children. We will not fail on account of such cowardice. The children are the most important,' Prandus repeated, looking directly at baby Efraim.

'I began to shake in fear. I could not even cry. Dizziness and nausea immobilized me. I felt helpless. Others were shrieking. I could see them flailing about in a frenzy of utter desperation. I could smell their fear. I could do nothing but look into the innocent eyes of my doomed child.

'Prandus walked among the remaining family members, inspecting each of them. He stopped in front of Sarah Chava and signaled one of his militiamen, who grabbed her forcefully by the arm and led her to the truck. 'She will be spared,' Prandus said.

'Two Lithuanians then gently nudged my wife, Leah, who was screaming as she clutched the baby Efraim next to the pit.

'Grandpa Mordechai pleaded with Prandus, 'Please, I beg you. Shoot me first, so that I do not have to see my family killed. The Bible — the one that you believe in as I do — commands that when a person takes a baby bird, it must first send away its mother. Please send me away first.'

' 'No,' Prandus said flatly. 'Our orders are to kill the youngest first. They are the most important.'

'As Grandpa Mordechai began to cry, I thought about my grandfather's great love of *yichus* — of his family's contributions to the Jewish people over so many generations. Now it would all end, forever. It was like extinction.'

Max turned to Emma with an apologetic look. 'It may sound strange now that this is what I thought about, but it is true. There would be no one to carry on the family name. Grandpa Mordechai would have no afterlife through his descendants, because there would be no descendants. Maybe Sarah Chava, I remember thinking. At least there was some hope for her.

'Grandpa Mordechai understood there would be no survivors here on earth as he turned his head upward and began reciting the words *Ani ma-amin, b'emunah shlaima, beviyas ha-Mashiach*. 'I believe, with complete faith, in the coming of the Messiah.' I looked into my grandfather's eyes and saw belief. I looked into my father's eyes and saw terror. At that moment, I understood the power of faith. At that moment, I also

62

understood that I could never again believe. I felt the same terror as my father, when I saw Prandus aim his rifle at my wife.

'It all happened in quick succession, amid screaming, shrieking, and futile attempts to resist or run. First Prandus shot my wife, Leah, in her pregnant stomach. Efraim fell to the ground. I covered him with my body. Prandus kicked me away with his heavy boot and aimed the rifle at the crying baby. I reached for Efraim, shouting, 'No, no!' as Prandus shot him in the head. I saw his tiny skull explode. An instant later he pointed the gun at my head and fired. The last word I heard was my grandfather shouting, '*Nekama!*' '

7

Cambridge
The Same Night

'He shot you, Uncle Max? How did you survive?' Emma asked, her eyes filled with tears.

'I tried to save him. I did everything I could. But it wasn't enough,' Max cried, not even hearing Emma's question.

'There's nothing more you could have done,' said Abe.

'But I lived and he died. Everyone else died.'

'How did you survive?' Emma persisted.

This time Max heard her question.

'If I believed in God, I would tell you it was a miracle. But it was just dumb luck. That is how most survivors made it — by luck.'

'What about Sarah Chava?'

'I don't know. I never found out what happened to her.'

'So it is possible,' Emma exclaimed, 'that she may have survived?'

'There is always the possibility of survival.

I have never given up hope,' Max said, shaking his head and staring beyond Emma. 'She would be an old woman if she did manage somehow to survive, maybe even a grandmother. I cannot imagine her as an old woman. Maybe . . . '

As he said these words, Max again began to sob.

'If that bastard Prandus walked through the door now, I could kill him with my bare hands,' Emma said, her face contorted.

'And I would help you,' Jacob said, his voice shaking with emotion.

'He, too, would be an old man,' Max said. 'It is harder to kill an old man.'

'It wasn't hard for that monster,' Emma replied.

'Did they catch him after the war?' Abe asked.

'I don't think so,' Max replied. 'I have heard nothing of what happened to him. He's probably living somewhere in Vilna. Maybe he died. I do not know.'

'What was that word your grandfather shouted?' Emma asked.

'*Nekama*,' Max replied. 'It means take revenge. I later learned that the word *nekama* was written on the walls of the death camps and the ghetto bunkers. I do not know whom my grandfather was telling to take revenge, since he believed none of us would survive. Maybe he was pleading with God.'

'What happened after you were shot? How did you escape?' Rendi asked softly, uncertain if Max could continue.

8

Resurrection
Ponary Woods: 1942

'I remembered nothing after being shot until I felt the dirt hitting my head. Someone was shoveling dirt over my body. Though my head was pounding with pain, I began to wonder whether I was alive or dead. I knew I was being buried. Buried alive? Maybe that will be worse than a quick death. Should I move and thus assure a coup de grâce? Or should I remain motionless, feigning death? I remembered the shallowness of the hole I had dug. Maybe I could survive the burial.

'I remained still until I could breathe no more. And then I held my breath as long as I could. When I began to feel faint I knew I had no choice. I pushed my head to the surface, certain I would be shot.

'I tried to see, quietly shaking my head to dislodge the dirt that caked my eyes. I could make out the moving figure of a tall Lithuanian with a shovel in one hand and a gun in the other. Because only one eye was open, I could not tell whether

67

the Lithuanian was moving toward me or away from me. After a terrified moment, I managed to open my other eye and saw that the Lithuanian was moving toward another family's burial pit. I lay still for what seemed like an eternity, quietly blowing dirt from my nostrils, until I finally heard the truck engines turn over and leave. Then I tried to get up. I could not move my legs, or even feel them. I willed my legs to free themselves from their mud-packed crypt, and after a few moments of uncertainty, they broke through. I staggered, holding on to a tree until I could steady myself. Then I took my first full breath of the night's air, rancid from the smell of death and blood and flesh.

'The glen was quiet. No one was visible. I could see mounds of dirt all around. I could also see rivers of blood and particles of flesh in the pale moonlight. Then I heard a sound. It was a gurgle. It came from my pit. It recurred. I dug quickly with my fingers in the direction of the sound. I felt a human body. I dug furiously, uncovering the body of my grandmother Blima. She was dead. The blood flowing from her chest wound was making the gurgling sound. It was a sound that would awaken me at night for years. Though I knew they were all dead, I continued to dig, then I heard the sound of an approaching truck. I had to escape.

'I ran in the direction of a stream in which my friends and I used to swim. I cleaned my wound — the bullet had entered the back of my head and exited below my ear. It had caused great pain, but remarkably little damage or bleeding. I used my white *kittel* to make bandages. I remained in the woods all the next day, my head wound causing such excruciating pain that I feared blacking out.

'At nightfall, I decided I had to take a chance and approach a farmhouse, hoping the occupants were not Nazi sympathizers. Considering the pervasiveness of pro-German feelings, I knew how risky it would be, but I had no choice. Before deciding whether to knock on the door, I watched the woman and her son through the window. I saw them at dinner, eating a simple meal of soup and bread. There was something about the woman that led me to trust her. Maybe it was that she prayed with such devotion both before and after the meal. Maybe it was that she treated her son lovingly. After watching the son go to sleep, I waited until the woman went alone to the outhouse. I did not want to alarm her, so as she left the outhouse, I whispered, 'I'm hurt. Will you please help me?'

'The woman was startled but not frightened

69

by the sight of me with a bandage wrapped around my head. 'Come in,' she said. 'I will try to help you.'

' 'I am a Jew,' I blurted out.

' 'I know that,' she said, looking at my sidetale earlocks. 'It is my Christian duty to help anyone in need.' And with that she led me inside her house.

'Katrina Liatus was a forty-year-old widow who worked the land. My grandfather would have looked down on her as a peasant. Katrina would not have denied that she was a simple woman. She could not read or write, but she could certainly think. Every decision she made about me — and necessarily about herself, since if I were caught, it could mean the end of her — turned out to be brilliant. She knew exactly whom to trust, whom to flatter, whom to deceive, and even whom to kill. She lied to the local priest, describing me as a cousin from Kovno. She trusted the constable, even though he was friendly with some of Prandus's men. She flattered the landlord. She killed a drunken neighbor who discovered my secret and threatened to disclose it unless Katrina submitted to his sexual advances. Pretending to agree, she invited him to her house, stabbed him through the heart, and told the police that he had tried to rape her. Since the drunk had a reputation for such conduct, no one made a fuss. If the constable suspected what happened, he never let on.

'Katrina also knew how to treat my wound, using folk remedies — boiling hot rags, mustard plasters, leeches, and a heavy dose of prayer — to avoid infection. I can still feel the hot mustard against my throbbing wound.

'Katrina gave me a haircut and my first shave. 'You must not look Jewish if you are to remain here.' I agreed and dressed myself in Lithuanian peasant clothing. Katrina gave me a cross to wear around my neck. I was nervous as I put it on.

'I lived with Katrina and her twelve-year-old son, Lukus. Our cover story was that I was a cousin from Kovno serving as a companion for Lukus, and indeed I did so for more than six months. I might have remained with Katrina and her son indefinitely, had a group of Lithuanian partisans not broken into the Liatus house one night to steal food. I woke up and heard them. I crept into Katrina's room to warn her. 'Let them have the food. They're just children like you and Lukus,' she said.

'I peeked into the kitchen and watched. A young man, who was younger than me, took some food. Suddenly I recognized a woman in the group. She was a Jewish student named Miriam who had studied with my father. Frightened, I walked into the kitchen and introduced myself. I told her of my father's murder, and she hugged me and asked me to join them. I thought hard about what to do. I had no experience that would suit me as a partisan. But I felt I had no choice. They were fighting against the people who had killed my family. I agreed to join the group, and I bade Katrina and Lukus goodbye.

'I took the cross from around my neck and put it in my pocket as a reminder of Katrina Liatus. I still have it in a drawer at home.

'I knew nothing of fighting or guns, but I learned. During the ensuing years until the liberation, I fought the Nazis and, when I could, searched for my sister. I did not recite the Kaddish. I did not grieve. I slept so little that I did not give myself time to dream. The nightmares came later. Then it was a struggle to survive. I did not expect to live for long. The Nazis were invincible. Every day, it seemed, one of my friends was found dead, or failed to return after a mission. Miriam was blown up by a German grenade a few months after recruiting me.

'I had several miraculous escapes from almost certain death. Yet even these did not persuade me that it was my 'destiny' to live, for to believe that would require me to believe that it was the rest of my family's destiny to die. I could not believe in a power that was capable of abetting such evil for His own unknown purposes. I preferred to believe in the unmitigated evil of nazism and the unqualified need to fight it.

'I fought for almost two years in several ragtag partisan units. I shot one German soldier during an attack on a troop train, but I don't know whether I killed him. I hoped that I had, though now I realize that he might just have been a youngster who was drafted into Hitler's army.

'In these days following the liberation, I wandered through the streets of Vilna in a daze. I asked everyone if they had seen a girl who fit Sarah Chava's description. I kept looking for something, someone from the past.

'Suddenly I found myself in front of the old Menuchen house. It looked exactly the same as it had on the Passover night when Marcelus Prandus came to the door and murdered my family. Even the large wooden mezuzah was still there. Everything the Menuchen house had represented, however, was gone. It was hard to believe that so much had changed in just three years. I walked up to the front of the house and stood there — remembering. A man opened the door and asked what I wanted. When I told him it was my family's home, he said, 'Not any longer,' insisting that the house had been given to him. He threatened that if I ever came to the door again, he would call the police, who would finish what Hitler had started.

'Despite the threat, I sneaked into the house one afternoon to see if I could retrieve any mementoes of my family. I climbed to the attic in search of Reb Mordechai's Passover box, but it was gone. The library, too, had vanished. I searched everywhere — for something, anything that would connect this house to its long heritage. Nothing. As I was about to leave, I spotted my old chest of drawers. I pulled frantically at each drawer. As I opened the bottom one, it broke apart. Beneath the rotting wood, I saw a single family photograph, which had fallen behind the drawer. It had been taken at Efraim's circumcision party, less than a year before Ponary Woods. It included a smiling Sarah Chava. On the back was a note from my sister wishing Efraim *mazel tov*. I slipped the photograph in my pocket and climbed out the window.

'I slept in the Jewish graveyard, which had several old family mausoleums. Other

Jewish survivors also found their way to the graveyard. I went up to each of them with my photograph. I didn't have to say a word. I just pointed to my sister. The other person looked and shook his head. It became a ritual. There were rumors of Jews who had passed for Christians, or who had been hidden by Christians. Perhaps Sarah Chava. I asked everywhere. I showed everyone the picture. But I met no one who knew anything about the fate of my little sister. Finally, after a week of sleeping in the old Jewish graveyard, I met a friend from my religious school. His name was Chayim, and he, like me, had been in a partisan unit. I showed Chayim the photograph of Sarah Chava. Chayim shook his head.

'Chayim invited me to join his tiny group of survivors. 'We need you for a *minyan*,' Chayim joked. They were planning to blow up the prison that was holding the Gestapo and SS prisoners.

'I was sorely tempted, especially if Chayim's group could help me find and kill Marcelus Prandus.

'Even so, I turned down Chayim, convinced that the Nazis would be severely punished by the Allies. Besides, in the weeks following the end of the war, I found it difficult to think about punishment. There was so

75

much misery, poverty, and death all around that nature seemed to be exacting its own punishment. Sixteen-year-old Lithuanian girls, wearing crosses, were selling their bodies for a loaf of bread, a bottle of milk, or a chocolate bar. The Communists in Lithuania were exacting their own cruel revenge. There was talk of trials.

'I hoped that maybe someone had taken revenge against Marcelus Prandus. I looked for Prandus — not sure what I would do if I found him. I never did. Vilna is a large city, and in the months following its liberation, it was in turmoil. On several occasions, I thought I saw Prandus — on a bus, in a market, at a checkpoint — but it was always some other tall, blond-haired, blue-eyed Lithuanian. Soon all tall, young Lithuanian men began to remind me of Marcelus Prandus. I left Vilna without learning anything about Prandus. But somehow I knew that Marcelus Prandus was still alive. People like him survive.'

9

Cambridge
The Same Night

'Did many Jews seek revenge after the war?' Emma asked.

'A few, like Chayim. There was a small revenge movement — a few assassinations, nothing more. I sometimes wish there had been more,' Max said in a voice of frustration and mounting anger. 'We were in shock. Actually, there was more revenge in the displaced persons camp to which I was sent a few months after the liberation.'

'There were Nazis in the displaced persons camps?' Abe asked incredulously.

'No. No. Of course not. Only Jews. The revenge was taken by Jews against Jews. Here, let me give you an example. The first week in the camp, I went to Sabbath services — to see if I could still pray. In the middle of the Torah reading, I noticed the man to my left, a Polish Jew, looking intently into the face of the man to my right, a Czech Jew. The man to my right turned away, as if to hide his face. Suddenly the Polish Jew let out a bestial shriek. Flinging his entire body over mine and shouting, 'Capo, capo!' he bit the Czech man on his throat, like a wolf trying to kill his prey. I tried to separate the men and, in the process, had my hand bitten by the Polish man. The Czech man was carried to the hospital, bleeding profusely from his neck. After receiving several stitches, he left the camp and was never heard from again.

'Almost every day one survivor of a death camp would identify another as a capo or collaborator. There were shouted accusations, heated denials, beatings, and even one killing.'

'Why was so much anger directed against fellow Jews? Weren't they victims, too?' Rendi asked.

'You must understand,' Max continued in an explanatory tone, 'the Nazis were distant, abstract figures, whereas the collaborators were flesh-and-blood neighbors. It was easier to feel passion against someone with whom you could personally identify.'

'Were there any happy encounters at the camp?' Emma asked. 'Did anyone ever find a loved one?'

'A few. Every so often a friend or relative who was presumed dead would appear. These occasional reunions encouraged me to continue my search for Sarah Chava, though I knew the chances that she had survived were slim. Every camp had a bulletin board on which photographs and descriptions of lost loved ones were placed, with pleas for information. Newsletters were circulated among the camps. But good news was rare. Even bad news was rare. Mostly, there was no news of missing loved ones.'

Max sat silently as his thoughts turned to his sister. He tried hard to mask his growing distress. It was a mistake to tell the story, he now thought. It had brought back not only the pain, but his long-suppressed need for justice — even revenge.

He had to get out of there, to be alone. He could not let his friends see his true feelings. He was ashamed of what he was thinking. He needed to say something more uplifting.

'We heard stories of incredible bravery by some young women who had been spared from death only to face sexual humiliation by Nazis. They told us of an entire class of high school girls who took poison together rather than submit to their Nazi tormentors. When I heard this, I wondered whether Sarah Chava had faced a similar choice. I dreamed of Sarah Chava, mostly nightmares, but I heard nothing about her fate. I can only hope,' Max said, looking off in the distance.

'There was one other happy encounter,'

he added, 'but it was short-lived. I met a boyhood neighbor in the camp. Dori Bloom. We became close friends. We traveled to Palestine together. We fought in the army together. We even went to Germany together.' Again Max began to cry. 'I cannot go on. I have subjected you to enough sadness for one night. I must stop now and go home. Please excuse me.'

Abe put his arm around Max's shoulder as the old man made his way to the door.

★ ★ ★

It was past midnight when Max finally took leave of the Ringel home. He felt as if an enormous weight had been lifted as he made his way to his Cambridge home.

As Max walked along Brattle Street, where he had lived for nearly forty years, he thought about his life in Cambridge. His career as a Harvard professor had been as close to perfect as possible, with respect, admiration, and honors. His innovative work on the Book of Ecclesiastes, which began as his Ph.D. thesis at Hebrew University, had made him one of the leading biblical scholars in the world. He had drawn on both the religious teachings of his grandfather and the secular research of his father to help create a new genre of scholarship. But his personal life in America had been incomplete. A few friends, like Abe and his family and — of course — Haskell, but no intimate relationships. No real love. No peace of mind. Then there were the memories. During the day his work kept his memories away. At night they filled his mind. Max had never had a good night's sleep, never experienced complete happiness even for a day. He obsessed about Marcelus Prandus, wondering whether he was alive or dead, whether he had children, whether he ever felt guilt over what he had done. Had Prandus become like Dostoyevsky's fictional Raskolnikov, his unpunished crimes eating at him and destroying his life? Or, like the real-life Stalin, had he never given them a second thought?

About once a month, Max 'saw' Prandus — in a crowd, on television, in a mirror, even in his classroom. It was always his imagination, but every time he 'saw' his family's killer, his heart skipped a beat.

Barely noticing where he was walking, Max recalled the worst Prandus 'sighting', which had occurred one evening a few years earlier. Max was soaking in the bathtub and was flipping the channels when he heard the name. He had gone past CNN before the name registered. Then it had struck him like a kick in the groin. For an instant he was immobilized, staring at the shopping channel as the name of the devil pulsed through his brain in a pounding rhythm: Prandus, Prandus . . . a name that had brought terror to thousands and that was still capable — fifty years later — of making Max lose control over his bladder.

By the time he regained CNN, the announcer was on to another story. A phone call to CNN confirmed that there had indeed been a story about a Nazi collaborator named Prandus, who was deported back to Lithuania for lying about his wartime role in dealing with the Jews of Kovno. On his immigration form Prandus had claimed to be a grocer, but the Justice Department Office of Special Investigations had proved he was a death camp guard at Sobibor.

The intern at CNN had been kind enough to fax Max a sheet from the Internet newsline that contained a picture of the seventy-seven-year-old Prandus outside his modest home in a Chicago suburb. A quick look at the grainy photograph of the short, dark-complexioned old man was proof enough that this Prandus, whose American name was Michael, was not the Marcelus Prandus who had murdered Max's family. This Prandus had murdered other Jewish families. Perhaps he was even related to Marcelus. But he was not the object of Max Menuchen's obsession.

This false sighting turned Max into an emotional cripple for several weeks, as he obsessed anew over whether his life might have been different had he managed to take revenge against Prandus.

Max had tried to combat this emptiness by occupying every waking hour with his work. Instead of thinking about his own lost family, he was content to serve as mentor to the many students who regarded him as their academic father. This he could do, because it did not require emotional involvements or sharing his personal life. His students knew not to probe too deeply — all but one: Danielle Grant, who was, ironically, his most brilliant protégée. As his thoughts returned to the present, Max wondered with a tinge of regret how his former student was faring — never imagining that she would soon become an integral part of his quest for revenge.

Part Three

Confronting the Truth

10

The Chance Encounter
Cambridge, Massachusetts,
Six Weeks Later: Mid-May 1999

It was a beautiful Sunday morning, an ideal day for a walk along the Charles River. Max was out walking by eight-thirty. As he reached Memorial Drive, he encountered an AIDS walk-a-thon. The participants were wearing T-shirts carrying the logo 'Fight AIDS, Not Gays.' Small groups of walkers represented various institutions — corporations, schools, churches. There was a Harvard Divinity School contingent, in which Max spotted Danielle Grant. They greeted one another warmly, and she asked him to join her. Max demurred. He decided to sit on one of the benches until the walkers passed, and then he would continue his stroll.

Had Max turned his head during the next few seconds — perhaps to observe a robin in a tree — he might have missed the sight that was to reshape his future. His life would have continued on its well-trodden path to a comfortable retirement and an uneventful death, with a respectable obituary commemorating his successful career as a professor of Bible studies at the Harvard Divinity School. If their spirit of generosity prevailed over their usual academic competitiveness, colleagues might even have acknowledged that it was Dr Max Menuchen who had finally uncovered the mystery of how the iconoclastic Book of Ecclesiastes had come to be written.

Max did not turn his head. Hence his obituary would be quite different from those accorded successful, but otherwise unremarkable, academics. His academic career, his books, his teaching — they would all be squeezed into a short paragraph at the end of the kind of obituary reserved for infamous men who have made their mark on history by one terrible crime.

Max looked straight ahead at the marchers in the walk-a-thon. Suddenly, out of the corner of his eye, he noticed a profile — it was just a fleeting image, yet it immediately conjured in his mind the face that had filled his nightmares for half a century. The marcher turned his face in Max's direction — a face with characteristic Lithuanian features and the steel-blue eyes that had peered deeply into his as Marcelus Prandus pronounced the death sentence on his family. He was tall and well built. Like Prandus. Yet it wasn't a particularly close resemblance. This man wore glasses, had a different hairstyle and a slimmer face. For an instant, Max fought to ignore his shock of recognition. After all, he had 'seen' Marcelus Prandus so many times over the years — in bathroom mirrors, on television, and in his nightmares. Maybe this man was just another tall, blond Ukrainian. He remembered that at the trial of Ivan the Terrible of Treblinka, the defense had argued that to Jewish victims, all Ukrainians looked alike. This time, however, Max was 'seeing' something else about this face in the crowd. This time there was no mistaking his visceral certainty that a trace of Marcelus Prandus was near at hand. Marcelus Prandus would be a bit older than Max — late seventies. This man was in his forties. Could he be a relative? The man was walking behind a banner bearing the words 'Social Gospel Group, Lithuanian Church of Salem.'

Almost automatically, as if his legs were making the decision for him, Max walked behind the group of marchers. He kept a discreet distance between himself and the man he was following. Suddenly, they stopped for a light at the Western Avenue Bridge. Impulsively, Max tapped the man on the shoulder.

'Excuse me, sir. I hope you do not think me presumptuous. But you look familiar. Might I please inquire as to your name?'

'Paul Prandus,' the younger man responded in a soft voice, extending his hand politely for a shake. 'Do I know you?'

Instinctively, Max pulled away as the reality set in. His heart was racing. His hand began to shake. He felt dizzy. Yet he marshaled the courage to proceed.

'No, I do not think so. I used to know a man named Prandus in Vilnius, Lithuania. And you bear a resemblance to him.'

'That's where my father is from. Maybe your friend was Papa's cousin or something. What was his name? I'll ask my father when I see him tonight.'

'His name was Marcelus Prandus.'

'Hey, that's my dad. You knew him?'

Now Max was shaking visibly. He could barely speak. But he got out the words, trying his best to hide his anxiety: 'Yes, I did. I gather he lives nearby?'

'In Salem. Why don't you call him? I'm sure he'd love to hear from someone back in the old country. What's your name?'

Max froze. What should he say? He was

90

not a good liar. But he needed to continue the conversation.

'He wouldn't know me by my current name. I changed it when I came to America after the war.'

'Lots of people did. We kept ours. What was your name in the old country? I bet Dad will remember. He's still as sharp as a tack.'

'Lukus Liatus,' Max replied, conjuring up the name of the boy he had taken care of during his recuperation.

'I'll ask Papa. Here's his phone number,' the younger man said, scribbling on a business card. 'He loves talking about what he calls the 'good old days' back in Lithuania. Dad's spirits could use a lift. I'm afraid he's quite sick. Pancreatic cancer. Not a good prognosis.'

The word *cancer* sent a shock through Max's entire body. How many times had he wished for Marcelus Prandus to die a lingering death from a painful illness. But not now, in his late seventies, after living a long, happy life surrounded by his family. That was too good a way to die.

'I'm sorry to hear that,' Max said, only partially dissembling.

'We're all sorry.'

'You have a family?' Max asked, trying not

to think of his own lost family.

Paul nodded. 'The grandchildren are taking it the hardest. They love him so much. My son, Marc, is named after him. He's the apple of Papa's eye. His life is his children and grandchildren. We all live near each other in Salem. Papa's a real family man. I bet it's the same with you,' Paul said, smiling.

'Yes, it is,' Max lied.

'I have to be walking,' the young Prandus said. 'I'm leading this motley group. It was really fortuitous running into you, Mr Liatus. I know it will make my father's day.'

'Thank you, Mr Prandus. Send my best to your father,' Max said, grasping the business card with the phone number of his family's murderer and turning in the direction of Abe Ringel's home.

11

Seeking Justice

Abe heard the pounding as he was completing a running program on his treadmill. He came to the door, huffing and puffing, in his sweatsuit and sneakers.

'Max, is everything okay?' Abe said, showing the old man in.

'I don't know. I'm dizzy.'

'Sit down. I'll get you some seltzer.'

When Abe returned with an old-fashioned seltzer bottle and a glass, Rendi was with him. 'You don't look good,' Rendi said to Max. 'Should I call a doctor?'

'No, I'm fine. I just learned something that is making my heart race.'

'What is it?' Abe and Rendi asked in unison.

'He is alive,' Max declared slowly.

'Who's alive?'

'Marcelus Prandus. The man who killed my family.'

'How do you know he's alive?'

'I saw his son.'

'Where? How do you know it was his

son?' Abe demanded in his staccato style of cross-examination.

'Right here in Cambridge,' Max said, pointing to the door. Now he was speaking very quickly. 'In a walk-a-thon. Something about him reminded me of his father. I asked him. He told me. He is the son. He wrote his father's phone number on his card. Here, look.' Max produced the crumpled card. 'Marcelus Prandus has been living in Salem for years. Now he's dying of cancer.'

'Divine justice, I guess,' Rendi observed. 'No one is going to be shedding any tears.'

'No. No. That's exactly the point. He has lived a happy life. He had children and grandchildren. They will miss him. He will die content. We must do something before he dies,' Max demanded, grabbing Abe's arm. 'Can you get him deported? That way he will die alone.'

'Settle down,' Abe said reassuringly, loosening Max's grip. 'I know how traumatic this must be for you. I will do everything possible.'

'So will I,' Rendi added. 'I have some sources. I'll find out everything I can.'

'Will you get him deported?' Max persisted, his voice rising.

Abe placed his arm around the old man

and said: 'Look, the legal system works slowly. It could take some time to undertake an investigation. How sick is he?'

'Pancreatic cancer.'

'I don't know whether he will live long enough to complete an investigation. I'll make some calls — I know someone in the Justice Department who investigates Nazi crimes. Give me Prandus's phone number. I'll give it to my friend at Justice. It will be a start.'

'Yes, yes, a start,' Max said enthusiastically.

Abe worried that he might be creating unrealistic expectations. 'I must tell you, Max, it may be too late for legal justice. He's being punished. He's dying. Maybe you should leave it alone. Just let nature take its course.'

'Can they arrest him? Hold him while they investigate?'

'I'll try,' said Abe. 'But I can't promise anything.'

'You can get him deported, Abe. I know you can. You must,' Max said as he left the Ringel home.

12

Danielle Grant

Max knew there was still time for justice. As he walked toward his home, a sentence from Ecclesiastes popped into his head: 'All things I have seen in the days of my vanity; there is a righteous man that perisheth in his righteousness, and there is a wicked man that prolongeth his life in his evil-doing.' Max knew he could not be as accepting as the author of Ecclesiastes. He would have his justice. Now that he knew where Marcelus Prandus lived, he no longer had an excuse for postponing his revenge. It was as if fate had put Prandus so near to challenge him: can you satisfy your grandfather's last wish — for *nekama*?

Max had to accept the challenge. He had to act, whatever the consequences, and he had to act quickly, before Prandus's death deprived him of the opportunity. He would let Abe Ringel pursue legal justice, Max decided. Abe was a great lawyer. If anyone could bring about legal justice, he could. But if Abe failed, then Max would find his own justice. How does one achieve proper revenge against a dying man? Max wondered. He knew that there was only one person to whom he could turn. He also realized he could never ask for her help directly.

★ ★ ★

Danielle Grant had been Max's most brilliant student — before she broke his cardinal rule never to probe his private life, especially his past. Her brilliance was a surprise to Max, who at first could not imagine a southern girl from a fundamentalist Christian background ever becoming a scholar in his fashion. Max was an agnostic by professional training. According to Professor Menuchen, one must be a skeptic, a doubter, and an open-minded scholar in order to pursue biblical criticism. Although many of his colleagues were personally religious — why else would they be motivated to devote their professional studies to the holy books? — they maintained a healthy skepticism in their scholarship. Max was different. He was an atheist in his personal life, while his professional work allowed for the possibility of divinity.

From the start, Danielle simply would not abide by Professor Menuchen's rule.

'Tell me about yourself,' she asked him

during their initial meeting, when she was just a freshman at the college.

'Read my books,' he replied, taken aback by her audacity. 'And you will learn all you need to know about me.'

'I *have* read your books, and they are a wonderful window into your mind. But they reveal only your rational side. Now I want to learn about your soul.'

'My mind is your concern, as my student. My soul remains my own concern,' the professor said without a hint of harshness.

There was never any harshness in any aspect of Max Menuchen's affect. His face was round, with deep-set eyes, bushy gray eyebrows, and a warm, open smile. Despite its openness, however, it was a smile that seemed to hide a secret — as if he always knew something no one else was able to understand. And although there was certainly nothing sexual about Max Menuchen, there was passion. During the previous forty years it had been a passion for scholarship. Now, as Max walked back to his home, it was quickly becoming a passion for revenge.

He needed to talk to Danielle. She was now an assistant professor of Bible studies. Though they had grown apart over her persistence in prying into her teacher's private life, he had remained interested in her. It was Danielle's love of learning and her unique approach to scholarship that first distinguished Danielle. She believed strongly that scholarship could not be understood without a deep knowledge of the scholar. That was not an unusual *weltanschauung* in her generation, which was peopled with psychologically oriented literary critics, but it was a bit odd in a biblical scholar who believed — as Danielle did — that God wrote the Bible. Her special academic interest was in concepts of justice in the Book of Genesis. Danielle's graduate seminar on this subject was among the most popular in the department. She was being considered by several major universities — including Harvard — for a full professorship.

Danielle had another oddity: she managed to fit in a full-time hobby as a photographer of multimedia video collages. Danielle had shocked the rather staid Bible department with her collage of the creation. Employing images from outer space provided by NASA, time-lapsed photography from the nature channel of flowers blooming, and computer-generated art that she herself had designed, Danielle had managed to illustrate the biblical account of creation. Entitled '*Terem Kol*' — ancient Hebrew for the abyss before the time of creation — it was a tour de force

99

that even the most skeptical and the most fundamentalist members of the department had to admire. As Max had observed after watching it, 'This would surely win a prize *if* there were any category of art into which it fit.'

Danielle was utterly unpredictable. She talked with the urbane southern accent of her paternal grandfather, whose ancestors owned plantations on the outskirts of Charleston and had served in every political office from delegate of the Confederate Congress to mayor of Charleston. Yet she thought like her paternal grandmother, whose family had been southern Catholic abolitionists since the turn of the nineteenth century.

All in all, Danielle had quite a background. Max had never encountered anyone quite like her. Still, he would not give in to her polite demands that he bare his soul to her.

The conflict reached a head when Danielle decided to do her senior honors thesis on the scholarship of Max Menuchen. Her goal was to deconstruct *his* deconstruction of Ecclesiastes. In order to do this, she claimed, she would have to know a great deal about his background, his experiences, his family. Before confronting him with the project, Danielle did library research on the Menuchen family. She traveled to New York and went through the archives of the Jewish Research Institute, which had moved from Vilna to New York at the end of the war and which contained an extensive history of the Vilna Jewish community. She arranged for an Israeli friend to translate records from the Yad Vashem archives in Jerusalem. It was all very frustrating since there was scant documentation of individuals or even families, only of entire communities that had perished. After weeks of prodigious research, Danielle managed to come up with a description of the fate of Vilna's Jews and a sketch of what must have happened to the Menuchen family.

'Here it is, Professor,' she said proudly, handing Max thirty-five neatly organized pages. 'My memorandum on how your interpretation of Ecclesiastes reflects your own experiences as a young man in Vilna.'

Max quickly perused the first few pages, his anger growing silently. Finally he could no longer hold it in. 'How dare you pry into my private life in this way.'

'You are a public figure,' Danielle replied. 'I used only public sources. A scholar must do research on her subject, and you are my subject. I make no apologies.'

'How would you like it,' Max sputtered, 'if I did research on your background?'

'I am not a public person,' Danielle replied defensively, raising her voice a bit. 'At least not yet.'

To Max, Danielle seemed to be protesting too much, almost as if she had some secret in her own past that she did not want uncovered. He had no idea what it might be, and at this point he did not care. Still, he regarded himself as a pretty good judge of such matters.

'You have no legitimate reason for researching me,' Danielle continued, 'other than to satisfy personal curiosity.'

'But I *am* curious. Why are you so obsessed with a nobody like me? I sit in my study and write about an old, obscure book of the Bible. I bother no one. Why must you bother me?'

'Because I need to understand you, in order to understand your work.'

'My work stands or falls on its own merits or demerits,' Max insisted.

'I cannot believe that your past, with all of its tragedy, has no bearing on how you think and what you write.'

'I have no patience for such psychological speculation,' he said dismissively. 'The past is gone. We must not allow it to burden us with its sins. We must move on.'

Danielle could see that Max did not mean

what he was saying. She knew from her research that it would be impossible for him not to be burdened by his past. Just how burdened he was, she would later learn.

'I cannot help you,' Max said.

'You can, but you won't,' Danielle shot back angrily.

'I will not cooperate with your project,' Max insisted. 'I will not even read it.'

That had been Max's last serious conversation with Danielle. There had been polite hellos and cordial chitchat, but no substantive discussions. Max had followed Danielle's progress. How could he avoid it? She was the department's young superstar. Professors had competed to supervise her Ph.D. Though Max admired her work, he regarded her as eccentric. He was content to watch her from a distance — until today. Now he needed her, more than she could ever understand. He could not sort this all through by himself. He needed another head — dared he think, another soul — to help him puzzle through the justice of what he had to do. Of course, there was Abe Ringel, but he was a lawyer who always considered issues from a strictly legal perspective. Max needed someone who could go beyond legalisms — someone who could tell him whether a course of action might be just even if it were illegal. Max knew no human being more qualified to help him than Danielle Grant. Yet even he could not have foreseen that she would become so essential in plotting — and implementing — his revenge against the dying Marcelus Prandus.

13

The Team

Abe knocked on Emma's door, and a young woman wearing a 'Che Guevara' T-shirt appeared.

'Angela Davis Bernstein, I presume,' Abe said, extending his hand.

'Mr Ringel, what are you doing in New Haven? Is everything okay?'

'I'm here to take Emma out for a pizza at Pepe's.'

'Was she expecting you? I think she's out with Jacob.'

'I should have called. It was spur of the moment. I'm on my way down to New York. Do you know where they went?'

'I guess. They tend to spend their time at a European coffee shop on York Street. C'mon, I'll take you there.'

Angela got into Abe's car and they drove the five minutes to the Milano. 'So, are you applying for an internship with Cravath?' Abe asked with a smile.

'No, I'm suing them,' Angela replied dead seriously. 'They're representing the Swiss banks that kept all that gold that Jews left behind during the war, and our Lawyers Guild chapter is trying to attach their legal fees on the ground that it's blood money.'

'What's your legal theory?' Abe asked professionally.

'We're working on that.'

The conversation ended as they entered the café, where Emma and Jacob were deep in conversation.

'Hey, Dad, is everything okay?'

'Everything's fine, sweetie, but I need to talk to you. Actually, I can talk to all three of you.'

'Grab a couple of chairs and order a cappuccino. They make them great here.'

After the waiter took their orders, Abe began. 'It's about Max.'

'Is he okay? I worry about him,' Emma interjected.

'He's okay physically, but something has happened.'

'What?'

'Marcelus Prandus is alive.'

'Oh, my God. Did they find him in Vilna?'

'No. He's living in Salem, Massachusetts — just a few miles from Cambridge.'

'But he's a war criminal. A mass murderer. How can that be?'

'That's what I'm here for. When are your finals over?'

'Two weeks.'

'Would the three of you consider working on this case for a few days?'

'I will!' Emma shouted.

'But we're supposed to go to Amsterdam, to meet my parents,' Jacob whispered.

'We'll go after we finish this. I want to nail that bastard Prandus. Please, Jacob, for me?'

'Yes, yes, I will do it. My parents will understand,' Jacob said.

'How about you, Angie? You would be great. We'll be a team, please,' Emma pleaded.

'Hey, I got nothing better to do. No boyfriend is taking me to Amsterdam or anything. I'm in.'

'We're a team. What do we do? How do we get Prandus's ass in jail?'

'It's not going to be easy. And there is a big timing issue. He's got cancer, and Max wants to see him deported and prosecuted before he dies.'

'I can cut classes and start today,' Emma said.

'No need, sweetie. We have to start with some library research, and there are few better places for that than the Yale library.'

'What should we be looking for?' Jacob

asked. 'I have a lot of experience in research, since I'm working on my thesis.'

'We need several things. First, we need proof that Prandus killed Jews. Max will identify him, but he hasn't seen him in more than fifty years. His ID will have to be corroborated. I'm on my way to New York, where they have files on every European city in which Jews were murdered by the Nazis. I don't know what I'm going to find in those dusty old files. I need your help.'

'What can we do?' Angela asked.

'You kids know how to use computers, and there must be loads of stuff on the Internet. Rendi is going to do some snooping around Salem, where this man lives. But Prandus can't know we're tracking him — not yet. By the end of next week, I want to know more about Marcelus Prandus than his children know.'

'That may not be very much,' Jacob said. 'There are still lots of Nazi collaborators in Amsterdam, and their children think they were all doing ordinary jobs during the war.'

'Find out everything you can. Here's his home phone number. So far that's all I have.'

'It's a start,' Emma said. 'Let's nail the son of a bitch before the angel of death beats us to him.'

14

The Evil King

'What an unexpected pleasure,' said Danielle. 'After so many years. I rushed straight over here after getting your message.'

'Thank you,' said Max. 'I need your help.'

'My help? I know very little about Ecclesiastes. Even after reading your books, I have great difficulty understanding how it made it into the canon.'

'So do I. So do I. We don't know all we should about the canonizers.'

'Is that what you summoned me for? To discuss Ecclesiastes?' Danielle asked.

'No. I need your help with an intellectual puzzle that I am trying to work through. It's in your area of expertise.'

'My area is a three-thousand-year-old book called Genesis. I remember you once lecturing me about not wallowing in the past.'

'Can we put that behind us? I was insensitive. You touched a raw nerve. I would like to move on.'

'That's okay with me. What can I do to help you?'

'Here is the intellectual challenge. It's rather simple. But I don't know that it has ever been adequately addressed by the biblical commentators or even the philosophers.'

'Quite a compliment. Asking me to go where none have gone before,' Danielle said, twisting her ring nervously.

'Here is the question,' Max began in his academic style. 'An evil king orders the killing of an entire village — men, women, children, infants.'

'An all too frequent occurrence in history,' Danielle interjected.

'Yes. The king's evil command is carried out, and the village is destroyed. Then the king is defeated in battle, captured, and put on trial.'

'Before a court, like the Sanhedrin.'

'Precisely. But there is a catch. The king is dying of a painful illness. He laughs at the prospect of execution. What can the court do to punish him?'

'I guess they could torture him. Make it a lingering death.'

Max shook his head in dissatisfaction. 'That would just allow him to become a martyr, enduring pain. It still would not be proportional to the king's evil act of

110

murdering innocent children.'

'What are you driving at, Professor?'

'This. Would it ever be just to hurt the king's children, as a way of taking revenge on what the king did to other people's children?'

Danielle raised her eyebrows in apparent shock over Professor Max Menuchen's suggestion that it might be appropriate to hurt innocent children in order to punish their evil father.

'Well, there is certainly enough historical precedent for killing the children of kings,' Danielle replied. 'The Russian revolutionaries executed all the czar's children to assure that there would be no claimants to the throne. Plenty of other regicides killed the princes and princesses.'

'Ah. But those killings — whatever one should think about them — were designed to prevent future claims, not to punish the king for his past evil.'

'Does that make a difference?'

'To me it makes all the difference in the world. My question is whether it can ever be just to kill an innocent child solely in order to punish his evil parent for killing someone else's innocent child.'

'It does not sound just to me, although history is full of examples of using children to take revenge against parents. In some Arab countries, even today, the blood revenge requires a father whose son was killed to kill the son of the killer. God himself kills Pharaoh's firstborn son — and the firstborn son of every other Egyptian — in order to get at Pharaoh. He kills the innocent child of David and Bathsheba's illicit relationship in order to punish David. But that's God's way. We can't always understand divine justice. For humans, there must be a fairer way than to kill innocent children. Remember Camus' just assassin, who refused to blow up the evil duke's carriage when he saw an innocent child sitting alongside the duke?'

'Ah, yes,' Max replied, 'but he thought he would have another chance to kill the duke when he was alone. What if there is no other chance, no other way? What if the *only* punishment that will be painful to the evil king is to hurt his children?'

'Kant would say it is never proper to use one human being as a means toward achieving justice toward another.'

'Yet he also demanded that every murderer on an island kingdom be put to death before the kingdom disbands so that injustice will not remain unpunished,' Max said in a frustrated voice.

'It seems obvious that human beings are

incapable of solving this problem. It must be left to divine justice,' Danielle snapped in equal frustration.

'But I don't believe in divine justice. After what I saw during the Holocaust, it would be insulting God to believe in him as an omniscient and omnipotent power. It would mean that he had the power to intervene, yet he chose not to.'

'How can you not believe in divine justice?' Danielle asked angrily. 'If you don't believe in God, why do you remain Jewish?'

Max stood up, took a few paces, and then replied in a soft tone, as if he were speaking to himself rather than to Danielle. 'After the Holocaust, it is imperative for a Jew to remain Jewish, even if he has lost faith in God. I still admire many of the teachings of the Bible. As Ecclesiastes says: 'All go into one place; all are of the dust, and all return to dust.' The author of Ecclesiastes was a Jew who also did not believe in divine justice.'

'I know what you don't believe in,' Danielle said stridently. 'Tell me, Max, what you do believe in. Do you believe in human justice?'

'Not after what I have seen humans do to each other without other humans intervening.'

'So you don't believe in divine justice or in human justice. Where does that leave you?'

'It imposes on me a great responsibility to think for myself about personal justice,' Max said, shaking his head. 'That is why I am writing about this intriguing problem.'

'If you did believe in God's justice, you wouldn't have the problem you now face,' said Danielle as if she were trying to convert a young friend.

'Perhaps, but it is *my* hypothetical,' Max responded gently. 'Please try to help me on my own terms. What is personal human justice for my king?'

'I am not certain there can ever be human justice in the case you pose. Perhaps you have to wait for what Isaiah called 'the day of vengeance of our God.' '

'That may be acceptable to you as a believing Christian, but I cannot accept that answer. Please think some more about it. See if the commentators discuss it. Try to come up with something better, please.'

There was a desperation in Max's voice that belied the academic nature of his question.

'Of course,' Danielle said as she turned to leave. 'It's a fascinating hypothetical.' She paused, fixing Max with a penetrating stare. 'A real mind twister,' she continued with a tone of academic cynicism. 'I'll come back in a few days with some research and maybe even an idea or two.'

'I really do value your insights,' said Max. 'This problem is keeping me up at night.'

'I can see that,' Danielle said as she walked into the chilly evening.

15

Doubts

As Danielle pondered the abstract discussion about the hypothetical king, Max's thoughts turned to the real subject.

He knew that Marcelus Prandus did not deserve to die a natural death surrounded by loving children and grandchildren, as so many Nazi murderers had.

Prandus, like Max's hypothetical king, would welcome death. He was dying anyway. A quick execution would spare him and his family the pain of cancer or the religious purgatory of suicide. If Max killed him, he would become his Dr Kevorkian. He recalled an old Yiddish blessing: 'May your family die in the correct order.' Prandus was about to experience this blessing, though he had denied it to so many others, including Max's family.

Max wondered if he was capable of torturing Prandus. He decided he was. All he would have to do was think about the scene in the Ponary Woods, and he would become capable of the most barbaric behavior. As soon as he thought these words, Max realized that even Prandus had not tortured, except perhaps when he'd refused Grandpa Mordechai's request to die first. There seemed to be no hatred in Prandus, Max recalled. Only a maniacal obsession with seeds and genes.

No, he would not torture Prandus. He would not kill him. That was too good for the man who had murdered his family. There was only one just punishment for Marcelus Prandus. Max shuddered as he silently pronounced sentence on the man who had shot his child: Max Menuchen would kill one of Marcelus Prandus's grandchildren. A chill ran through Max's body as he pictured himself killing an innocent child. Could Max Menuchen, a just man, actually murder an innocent child? He thought of Ivan's abstract question in *The Brothers Karamazov*: would it be just to kill a little child if that were the only way to create a happy world? Then he thought of the very real question confronted by Jews hiding from their Nazi pursuers: would it be just to kill a child whose cries would endanger an entire family? Many families had had to answer that excruciating question by smothering an innocent baby.

Max began to consider how he might go about killing Marcelus Prandus's grandchild. He could run him down with his car, killing him instantly and painlessly. The child would never know what happened. The child would not suffer. Marcelus Prandus would suffer, because he would know *why* his grandchild had been killed. Prandus would know that it was his own fault his grandchild's life had been taken. That would be just punishment. It would not be quantitatively proportional to the evils he had inflicted, but it would be qualitatively proportional.

Max understood that others would suffer — the murdered child's innocent parents and siblings. But suffering by innocent loved ones was an inevitable by-product of justice. Besides, the family would blame the old man and his evil past for the death of their child and brother, which would increase the suffering of Marcelus Prandus, and that would make it worth it. Marcelus Prandus would die miserable and unhappy, cursing the day he was born. That would be exquisite justice.

There was only one way for Max to learn whether he was indeed capable of killing a Prandus grandchild. He would have to see him with his own eyes, confront him, follow him — stalk him. But first, of course, he would have to be sure that this Marcelus Prandus was the right one, not like the other Prandus he had seen on TV.

* * *

It was a simple matter for Max to get close to Marcelus Prandus. He found out where he lived by calling the phone number given to him by Paul Prandus, pretending to be a visiting priest from Lithuania who wanted to put Marcelus Prandus on a mailing list for free religious books from the old country. Max then walked up and down English Street in Salem, the block on which Prandus lived, until the old man emerged for an afternoon walk to the Lithuanian-American Social Club. As soon as Max saw him he knew. Though he was stockier and grayer, there was no mistaking the face — the face Max had seen a thousand times in his dreams. Max began to shake in fear and anticipation. It took all of his self-control not to attack the tall man in the street, but he knew that giving in to his impulse for immediate gratification would prevent him from exacting the revenge he needed. Max thought of Goethe's admonition to act 'Without haste, but without rest.'

Max realized that he could no longer

postpone the deed. He must act — soon, this week. Time was running out on Marcelus Prandus. Who could say when he would die of the cancer? He must not be allowed to die without experiencing at least part of what Max had experienced in the Ponary Woods.

It was easy for Max to locate the school attended by the eight-year-old Marc Prandus. It took only a couple of days for Max to figure out Marc's routine. He walked four blocks to school every morning — alone. He had to cross one major intersection with traffic lights and a crossing guard. How easy it was, Max thought, to plan, even rehearse, a murder. Surprisingly, it all came so naturally to Max, the most unlikely of criminals. As he drove his ageing Volvo back to Cambridge, Max could almost hear Reb Mordechai whispering, '*Nekama, nekama*,' giving him instructions. The real test, however, was still a few days away. Like Raskolnikov, Max would not know whether he could actually kill an innocent human being until the moment was at hand.

That evening Max was to learn something that resolved all of his doubts in favor of even more deadly action.

16

Tracking Prandus

'All right, what have we got?' Abe asked as he paced around his large work office with the picture windows facing the Charles River. The room was sparsely furnished. A large stand-up desk faced the window. Because Abe rarely sat when he worked, there were no chairs around. He would see clients in the library, around a large oak table. Rendi was perched on a low file cabinet. Emma, Jacob, and Angela sat on the floor.

Rendi began. 'We know where he lives. He has two children — one a lawyer, the other a stockbroker. He belongs to some Lithuanian social club. Votes Republican. Doesn't like blacks or gays. Goes to church. Used to be a mechanic. Retired. A widower. Two grandchildren. Belongs to the Rotary Club. No criminal record. He's a regular Archie Bunker.'

'What about Vilna?'

'I researched that,' Emma said, looking at her notes. 'It turns out that it was really two cities living together in an uneasy

121

proximity. Vilnius, the capital, was a hotbed of nationalism and fascism. Vilna, the city's Jewish name, was called 'the Jerusalem of the North,' because of its large number of highly educated Jews.'

'What happened to them?'

'Even before the Nazis occupied Lithuania, the nationalists targeted the Jews. Here, let me read from a directive issued by their leader: 'There must be no possibility of continued Jewish existence in Lithuania.' '

'Haskell told me they accomplished their goal,' Abe noted.

'Haskell was right,' Emma continued. 'Here is an account I found in the *Los Angeles Times*: 'While the Germans were fighting the Soviets for control of Lithuania, Lithuanian nationalists formed para-military units and killed thousands of Jews in a matter of days. After the Nazis took power, many young Lithuanians volunteered for the execution squads in killing fields such as the Ponary Woods. Within months, 95 percent of Lithuanian's nearly quarter of a million Jews were dead. Most weren't even sent to the death camps. The Lithuanians couldn't wait to kill them. They were taken to the woods, lined up beside pits, and shot.' '

'How did they manage to kill so many Jews in so little time?' Rendi asked.

'I want you to look at this segment from *Sixty Minutes*,' Emma said. 'It will shock you.'

Emma popped a video into the office machine that hung from the ceiling. The face of Antanas Kenstavicious flashed on the screen. He had been a former police chief in Lithuania who had moved to Canada after the war.

He had a warm smile and a large, gentle face. He could have played Santa Claus in the local Christmas pageant. But then the old man described what the militia had done to the Jewish families he helped to round up during that April of 1942:

We commanded them to lay down, and Jews would come and lay down . . . no screaming. They was like a sheep. And then coming the commander, they shoot, bang, and they fall down . . . they fall in the ditch . . . One o'clock finished. No more Jews[1].

Emma began to sob softly. Jacob put an arm around her shoulder.

---

[1] *60 Minutes*, Feb. 2, 1997 (vol. XXIX, No. 20): 'Canada's Dark Secret.'

'How did that bastard escape to Canada?' Angela asked.

'It was easy right after the war. Canada welcomed Nazis without asking any hard questions, as long as they were anti-Communists,' Rendi replied.

'After the *Sixty Minutes* piece, didn't they try to deport him or prosecute him?' Abe wondered.

'He died shortly after the piece aired. He was eighty-five years old,' Emma said. 'That's what I'm afraid may happen to Prandus.'

'How did Prandus get into America?' Abe asked.

'I checked into that,' said Rendi. 'He swore under oath that he had been a professional soccer player during the war years. Not a word about any militia.'

'That's great!' Abe exclaimed, pounding his desk. 'If we can prove he killed Max's family, we can get him deported for lying on his visa application.'

'Like Al Capone was convicted for lying on his tax return,' Angela interjected.

'Yeah, but even if that were to happen, he would go back to Lithuania and be treated as a hero. There's a story on the Web about Nazi mass murderers living the life of Riley in Vilnius, even now,' Emma said.

'At least he will die apart from his family — if we can prove he was a killer. Any luck on that?'

'I haven't found a single reference to Marcelus Prandus in all the files I accessed. There are other names of Lithuanian collaborators, but Prandus's name is absent. Is that bad, Mr Ringel?'

'It's not fatal. Remember that absence of evidence is not necessarily evidence of absence,' Abe said pedantically, repeating an argument he frequently made to jurors. 'Keep looking.'

'I have one good lead,' Jacob said. 'The Russians have begun to open their wartime files, and I have a friend who is studying in Moscow for the year. I asked him to look through the war archives. I should have something in a week.'

'Tell him to make it a day,' Abe demanded. 'This guy Prandus may not live that long.'

'I'll try.'

'What else?' Abe asked.

'How is Max doing?' Emma asked.

'Not too well. Knowing that this murderer has been living nearby has really thrown him for a loop. We have to do something soon.'

'Can you go to Washington with what we've got?' Emma asked impatiently. 'Max can ID Prandus.'

'Still, we're going to need corroboration. After the Demjanjuk fiasco — remember, Ivan the Terrible? — they're a little gunshy down there about uncorroborated eyewitness accounts. We're not ready yet. We need more.'

'What about his statement that he was a soccer player? Isn't that enough?' Angela asked.

'Not quite. Maybe he was a soccer player — in his spare time when he wasn't busy killing Jews. Unless we can find documentary evidence that he killed Jews, there is nothing other than Max's uncorroborated account to show he was lying. We're counting on your friend in Russia, Jacob. I hope he comes through — and quickly.'

17

The smoking Gun:
A Few Days Later

'Mr Ringel, Mr Ringel — we have it!' Jacob was running as he broke into Abe's office with Emma behind him. In his hand there was a sheaf of fax paper.

'These files just came in from Moscow over the office fax. I've glanced at them, and Marcelus Prandus's name is all over them.'

'Bingo! Quick, let me see them.'

Abe began to read as Jacob and Emma peered over his shoulder. 'It's the transcript of a trial, but the defendant is a guy named General Heinrich Gruber. So far no mention of Prandus.'

'Read on,' Jacob said breathlessly. 'Gruber was the German Gestapo chief in Vilna. At the end of the war, he was captured by Soviet troops and put on trial. The names of some of the Lithuanian collaborators were mentioned at the trial. Gruber's defense was that the Lithuanians did the killings themselves.'

'Here, here,' Abe said, pointing to the name of Marcelus Prandus. 'Here it is.'

Abe began to read from the transcript.

'On the morning of April 3, 1942, I received a report from Captain Marcelus Prandus of the Lithuanian Auxiliary Police about an action on the previous night. He reported that his men had arrested 126 Communists and traitors and took them to the Ponary Woods for interrogation. When they arrived at the woods the collaborators and traitors attempted to escape and to resist. They were all shot and buried in collective graves.'

'The bastard,' Emma exclaimed. 'Trying to blame the victims.'

'That was a standard claim,' Jacob said. 'I came across it many times in my research. Jews, no matter how young or old, were always referred to as Communists or traitors, and they were invariably trying to escape when they were shot. The Soviets rejected the claims after digging up some of the common graves and finding babies and close-up gunshot wounds to the back of the head.'

'Can anyone trust the Soviets? Remember this was the time of Stalin,' Abe commented.

'Most historians believe these findings were fairly accurate, especially when they were based on hard evidence such as pathology reports. When only confessions were relied on, they were suspect,' said Jacob.

'Okay, let me read on.'

Abe continued to read through General Gruber's testimony, finding reports of additional actions conducted by Captain Prandus.

'Here's something interesting,' Abe noted. 'Listen to this question and answer.

'Question: Do you know the whereabouts of Captain Prandus? Answer: I was told that he was living in Vilnius for a while after the war. But when I tried to summon him as a witness, I learned that he and his mother had escaped to America.'

'Well, this is certainly enough to take to Washington,' Emma said.

'More than enough,' Abe exclaimed enthusiastically. 'I'll make the call right now. In the meantime, you two star researchers read through the rest of the file and highlight every single reference to Prandus.'

'You got it. This is great. I feel like a real lawyer.'

'You are a real lawyer, sweetie. You too, Jacob. And this is a very real case. We're going to get this bastard deported — before he dies,' Abe said with a look of determination that Emma recognized from past cases. 'He's going to die alone, somewhere in Lithuania, or in handcuffs on the way there. Now you kids go back to the library, while I call my contact at the Justice Department.'

★ ★ ★

'Can I please speak to Martin Mandel in the Office of Special Investigations?' Abe asked, and waited to be connected.

'Mandel, OSI,' came the clipped response a moment later.

'Hi, my name is Abe Ringel.'

'I know who you are, Mr Ringel. Haskell Levine used to do some work with us. He told me about you. It's a pleasure speaking to you.'

'Well, I'm afraid I'm calling about a rather unpleasant subject.'

'That's all we deal with down here. What do you have?'

'A man named Marcelus Prandus. Lives in Salem, Massachusetts. Came to the U.S. in 1947, claiming he was a professional soccer player. My client, Max Menuchen — an old friend of Haskell Levine's by the way — will testify that Prandus was a captain in the Lithuanian Auxiliary Police and that he personally shot several members of Max's family, including his pregnant wife and baby.'

'Was he an eyewitness?'

'Yes. Prandus shot him, too, but he survived.'

'We need corroboration. An eyewitness who was shot isn't enough. Not after Demjanjuk.'

'We have corroboration.'

'What kind?'

'A Soviet trial transcript. Hot off the press. Just released in Moscow.'

'Fax it to me.'

'I will. But there's a rub.'

'There always is. What is it this time?'

'Prandus is dying of pancreatic cancer. He's probably got only a few months to live.'

'That's a serious rub. It takes time to put together a case, even as clear a case as this one seems to be. We need to get the transcript certified. With the Russian bureaucracy, it could take a few months.'

'Can't you speed it up? The guy is dying.'

'We can try, but it's still going to take some time. Prandus is going to get himself a lawyer. You certainly understand that. And his lawyer is going to play the delay game. You know about that, too, Mr Ringel.'

'Can you arrest him in the meantime?'

'Does he have a family, roots in the community?'

'I'm afraid he does.'

'No way a judge is going to deny him bail. He'll be allowed to stay at home.'

'Is there *anything* we can do quickly?'

'I'm afraid not. I have to be honest with you. There's no way we could get this guy in custody or deported in less than six months to a year.'

'He'll be dead by then.'

'I'm sorry. That happens to us all in time. Our colleagues in Canada just had a case — it was on *Sixty Minutes* — of another Lithuanian killer. He died at home with his family before they could make a case. And he confessed on television. I'm sorry, Mr Ringel, but it's probably too late for the legal system to do much to Captain Prandus. Let's hope there's a hell. It's the only punishment Prandus is going to get.'

'Damn!' Abe shouted as he hung up the phone. He ran toward the library.

'Bad news,' he exclaimed as he threw open the library door and saw Emma crying in Jacob's arms. 'What's the matter, sweetie?' he asked. 'Is everything all right?'

'No, it's not,' Emma said, unable to control her emotions. 'It's about Sarah Chava. We found out what happened to her. I'm going to kill that bastard Prandus. Don't ever let me near him. I'm going to kill him with my bare hands.'

'What happened to her, sweetie? We're going to have to tell Max.'

'He raped her,' Emma cried, remembering her own ordeal. 'Prandus raped her. Then he . . . ' But she couldn't go on. She began to cry as Abe tried to comfort her.

'Here,' Jacob said, pointing to a highlighted paragraph. 'It's the testimony of a member of Prandus's group who gave evidence against General Gruber. It's all right here.'

Abe read the page quickly, gasped, and said, 'I need to tell Max about this right now.'

He ran out of the office holding the transcript, trying to suppress his rage at Marcelus Prandus and his frustration at the inability of the legal system to bring him to justice.

18

Sarah Chava

Abe hurried to Max's house, clutching the files. He pounded on the door, wondering how he would break the terrible news to his old friend.

Max came to the door with a teacup in his hand.

'Abe, what's wrong? You look as if you ran all the way here.'

'I did. I have news. It's very bad.'

'They can't do anything about Prandus,' Max said fatalistically. 'It's too late. I expected that. You did your best — I appreciate it.'

'You're right. I spoke to the head of the Nazi-hunting unit in Washington. It would take at least six months.'

'Prandus will be dead by then,' Max said, raising his voice slightly.

'It's worse than that,' said Abe, moving nearer to his friend and looking into his eyes. 'I'm afraid I have some even more distressing information.'

'What could be more distressing?'

'It's about Sarah Chava.'

'She's dead. You have proof?'

'Here, let me read what Jacob just received from Moscow. Sit down. This is going to be very difficult.'

Max sat behind his desk and put his head in his hands as Abe began to read from the testimony of Jarus Plunk, a member of the Lithuanian Auxiliary Police.

'A sixteen-year-old girl, family name Menuchen, was raped by Marcelus Prandus and then turned over to the local German Gestapo chief, Heinrich Gruber, who also abused her and then sent her to Auschwitz to work as a prostitute for the German guards.' Abe then turned to a paragraph from the court's findings: 'Menuchen (female) was not among the prisoners liberated at the end of the war and is presumed to have been gassed after a few months along with other Jewish women who had been forced to work as prostitutes.'

Max cried out loud as he imagined what his teenage sister had been through in the months or years between Ponary Woods and the time she finally died. Did she try to escape? Had she become pregnant? Did she have an abortion? Did she contract a venereal disease? Had she been driven crazy by her tormentors? 'If only she had died along with the rest of the family,' Max moaned as these horrible images rushed through his mind. 'If only I had also died along with the rest of the family.'

Then he began to shake. He felt dizzy and nauseated, immobilized by fear and powerlessness. This feeling of paralysis was familiar. His mind went blank. Then, suddenly, he understood. His body was replicating the same feelings he had experienced as Marcelus Prandus pronounced the death sentence on his family.

Abe, concerned that Max might harm himself, tried to comfort him, but he could not allay the old man's anguish.

'Abe, I must be by myself now,' Max said, gasping for breath between his cries.

Abe walked toward the door, powerless to do anything, since it was clear that Max needed to be alone with his memories.

19

The Accident

After Abe closed the door behind him, Max felt himself losing whatever control he had been able to retain. He ran upstairs to his bedroom and found the old tea canister containing the photograph of Sarah Chava at the circumcision of Max's son. She was fifteen in the picture, and her smile was as sweet as Max had remembered it in real life. He rarely looked at the picture because it brought back such terrible memories. But now he could not stop himself.

He gazed at the photograph for what seemed like hours, imagining what his sister had gone through before her death. First he cried, then he screamed, and finally he pounded his fists against the table until they became swollen. It was as if he were compressing all his accumulated grief, anger, and frustration into one long night. He cried, screamed, and pounded until he glimpsed the first light of dawn. Then he took the picture of Sarah Chava and walked out of his house and toward his car. He was crying and shaking so severely that he was not certain he could drive. He carefully placed the picture on the visor above the driver's seat, turned the ignition key, and pointed his car in the direction of Salem. A few minutes later he was on Storrow Drive. As he looked down at the speedometer, he realized he was driving at seventy miles per hour. Never before had Max Menuchen exceeded the speed limit. As he drove, the bitter and confused ravings of King Lear rushed into his head: 'I will have such revenges . . . I will do such things, — What they are yet I know not, — but they shall be the terrors of the earth.' His grandfather's last word — *nekama* — pounded repeatedly in his head like a mantra.

The events in Ponary Woods were no longer a half century ago. They were now. Sarah Chava's rape and murder had just happened. What Max would do now would not be in cold blood. He would be like the avenger described in the Bible: 'If the blood avenger puts the killer to death, it is not an act of murder.' The Bible understood that hot-blooded revenge killings were part of human nature. The rabbis of the Talmud said that blood revenge was an obligation.

The fate of his little sister made it clear to Max that he was now capable of doing anything to Marcelus Prandus. The die had been cast. Max accelerated the car to seventy-five, to eighty . . .

* * *

The next day Max Menuchen woke up in his bed about noon — bruised and aching. He looked out the window at his old Volvo, and he saw that its front had been dented. For the moment he could not recall what had caused the bruises and the denting. Had he actually run down Marcelus Prandus's grandchild?

Then it came back to him in a flash. He had crashed the Volvo into a road barrier. He had not killed anyone. At least not yet. He had made up his mind. There was no turning back.

20

The Maimonidean Solution

At about the same time Max was waking up, Danielle was looking for him in his office. When she learned that Max had failed to show up for his morning class, she rushed over to his house. The discussion about the evil king had worried her. And now Max — who never missed class — was not at school.

At first Max refused to come to the door. He was so distraught over the events of the past eighteen hours — the news of Sarah Chava, his driving to Salem, his accident — that he did not want to see anyone.

Danielle persisted, standing outside and refusing to go away. Eventually, Max relented, after cleaning himself up and changing his clothes.

Max opened the door to Danielle. She gazed around his small home decorated with mahogany antique furniture from Europe. Max stood unsteadily, even paler than usual.

'I had a slight accident,' he explained. 'Now I need some rest. I appreciate your calling on me, but please allow me to be alone.'

'I think I've solved your problem of the evil king,' she said, ignoring his invitation to leave. 'Your instincts were right on target. I found the answer in a twelfth-century commentary on the Book of Job by a brilliant Jewish doctor who lived in Egypt. I call it the 'Maimonidean solution.' '

'I'm sure it is brilliant, but I have decided not to write the article after all. The matter has become moot. I'm sorry for having put you through the task of researching it.'

'Max,' Danielle began, 'you must stop insulting my intelligence. I know this has nothing to do with any article you are writing. Remember that I did research on you. I know what happened to your family. The terrible events are memorialized in Yad Vashem.'

'What do you know?' Max's tone was sharp.

'That nearly every Jewish family in Vilna was murdered. Yours had to be among them. I've known from the very beginning. All that stuff about an article — about justice — it's a rationalization. You need revenge. It's psychological. Revenge is the most powerful of human motivations. But you want to be able to rationalize it as justice.'

'I do want justice,' Max said defensively.

'Call it what you want. I think I have a solution to your problem. First you must trust me. You must tell me exactly what is going on.'

'I cannot involve you.'

'I'm already involved. I want to help you. I need to help you — as much for my own sake as for yours.'

'I found him,' Max blurted out. He told her about Marcelus Prandus, the murders, the rape.

'Oh, my God,' Danielle exclaimed, stepping back and placing a hand over her mouth.

Max was shaking again. He began to shout in Yiddish, *'Nekama!'* and, *'Ganze mishpoche!'*

Danielle grabbed the trembling Max by his shoulders.

'What are you saying?' she demanded. 'Tell me.'

'I have decided I must kill the entire Prandus family,' Max said intently, his eyes looking wildly past Danielle. 'I will wipe out their seed, as he wiped out ours. I have no choice. My grandfather's soul cries out for revenge. *Nekama* — 'take revenge' — was his last wish. My entire family cries out, especially Sarah Chava.' As he spoke his sister's name, Max began to sob. Then he wiped away his tears and looked into Danielle's eyes as he spoke.

'In two days it will be Marcelus Prandus's birthday,' he continued in a whisper. 'I found out from a shopkeeper in Salem that the entire Prandus family will be gathered together for dinner. Just like the Menuchen family was gathered for dinner on Passover in 1942. I will knock at the door, just like Marcelus Prandus knocked on our door. When it is opened for me, I will throw in a bomb. Originally I planned to kill his eight-year-old grandson. Now I believe that killing many people will be easier than killing one. The Nazis certainly understood that.'

Danielle held Max more tightly around his shoulder and looked directly into his tearful eyes. 'Max, you're not a Nazi. You're not a mass murderer. Your plan will not work. Please listen to me. I know more about firearms than you do. Guns have been in my family since the Civil War. I target shoot near my cottage in the Berkshires, and I make my own gunpowder. If you try to blow up the Prandus family, you'll only succeed in blowing yourself up.'

'That would not be so terrible,' Max said.

'Look,' Danielle said in her take-charge voice. 'Even if you were to blow up the entire Prandus family, that would not be proportional to what Prandus did to your family. They were forced to watch each other die. The patriarch — your grandfather — was forced to watch as each of his descendants died. Your plan will not achieve proportional justice.'

'I must do something,' Max insisted. 'Don't try to stop me.'

'I won't try to stop you. I have no such right. I will show you how to do it better. The Maimonidean solution is the perfect revenge. I will show you how to achieve proportional justice. On one condition. You must allow me to help you. I came here today simply to tell you about the solution I had found, but now, after hearing what happened to your family, especially your sister, I must help you.'

'Why would you be willing to risk your freedom, even your life, to help me?'

'I have my reasons.'

'Then you must share them with me before I decide. I have always believed that you are hiding something from me. Now I am certain. There must be something in your life that is pushing you into joining with me in this dangerous quest for revenge. Your abstract interest in biblical justice doesn't explain why you would be willing to risk everything to help me get revenge against a man who did nothing to you.'

'Please don't ask me,' Danielle whispered.

'Why not?' Max asked. 'You were prepared to probe my private life. Why do you shut me off from yours?'

Danielle looked deeply into Max's eyes and spoke gently. 'I see that I must tell you what I've never told anyone before, not even my mother. If we're to work together, you're entitled to know.'

Danielle paused for a moment. 'When I was fourteen years old, I was going out with a black boy in my high school. When my grandfather found out about it, he came into my room one night and threatened to kill me if I went out with a 'nigger' again. He slapped me. He demanded to know if I had sexual intercourse with him. I told him the truth — that I had not. He wouldn't believe me. He said he would see for himself.' Danielle looked away from Max as she continued. 'He started screaming that I was not a virgin. Then he raped me. My own grandfather. He said that I was too good for any 'nigger' and that it would be better to have my own grandfather's child than the child of a black.'

'Oh, my God,' Max said, placing his arms gently around Danielle. 'How could a grandfather do that to his own flesh and blood?'

Danielle began to weep. It was the first time Max ever saw her cry. 'I became pregnant and had an abortion. I did it all alone. It was against my deepest religious beliefs. I killed a child. My child. My grandfather's child. I justified it by believing that the child would have carried my grandfather's genes and would have been a monster like him. But it wasn't the baby's fault. My child could have lived.' She sighed, wiping away her tears. 'Then I became obsessed with my genetic heritage. If my grandfather was capable of such evil, was I? Could I become the Mr Hyde he had become? If the answer was yes, I was doomed. If the answer was no, I had killed my baby unnecessarily.'

'You are destroying yourself. You are not to blame.'

'Maybe,' Danielle said in a shaking voice. 'But like you, I need revenge. I could never take revenge against my grandfather. He died shortly after my abortion. He didn't even know I had become pregnant. He pretended that nothing had happened. He died peacefully in his sleep. I am taking my revenge against another rapist, the man who raped your sister. When I see Prandus suffer, I will see my grandfather suffer,' Danielle said, her fists clenched, her eyes glazed. 'Now do you understand my passion for what we are doing?'

'Thank you for helping me to understand not only you, but me as well,' said Max.

The two professors embraced, holding each other for a long time. Max broke the silence. 'Now please tell me about your plan — and then leave. I must do it by myself. I cannot involve you any further.'

'You can't do it by yourself. I have to help. It will take two people. I will merely be assisting. Give me until tomorrow morning to come up with a detailed scenario. I promise you it will work.'

Max was beginning to understand the apparent inconsistencies in Danielle's life: religious Christian, gun enthusiast, film-maker, granddaughter of a monster, believer in genetic destiny, incest survivor. It was a prescription for psychosis. Yet she had managed to keep it all together — at least on the surface. The rage, the hate, the pent-up frustration, all were being kept in check by her external successes. Now they would explode like the images of creation in her video, if Max were to refuse her request — her demand — to partake of revenge. Just as he needed his *nekama*, she needed hers. They were more alike than he had ever imagined.

'We will meet tomorrow morning,' Max said.

★ ★ ★

The next morning, when Danielle demonstrated the step-by-step implementation of her Maimonidean solution, Max agreed immediately, on the condition that if they were caught, he would shoulder the entire blame. After learning Danielle's brilliant plan, Max was now certain that with her assistance he could finally secure his just revenge. He was ecstatic.

For the next two days, Max and Danielle monitored every move made by the Prandus family.

Max drove his old Volvo up and down English Street in Salem, where Marcelus Prandus lived in a small bungalow, while Danielle videotaped the old man's routine. Max also did some shopping in the neighborhood stores, pretending to be a visiting relative and learning details of the Prandus family. They also stalked and videotaped the children on their way to school, to their friends, and to visit their grandfather. It was a simple task, since the Pranduses lived within a few blocks of each other. In the evenings, Max and Danielle reviewed the videotapes and planned the next step. Danielle had shown Max how to coordinate his actions with her videotaping during their planning sessions at Max's house.

Max was nervous as the time approached for the next, and most critical, phase of the plan. Danielle reassured him that nothing could go wrong as long as they stuck to the carefully worked-out blueprint. Max did not know whether he was more frightened at the prospect of failure or success. He did know that there was no backing out now; they must move on to the next step.

21

Worry

'I'm worried about Max,' Abe whispered to Rendi as they lay in bed. He sat up and said, 'I'm going to call him.'

As Abe started to get out of bed, Rendi tugged on his pajamas. 'Come back to bed. It's two o'clock in the morning. You can't call him. He's an old man. He'll have a heart attack if you wake him. Call him in the morning.'

'I can't sleep.'

'That's obvious. You've been tossing and turning all night,' Rendi said, sitting up.

'I think he may do something to himself. I can only imagine his frustration. I failed him, Rendi. God failed him. The legal system failed him. There's nothing we can do. It's so damned unfair,' Abe said, his voice cracking. 'I can't stand it. I feel like a helpless amateur. We've got to come up with something.'

'Can't we at least expose Prandus? Write a column. Call a press conference. At least his neighbors will know.'

'They'll all say he seems such a nice, quiet person,' said Abe. 'They won't believe it. Look at Demjanjuk. He became a hero to his neighbors.'

'Some will look at him funny. It will cause him some distress. His own children will wonder. He will suffer.'

'You're missing the point,' Abe said, getting back under the covers. 'I don't give a damn about Prandus. He's history, as far as I'm concerned. I care about Max. A press conference won't help Max. It will just make him more frustrated, especially when he sees that Prandus's neighbors say nice things about him.'

'Sometimes, Abe, the doctor can't save the patient. Don't blame yourself. You've left no stone unturned for Max.'

Abe didn't even hear what Rendi had said. 'I wish Haskell were still alive. He'd know what to do. I'm at a loss. First thing in the morning, I'll go talk to Max. Maybe he can stay with us for a couple of days.'

'Okay. At least you'll be able to get some rest with Max in the next room,' Rendi said as she put the pillow over hear head and tried to get back to sleep.

Part Four

Nekama

22

The Pranduses' Last Supper

'Marc, now that you're eight, you are old enough to say the blessing. Have you learned a nice prayer in school?' Marcelus Prandus, the patriarch, asked his grandson and namesake.

'Yes, Grandpa Chelli,' the blond-haired boy replied, calling his grandfather by his family nickname.

The old man listened proudly as the child recited a blessing.

Birthdays were Marcelus Prandus's favorite times. Birthday parties were so American, and Marcelus Prandus was an American patriot. He loved what America had done for his children. It really is, he often thought, the land of opportunity. His children had been educated and had succeeded beyond his wildest expectations. His two grandchildren were all-American kids, the boy playing baseball and excelling in computers, the girl playing with Barbie dolls and ice-skating. He had kept from his children and grandchildren his hatred of Jews and blacks.

He would complain about the 'Yids' and the 'niggers' at the Lithuanian-American Social Club where he gathered with his friends from the old country. In front of his children and grandchildren, there were no bad words about any group. This was America, not Lithuania, and such hatreds would be a barrier to achieving the American dream.

Not that it was all perfect. Peter, his younger son, rarely went to church and broke the family tradition by sending his daughter to public, rather than parochial, school. He was no atheist, just lazy about religion.

Paul, on the other hand, was quite religious, but in the wrong way. He sent his son to a progressive Catholic school. As far as Marcelus was concerned, he took the teachings of Jesus too literally. He was an active voice of criticism within the Lithuanian church, demanding more aggressive actions on behalf of the poor and the dispossessed. The conflict between Marcelus and Paul reached a head when Paul helped to organize an AIDS walk-a-thon. Marcelus was furious, arguing that AIDS was 'God's way of telling homosexuals that they were immoral.'

Still, Paul was Marcelus's favorite. Like his father before him, Paul had been a star athlete — football, baseball, soccer. Tall and strikingly handsome, Paul had worked out with his father at the local YMCA since he was ten years old. After school he would help out in the car repair shop his father owned. On Sundays they attended church together and then — when the Red Sox were in town — they would drive down to Fenway Park for an afternoon of baseball, beer, and hot dogs.

Marcelus had wanted Paul to become a policeman, and as a child Paul had had fantasies about wearing a uniform, carrying a gun, and catching the bad guys. Paul had belonged to the Police Athletic League, and Marcelus was an honorary 'pal' and a volunteer soccer coach.

During his high school years Paul was a mischievous adolescent, fistfighting, always getting in trouble over girls, and drinking. He was known for his short temper, loud voice, and cursing. At the slightest provocation his face would flush a bright crimson and the veins on his neck would protrude.

Marcelus knew that Paul had his first sexual experience at fourteen — with an older cheerleader — and it made him proud. Paul had his first suspension from school at fifteen. Nothing all that serious — at least in Marcelus's view. Just a fistfight with a classmate. In fact, Marcelus admired Paul's spunk. 'At least he's not a fag, like some of those kids with glasses who sit in the library all day,' he would brag to his buddies at the Lithuanian club.

Then everything had changed. Paul's high school coach arranged for a football scholarship to Holy Cross, where Paul played freshman football and studied history. Marcelus remained in close touch with Paul during his freshman year. In his sophomore year Paul registered for a class in twentieth-century European history. Halfway through the semester the teacher began to lecture on the Soviet and German occupations of the Baltic nations, including Lithuania. After the second lecture Paul dropped the course and told his father that he was changing his major to government. Soon thereafter he quit football and became a serious student. His interest was prelaw. He began to grow apart from his father. In the middle of his sophomore year he met his future wife, an Irish Catholic woman from South Boston, and went steady with her throughout college and law school, driving him even further away from Marcelus. He attended Boston College Law School and then opened a small criminal law practice in Salem. He married, bought a modest home, and settled down a few blocks from Marcelus.

Though Paul remained in close physical proximity to his father, it was not like high school. But even though he had taken a different path, the old man rejoiced that his son had chosen to settle down a stone's throw from his father, especially since it gave the old man the opportunity to see his grandson every day.

Paul was now a professional. He had a first-rate Catholic school education, which had emphasized the teachings of the social gospel. He dressed like a lawyer, talked with an educated accent, and reflected the progressive beliefs of many in his generation of Catholics. He was married to a woman who looked ten years older than she was, and he remained faithful to her despite her diminishing interest in sex and his many opportunities and increasing appetites. Countless times Marcelus had commented on his son's wasted opportunities, assuring him that 'what a man's wife doesn't know won't hurt anyone.' Yet something in his father's attitude made Paul steadfast in his own fidelity.

From the time he enrolled in law school, Paul always spoke in a near whisper, to the point where people had to cup their ears to hear him. It was almost as if he had adopted this manner of speech in reaction to his youthful bravado. Indeed, his entire adult personality seemed calculated to control his childhood exuberance. Even his clothing reflected restraint. He always wore a suit, usually with a vest. His bulging muscles made his clothing seem tight and constraining. He tried hard to look utterly conventional — well mannered, soft-spoken, modest, and conservative.

Beneath his three-piece suit, his lawyerly demeanor, and his close family life, however, there was a controlled rage. Women at work viewed him as virile but shy, waiting to burst out of his self-imposed constraints. He was never flirtatious and tried not to send any message of availability, though his good looks and athletic body made him a subject of water-cooler banter. Only Paul knew how tightly wound he was and how tenuous was his control over his inner turmoil. Something was eating at him, but he did not want to know what it was. He would never seek counseling. He was satisfied to live his life of external contentment — to control his passions — without addressing the internal conflicts. He feared that someday, something might happen that would cause the rage within him to erupt. He hoped to be able to postpone it for as long as possible. So far it was working tolerably well. His wife, his son, his friends, and his colleagues saw an apparently well-balanced, normal, contented man.

Marcelus knew that Paul was in conflict with himself. He had seen the change. He could feel the tension. He had loved the young Paul — the rambunctious Paul, the Paul who had been so much like the young Marcelus. He felt uncomfortable with the older Paul — the elitist who lectured his father about the 'true' teachings of Jesus and the social gospel, which Marcelus characterized as 'liberal bullshit disguised as Christianity.'

Birthdays were the favorite time for family gatherings. Christmas and Easter always ended in arguments over religion. There was nothing to argue about on birthdays. One of the children would recite a prayer, Marcelus would respond, thanking God for bringing him to America, remembering his parents, and hoping for a good year, and after that the subject of religion was closed. There were a few family traditions, such as the uncovering of the turkey. When Marcelus's wife, Greta, was alive, she always instead on a ham for birthdays, because she did not know how to cook a turkey properly. It always came out dry whatever she did, while her hams — made from an old country recipe — were succulent and flavorful. The year she died, Marcelus took it upon himself to learn to cook a moist turkey. Every year it got better, until by now it was 'restaurant quality', as Marcelus bragged. He loved to bring it in covered by a gigantic silver food warmer. Everyone at the table had to stand in rapt attention as Marcelus lifted the warmer, revealing the golden brown bird, which was then carried around the table to applause and oohs and ahs. The male grandchild was then honored by being invited to help Grandpa Chelli carve the ceremonial first slice of the breast.

'Come, Marc. You have the honor of the first slice. But be careful with the knife. It's sharp.'

There was another family tradition as well. Marcelus Prandus would produce an old chalice from Lithuania and drink a toast from it. It was some kind of secret Jewish chalice, he explained, that 'an old Jew once gave me for good luck.' Marcelus Prandus believed strongly in luck. After all, he was blessed with so much luck — a wonderful family, he knew he was leaving behind a great legacy. Marcelus Prandus drank from the old chalice and prayed quietly for a painless death for himself and long lives for his children and grandchildren.

As the old man replaced the beautiful old chalice in its box, Paul wondered again why an old Jew would give so valuable a gift to his father.

This birthday party for Marcelus was a particularly poignant one for the Prandus family. It was the first since he had been diagnosed with cancer. Though no one spoke of it, the adults knew that this birthday party would be Grandpa Chelli's last. He might make it to Christmas, his doctors told Paul, but it was unlikely that he would see Easter.

Despite this reality, or perhaps because of it, Marcelus Prandus was in a wonderful mood as he surveyed his family.

If his death proved painful, he could bear it. He was a strong man, a man's man. He did not fear death, though he knew that his entry through the pearly gates would not be an easy one. His priest, Father Grilius — the only person to whom he had confided his prior life — had assured him that salvation was possible for anyone and for any past deed, as long as he died in a state of grace. He was ready. He would spend his last weeks with his family at his side. Moreover, he would die well, no whimpering or complaining, an example to his children and grandchildren. This was important to Marcelus Prandus.

Now, however, he wanted to enjoy this last birthday party with those he loved most. This feast would be the most joyous and festive of his life. 'Drink up,' he demanded, passing around an old bottle of slivovitz, a strong Eastern European plum brandy. Paul sipped a bit and gagged at its 125-proof strength. Marcelus laughed. 'Too much for you, Paul? In the old country, my father would drink it by the glass. You're getting soft. That is not the Lithuanian way.'

Marcelus wanted his children and grand-children to remember Grandpa Chelli presiding over the last birthday dinner before his death from cancer. Marcelus Prandus might die a lingering death, but he would die happy, knowing that he had produced a wonderful family that would carry on his name, his heritage, and his memory.

The meal was now over, and it was time for the birthday festivities. The old man blew out the candles on his cake. Everyone sang 'Happy Birthday'. Marcelus sang a Lithuanian birthday song. It ended at six o'clock amid hugging and kissing. Marcelus left the house with a big smile, on his way to the Lithuanian-American Social Club a few blocks away.

The club was his link to the past, where

he could talk to trusted friends about the old country. When the talk turned to the war, they always used euphemisms. The roundups and executions were of Communists, traitors, and parasites. The word Jew was rarely mentioned, except to complain about how much power they still had. They never discussed the children whom they had slaughtered or the families they had destroyed. There were no feelings of guilt to expiate. They had done what they had to do, and they did not dwell on it. No nightmares, no regrets. Life was good in America. The children didn't have to be burdened with a past they could never understand. The world had quickly forgotten. Why should they have to remember? They were confident that the unpleasantness of the past would never rear its ugly head again.

Marcelus Prandus looked forward to an evening speaking Lithuanian with his old friends and reminiscing about the good old days when sons followed in their fathers' footsteps.

23

The Kidnapping

The time had now arrived to bring in Marcelus Prandus so that he could see what was going to happen to his family. The birthday provided the perfect opportunity. It was easy for Danielle to position her station wagon on his route to the Lithuanian-American Social Club with the hood up.

'Excuse me, sir,' she said to the man who was whistling, as he walked down the street. 'I seem to be having a problem starting my car.'

'Happy to give a look. I used to own a car repair shop,' said the old man, tipping his hat politely.

When Marcelus lowered his head to peer into the engine, Danielle stuck a target pistol to his ribs. 'Into the back of the car. Now. Don't make a sound or I'll put a bullet through this silencer.'

'Don't shoot. I will do whatever you say,' Prandus replied nervously as he opened the door and sat down. Danielle got in next to him, keeping her pistol in his ribs.

Max appeared from around the corner, climbed into the driver's seat, and turned the car in the direction of the Berkshires.

During the two-and-a-half-hour drive, Prandus kept asking what was happening to him. 'I'm old and sick. I don't have any money. You must have the wrong person.' It was dark, so Prandus could not get a good look at his driver.

Max didn't know whether Prandus would recognize him, but it really didn't matter. Danielle kept saying, 'We're not going to hurt you. We only want to show you something.'

At dusk they arrived at a small abandoned hunting cabin a few miles from Danielle's summer cottage. It was deep in the woods, far from its closest neighbor. As soon as Prandus entered the cabin, he realized that he was in for a prolonged stay. It had been carefully prepared for his arrival. Blackout shades would keep the inside light from showing outside. The windows were all bolted shut and barred. There were no phones or other means of communicating with the outside world. The only appliance in view was a small television set with a built-in video player. Prandus concluded with relief that he was not going to be killed. Otherwise why would they have taken such pains to make the cabin ready for a lengthy stay?

Danielle tied the old man to a large oak chair. When she was finished binding his arms and legs, she announced, 'It's showtime. Here is the master of ceremonies.'

Max walked into the lighted room and looked Prandus directly in the eye. 'Do you remember me?' he asked.

Marcelus Prandus looked at Max Menuchen for a full minute, racking his brain for a clue. 'Your face is familiar,' he said tentatively. 'Do I know you?'

'My name is Max Menuchen,' declared the man standing over the man bound to the chair. He paused, then, pointing an accusing finger at Prandus, he said in a somber voice, 'You murdered my entire family in the Ponary Woods on April 2, 1942.' His gaze was steely. 'You made us dig our own grave. Your only mistake is that you did not succeed in killing me. I clawed my way out. I have waited for more than fifty years to have my revenge. Now I will have it.'

'Oh, my God, I, I don't know what you are talking about,' Prandus stuttered in panic. 'You must have the wrong person.' Forcing a smile, he continued, 'Prandus is a common name. I had a cousin who was sent back to Lithuania. It was him, not me. You must let

168

me go. I will help you find him.'

'I could never forget your eyes!' Max bellowed as his hand, with a will of its own, smashed against Prandus's face. It was the first time Max had ever hit anyone in his life. Prandus cringed in fear, not from the force of the blow, but from Max's words. As he watched the powerful man's face twitch, Max heard King Lear's terrible words: 'Tremble, thou wretch, that hast within thee undivulged crimes unwhipped of justice . . . '

'It wasn't me. My cousin looks just like me, and he has the same name. I helped the Jews during the war. The Greenbergs, the Levines, the Blooms. I helped them. Please. Please. Don't hurt me.'

'We are going to hurt you, more than you can imagine. We are going to make you feel what I felt. You will suffer as I did, as we all did that terrible night.' Max's booming voice was like a judge's pronouncing sentence.

'I'm dying of cancer,' he cried. 'It's only a matter of months, and I'll be dead. Can't you show mercy for a dying man?'

'Did you show mercy to my family?'

Max could see that Prandus was frightened, but he could also see that his fear had not yet escalated to terror, which it soon would when Prandus realized that the stakes were higher — much higher — than his own brief remaining life.

Prandus shifted under the strain of the ropes. He was like a trapped rat with no escape. Obviously, there was no use denying his identity. In apparent desperation he tried a different tack. 'I was wrong. It was terrible what I did. I was so young. Please forgive me.'

Max heard remorse in Prandus's voice — but it was the remorse of the caught criminal.

Prandus begged, 'Let me die in peace.'

'Remember my grandfather who begged you to let him die first?'

Until now Marcelus Prandus had no distinct memory of the Menuchen family. He had participated in so many *aktions*, had killed so many families, that it was all a blur. Yet the mention of the grandfather who had asked to be killed first brought back a picture of this one family. It was the first time Prandus had thought about it since that night more than fifty years earlier. For Prandus, Ponary Woods was one incident among many, each quickly forgotten. For his victims, it was forever. All Prandus could whimper was, 'I'm so sorry. Please don't kill me.'

'I won't kill you. I will do to you what

you did to my grandfather.'

'What do you mean?' Prandus asked as it began to sink in what might be in store for him. 'What do you mean? What do you mean?' he demanded, his voice shrill with terror.

'You have a grandson named Marc?'

'Oh, my God. Please don't hurt my Marc,' Prandus cried in shock as a feeling of nausea came over him. 'What do I have to do to stop you from hurting Marc? I'll pay you anything. I have some money in the bank. Take my house, my silver.'

'I don't want your money.'

'Oh, my God. Then take my life. Torture me. Do anything to me, but please don't touch Marc. Please. He's only a child. He didn't do anything. It's not his fault.'

'Those were my words to you that night. Before you killed my baby son. Do you remember what you said?'

'No. I'm sorry for whatever I said. Please forgive me.'

'I remember every word you said. 'It isn't his fault, but the fault is in him. In his seed, in his genes.' '

'No, no, please. Don't hurt him,' Prandus cried, tugging at his restraints. His arms turned red as he flexed his large muscles against the strong ropes. The veins on his

171

forehead began to protrude. It looked as though he might be having a stroke. Then exhaustion took over as the old man realized he could not break free.

'This time *you* are powerless,' Max said with an air of satisfaction.

'Take me to my grandson,' Prandus pleaded, hoping against hope that he might be able to warn him or otherwise save him. Again he strained against the ropes.

'You will never leave this room. We will bring Marc here, and you will see him die before your very eyes.'

'No, no, please, no. Anything but that. I can't stand it. I will die first.'

'You will not be so lucky.'

'I am a different person today. The man you are punishing is not the same person who did those terrible things in the woods. For fifty years I have led a good life.'

'The fifty happy years you spent after what you did make you even more deserving of punishment.'

'I was so young,' Prandus said, sobbing. 'Is there no forgiveness?'

'It is not for me to forgive, only to avenge.'

'An eye for an eye?'

'If I wanted an eye for an eye, I would first rape your grand-daughter. Do you remember my sister, Sarah Chava?'

'No. I never raped anybody.'

Max slapped him again, this time drawing blood from his lip. 'Do not deny what you did. It will do you no good,' he said sternly.

'We were following orders,' Prandus whimpered.

'You gave the orders.'

'But others gave me orders.'

'You agreed with their orders.'

'I was wrong. And I will probably burn in hell for eternity for obeying those orders. And so will you if you hurt my innocent grandchildren. Do you want to burn in hell?'

'The Ponary Woods were worse than any hell. I can take hell, if that's what is in store for me,' Max said.

'You don't believe in hell, do you?'

'Do *you*?'

'I didn't when I was young. When I did what I did. Now I do. My priest has forgiven me for Ponary Woods, without promising salvation. He says God will judge me harshly, but only at the end of my life.'

'Well, I am your judge and jury, just as you were my family's judge, jury, and executioner. I condemn you to watch the revenge killing of your grandchild. As you watch, you will know that he is being killed for only one reason: because of what you did in Ponary Woods. A philosopher once said that he who kills another must be considered as if by that act he has willed his own death. By killing my family, you willed the death of your family. *You* are their murderer.'

'They are innocent.'

'Then they will go to heaven, where you will never again see them, because whatever your priest has told you, you will certainly go to hell.'

'How do you know?' he asked wildly.

'If there is a hell, it is surely reserved for people like you and me, who are prepared to kill innocent people, especially children, in cold blood. I am prepared to spend eternity in hell for what I am about to do. Are you prepared to spend eternity in hell because of what you did?'

'If I could save my family by spending eternity in hell, I would do it.'

'I was never given that option.'

'You are not God!' Prandus shouted, looking upward.

'Neither were you. But you held the power of life and death over my family. And you chose death. I have the same power now over your grandchild. Now I must choose. Do you remember my grandfather's last word?'

'No, I don't.'

'It was *nekama*. That means take revenge. I must obey his last command.'

Danielle had listened silently to the dialogue between Max and the man who had killed his entire family. At various points she had wanted to interject her own feelings. She realized, however, that her feelings related to her own grandfather, for whom Prandus was merely a surrogate. This was Max's moment. The Maimonidean solution was her idea, but Max was in charge of his prisoner.

At a signal from Max, Danielle placed a gag over Prandus's mouth as the old man shook his head frantically from side to side and pressed against the ropes. 'Marc will be dead by tomorrow,' Max said as they left a whimpering Marcelus Prandus tied helplessly to the chair.

24

Max is Missing

'He's not at home and he's not in the office,' said Abe. 'No one knows where he is.'

'Has anyone checked inside the house?' Rendi asked.

'Yeah. I have a key. Nothing unusual. I even checked his luggage. It's all there. I'm worried.'

'He's probably at the library or on a walk. How long has he been unaccounted for?'

'Only today. Yesterday he spoke to his secretary. Asked for some books on the Bible. The usual stuff.'

'Look, I'm concerned, too. There's nothing we can do. It's too soon. The cops aren't going to start looking for someone who's been missing for a day.'

'You're right, but that doesn't make me feel any better. I'm going to try the hospitals.'

'Then I'll help you,' Rendi said. 'I'll try Mt Auburn. You call Cambridge City. After that we'll cover Boston.'

As Abe and Rendi called each of the hospitals, another family, several miles to the north, was looking for another old man who had disappeared at about the same time.

25

Paul Prandus

'My father never made it to the Lithuanian-American Social Club,' Paul Prandus told his friend, investigator Freddy Burns.

'What do you mean, he never made it? Maybe he went somewhere else.'

'You don't know Papa. He always goes to the club. It's his second home. He told us he was meeting his friends over there. They were expecting him. He never showed. He's missing.'

Although Paul spoke in his characteristically soft voice, his desperation was obvious.

'He's not missing,' Freddy said reassuringly. 'I've seen a million disappearances like this one. They guy comes home the next day. Sometimes with a black eye. Sometimes with a hangover. But he always comes home.'

'Papa always goes to the club. He left the house at six o'clock. It's a ten-minute walk. I'm worried that someone may have kidnapped him. We've got to find him.'

'Paul, you're watching too many movies. What would anybody want with your old man? You're not exactly Bill Gates, you know. You couldn't even pay a ransom that covered the costs of a decent kidnapping.'

'Maybe it's not about ransom,' Paul said, his voice getting even lower.

'Then what is it about?'

'I don't know.'

'How about the obvious? A heart attack? A girlfriend? A breakdown?'

'He's too old for girlfriends now. And he is not the type for a breakdown. Not yet. He's as strong as a horse, both mentally and even physically, despite his cancer. His heart's perfect. He was snatched — without a trace.'

'Okay. I'll work on that premise. Where do we start?'

'I have no idea.'

'Well, that's a hell of a lead. Let's start by checking the hospitals, the police station, the church, old friends, the park — the morgue. You take the police station and the church. I'll take the others. We'll exclude all the obvious places. Then, if he hasn't shown up — which I'm sure he will — we can look at the less obvious possibilities, like your snatch theory.'

'Please, find him. He's dying. I want him to die at home with his family. Not alone, in some strange place. My son needs to see him again,' Paul said, flipping open his wallet to show Freddy his son's picture. 'He loves him. Please, Freddy.'

Paul knew that his father would not be found in the obvious places. He knew, though he couldn't articulate it, that there was nothing obvious about his father's disappearance.

★ ★ ★

Freddy Burns certainly didn't look like a personal investigator. Maybe that was why he was so successful at his work. There was a time, now long gone, when he had looked the part. In the days he worked as a Boston police officer, he was trim and almost good-looking. But since he took the bullet in his groin, he had let himself go.

The bullet had come from a shoot-out with a Russian immigrant who was holding his own wife and children hostage, threatening to kill them unless his wife agreed to return to Russia. Both Freddy and the Russian were rushed to the emergency ward, where the criminal was treated before the cop because his wounds were more serious. When they finally got around to Freddy, they weren't able to restore him to his previous self, even after rehabilitation.

Freddy would never forget the first person who visited him in the hospital: it was the well-known Cambridge defense lawyer Abe Ringel, who had cross-examined him on many occasions, always trying to discredit his testimony. Freddy had a warm spot in his heart for the defense attorney. If he ever got in trouble, Freddy thought, he knew whom he would call to defend him.

When he finally left the hospital, they put him behind the desk, first as a dispatcher and then as a spokesman for the precinct. Freddy hated it. He felt cooped up. He described his job as a 'mercy fuck,' and he quit after a year on three-quarters disability. The pension was enough to pay his alimony and child support, but it left him with nothing. So Freddy Burns opened up the 'B and B Agency,' specializing in personal security and discreet inquiries. The second 'B' was part of his fantasy — never realized — that he would someday meet a woman who would be both his partner and his wife.

The first lawyer to hire Freddy was a recent graduate of the Boston College Law School who had just opened a practice in Salem. His name was Paul Prandus. He was a serious, somewhat rigid man who spent much of his time on church-related activities. Freddy had remembered Paul's name from his days as a local football star. Despite his athletic build, Paul didn't carry himself like a former athlete — no swagger, no jock talk, no carousing. Now he acted every bit the lawyer. Paul's client was a local high school senior who was facing homicide charges in a bizarre case. The boy had been in a schoolyard fight with the class bully and had caught him with a lucky punch. The bully's head hit the pavement at a sharp angle, putting him into a coma. He was kept alive by a respirator, and after ten months his mother was thinking seriously of pulling the plug. Paul said he identified with this young client because of his own youthful fistfights. 'We've got to help this kid,' he told Freddy.

Freddy happened to have been in the same hospital as the comatose kid, and the case was the talk of the wards, since under the law, if the victim of an assault dies within a year and a day of the assault, the crime is homicide. If the victim lives for more than a year and a day, the crime is merely assault. The defendant hired Paul Prandus to try to prevent the mother from pulling the plug on her son, thereby not turning an assailant into a murderer. Freddy called Prandus and offered to do some investigatory work, since he was already familiar with the case. Prandus hired him, and Freddy snooped around the hospital with ease, since he had been a familiar face there for months. He discovered that the injured kid's mother had never visited her son, that she had been estranged from him for several months before the coma, and that she had taken out several of those TV 'no physical exam required' insurance policies on her comatose son's life. This information gave Prandus a leg up in his negotiations and resulted in a plea of attempted manslaughter and a suspended sentence.

From that time on Paul Prandus always used Freddy Burns as his investigator.

★ ★ ★

Freddy and Paul quickly checked out all the leads and came up empty.

'Someone snatched him — or killed him,' said Paul. 'I know. I can feel it in my bones.'

'I don't think so. My gut tells me he's out somewhere with a broad, no matter what you say. No one's ever too old for a little hanky-panky. But he's your father, so we'll go with your bones over my gut.'

'I don't know where to begin,' said Paul.

'Let's start out with you. Is there anyone who would want to take revenge against you by hurting someone close to you?'

'I am a defense lawyer. We're not the most beloved species in the world.'

'Believe me, I know. You guys rank somewhere between skunks and poisonous snakes. Closer to the snakes. But why you in particular?'

'I don't know. I've defended some pretty bad characters. Lost my share, won my share.'

'And every time you lose, the guy who goes to jail has it in for you?'

'Could be. But every time I win, the victim's family has it in for me.'

'That doesn't narrow the list of suspects much. What you're telling me is that every criminal case you've been involved in provides a possible motive!'

'When a criminal lawyer is killed, everyone's a suspect. Even strangers despise us. You should read my anonymous hate mail.'

'I will. You never know where you'll find a lead.'

'I really don't think that anyone has it in for me enough to risk a long prison term and become a murderer.'

'What do you mean, *become* a murderer? Some of your clients had achieved that distinguished status even before they met you. It's a hell of a lot easier to kill your second victim than your first. Got any candidates?'

'I recently lost a big one involving a Mob guy with a rap sheet from here to Cape Cod. I have to tell you, though, it just doesn't sound right to me. I'm not the kind of lawyer who arouses those kinds of passions. I'm a pretty straitlaced guy. I've never even been so much as threatened. Hated, yes — threatened, no.'

'That makes it even more challenging. The threateners never kill. It's the quiet, resentful ones you've got to watch your back for. Tell me about this Mob guy.'

'He's in Walpole for life, but he's got friends.'

'Get me a list.'

'It would be a telephone book,' said Paul. 'We're talking about the Mafia. They've got hit men from all over.'

'Yeah, they play crisscross.'

'Huh?'

'They bring in a guy from Kansas to take out a guy from Boston, and a guy from Boston to go after a guy from Kansas. Crisscross.'

'I still don't know where we begin.'

'I begin with my knowledge of the Mob,' said Freddy. 'This doesn't look like their MO to me. They don't go after lawyers who blew

185

a case — unless it was a sellout. And they don't go after family members. They value family too highly. Not like the druggies in Miami. If the Mafia had it in for you, it would be you who would be missing, not your dad. This is not the Mafia.'

'I agree.'

'Is anyone else out to get even with you?'

'I can't think of anyone with enough of a motive. Well, maybe Scooter.'

'Who's Scooter?'

'Scooter Scott. Drug pusher from Malden. My client ratted him out. He got ten in federal prison. I made the deal.'

'Tell me more.'

'Scooter was not a happy camper. He did threaten my client. I used the threat to get my guy a suspended sentence. I argued that sending him to jail with a snitch jacket would be a death sentence.'

'So where is your little angel?'

'Witness protection program. Somewhere in the Midwest — Boring-town, U.S.A., where they send all the stoolies.'

'Did Scooter threaten you?'

'No. Just a dirty look.'

'How dirty?'

'Par for the course, nothing special.'

'Is Scooter connected?'

'Not that I know of. Pretty much of a loner.'

'He doesn't sound like the guy. Anyone else?'

'No. I don't think it's me.'

'Okay, let's say it's not you they were trying to get even with. Who else in your family?'

'The only other person I could think of would be Papa himself.'

'Your old man? Who did he ever hurt?'

'I don't know, but it could be him.'

'Wasn't he some kind of mechanic or something?'

'He was a lot of things since he came to this country. Security guard, auto mechanic, handyman. He's been retired for a few years. Mostly hangs around the Lithuanian-American Social Club with his buddies from the old country.'

'What did he do in the old country?'

'He never talked much about it. I know he was in the war. He fought against the Communists. That's why he left. Stalin wasn't happy with him.'

'Well, at least we know it's not Stalin who's out to get revenge. That bastard was tough, but even he couldn't get revenge from the grave.'

'Papa was in some kind of militia unit.

187

They rounded up Communists. He never wanted to talk about it. Maybe someone he rounded up held a grudge?'

'For fifty years? No way. Even the Mafia has a statute of limitations. Naw, that's a dead end. I have a rule about motives. Passions cool quickly. Look at yesterday, not last month. Let's focus on more recent events.'

'I have a weird feeling that Papa's disappearance may go back to the old country. What happened there produced some pretty strong feelings. I learned a little about it in college. It was pretty awful. Could you do a little checking? But don't talk to anyone in the family. At least not yet. Everyone's in shock. I don't want to get anyone riled up unnecessarily. Can you do a little snooping on the q.t.?'

'Is it okay if I go down to the Lithuanian-American Social Club and talk to some of his friends from the old country?'

'They'll never talk to you. They're a bunch of very narrow-minded old guys. Only Lithuanians count. An Irishman like you is from Mars. I'll go with you. They'll talk to me and maybe let you listen.'

★ ★ ★

Paul and Freddy walked the few blocks to the storefront social club. Half a dozen men, all in their seventies, were sitting around playing cards and speaking Lithuanian. One man was in a wheelchair, reading a book. The walls were covered with photographs and travel posters of Lithuania and faces of Lithuanian political and sports figures.

'Paulus. I ain't never seen you here before,' said Peter Vovus, one of Marcelus's friends. 'Is everything okay at home? I haven't seen your papa today.'

'Or yesterday,' chimed in another man. 'He was supposed to come by yesterday, but he never showed. Is his cancer acting up?'

'That's what I came to talk to you about. Papa's missing. Disappeared. This man, Freddy, is my investigator. He has reason to believe somebody may have snatched Papa or hurt him.'

'Oh, my God. Your father never hurt anybody. He's a good man, a family man.'

'Freddy here thinks it may go back to the old country, to Vilnius during the war.'

As Paul uttered these words, there were audible gasps from some of the old men. One by one they put down their cards and looked at Paul. The man in the wheelchair closed his book and moved closer to Paul as he continued.

'We need your help. We have no time to lose. If my father is still alive, we may have only hours or days to find him. We must find out the truth about Papa. Even if it's painful. So no bullshit. Please. We came here to ask you all one question: what did my father do during the war?'

Stunned silence. No one had asked these old men about the war years since they came to America in the 1940s.

Paul remembered how, at home, his father had never spoken of the war years. When he had asked him questions, he said he had been a policeman who helped in the roundup of Communists. Now Paul could not be satisfied with these answers.

'I've got to know, damn it,' Paul said emphatically, but without raising his voice. 'You're not helping Papa with your silence. You know what he did. Tell me. Did he help in the roundup of Jews? I must know. Then maybe we can figure out who took him.'

'It's a complicated story, Paulus,' said Peter Vovus. 'No one who wasn't there could possibly understand it. They were terrible times, and some very bad things happened — to Lithuanians and to others. You could never understand, you who were born in America.'

'That's what Papa always says. I must

hear the facts, even if I don't understand everything.'

'We never talk about it. What we did would be misunderstood.'

'This is not about judging you, Mr Vovus, or even about judging my father. It is about saving him, please. We will never repeat what you tell us. We have to know.'

'All right,' said Peter Vovus. 'I must give you some background first. About your grandfather, whom you didn't know. Sit down and listen. Your father told me this story many times.'

Paul and Freddy sat down as Peter Vovus began the story.

★ ★ ★

'It started with a stupid argument about soccer, which turned into a barroom brawl. Your grandfather, Paulus Prandus, hit Matius Plusk. Plusk picked up a vodka bottle and bashed your grandfather over the head. Your grandfather staggered toward the door. Plusk followed him, cursing. Several regulars at the Wolf Tavern, including my uncle, tried to break up the fight, but Plusk managed to hit him once more, this time with a heavy lantern. Your grandfather fell to the ground, dead.'

Peter Vovus shifted uncomfortably in his chair and downed a shot of vodka as he continued the story.

'Your grandmother always believed that the Jews had caused her husband's death. It was a Jewish-owned tavern — as many were in those days. The owner, Shmulka Grossberg, had not intervened in the fight. He never did. He would always say, 'Let the drunken *goyim*' — that's what he called us — 'kill each other if they want to. That is their way. They are always getting drunk and fighting.' This time, your grandfather was killed. A freak death — generally it takes more than a few blows to the head to kill. Nobody pressed charges, since everyone had seen Paulus strike the first blow. But at the funeral, the priest made it clear who was at fault. 'The Jews fill us with alcohol for their own profit,' Father Grekus preached. 'They care only about other Jews. We are just sources of their profit.' Everyone knew that Grossberg kept a gun behind his bar, in case of robbers, but he didn't use it. 'A Christian life is worthless to the Jew. It says so in their Talmud,' the priest told us.

'Even before your grandfather's death, your father had been taught — by his parents, priests, neighbors — that the Jews and Communists were the enemy of their way of life, and that the Jews created communism. We were all taught that.'

'It is true,' the man in the wheelchair interjected. 'I don't care what anyone says today. It is still true.'

'Shut up, Oleg. They're not here to listen to your opinions. They want facts,' Vovus said, shrugging his shoulders apologetically as he continued.

'Your father always loved authority, rules, order. His choice to become a policeman suited him perfectly. He loved the Fascists, even before they rescued our country from the Communists. After that, everybody loved the Fascists. As soon as Hitler's army liberated Vilnius, your father — he was twenty-one then — volunteered for duty in the operations against the Jews. He knew the Jews of Vilna. He understood them. They had killed his father. He knew they had to be destroyed.

'The chief of the local Gestapo, General Heinrich Gruber, knew about Paulus Prandus's death, and he entrusted your father with responsibility for conducting the roundups of Jews. Your father idolized Gruber, because he was the first German Nazi he knew.

'In less than six months, your father had risen through the ranks. His physical bearing and strength made him a commanding figure. I remember how good he looked in a black uniform of the militia,' Vovus said in a tone of nostalgia. 'His intelligence, charm, and good manners had earned him the respect of both his colleagues and his German superiors. Soon he was made a captain in the Lithuanian Auxiliary Militia. His mother was proud. That was important to him. He was a family man.

'After the war, the Communists were again in charge. There was talk of trials for collaboration, though he couldn't see how that would be possible, since everybody had collaborated. We agreed with the Nazis. They were on our side. It was those who had supported communism — the so-called partisans — who had collaborated. But all that was beside the point now that the Russians had occupied Vilnius, and Marcelus learned his name was on a list of suspects compiled by the Red Army.

'Your grandmother had some relatives in Boston, so that is where they fled. Later they moved up here. Coincidentally, my parents knew some people in Salem, so we moved here, too.

'You know the rest of the story, Paul. Your father lived an exemplary life after the war. Besides his family, his life was the Lithuanian-American Social Club. He was our president.

'I do not expect you to understand, but I hope that information is helpful to your investigator. It is the first time I have talked about it in many years.'

Paul sat there, stunned. He had always suspected that there was more to his father's past than rounding up some Communists, but even in his wildest fantasies he could never imagine his father as a Nazi.

'My father didn't actually kill any Jews, did he?' Paul asked weakly, knowing the answer.

'What did he tell you?'

'That he never hurt anyone.'

'Then let us leave it at that.'

'We can't. I must know. Did he kill any Jews?' Paul demanded, his voice rising.

'Everyone did. They were the enemy. Your father just followed orders. He got no pleasure from rounding up traitors. He was just doing his job.'

'Do you know the names of any specific families?'

'There were so many. I can remember a few names.'

'Please tell us.'

'In the beginning, they rounded up prominent families. The Blooms, the Solevichicks, the Kaplans, the Menuchens, the Glassmans.'

Freddy wrote down the names as Vovus recalled them.

'It's a start,' said Freddy. 'Let me work on it.' After what he had just heard, he was prepared to believe that Marcelus might have been abducted. He remembered the first rule of police work: if you don't find the missing person within the first couple of days, you're probably not going to find him alive.

26

The Children

The following morning, Max did exactly what he set out to do, methodically, systematically, and without any guilt or hesitation as Danielle videotaped the death scene for Prandus to see.

At midday, Max and Danielle returned from Salem to the cabin in the Berkshires, exhausted but satisfied that they had achieved the next step in their plan. This time there was no ambivalence and no accident.

'Is Marc here? Marc, Marc, run for your life!' Prandus screamed, his face turning red.

'He can't hear you. He's already dead,' said Max somberly.

'No, no, you said you would bring him here!'

'We killed him in Salem, and videotaped his death for you to see. Watch the TV screen.'

Danielle turned on the video machine and inserted the tape. A happy, playful Marc was skipping on his way to school. As he approached the intersection, Prandus could see a car waiting. The zoom lens focused on the driver. It was an old man. As Marc crossed, the car accelerated in the child's direction.

'No, no, watch out, Marc!' Prandus shrieked as the car crashed violently into the young boy's body, throwing it thirty feet into the air.

Prandus lowered his eyes and wept.

'I'm afraid Marc never made it to school this morning. Would you like to see it again, in slow motion, to be certain he is dead?'

'No, no, my God, no.' Prandus said, sobbing. 'You are so cruel. How could you have done this?'

'It's only the beginning, Mr Prandus. Next comes your grand-daughter and then your sons. The children must die first. They are the most important. And you must watch, as I eradicate the Prandus seed from this world, just as you eradicated the Menuchen seed!' Max said with a determined look.

'No. No. Please don't. You killed my grandson. Isn't that enough?' Prandus pleaded.

'None of your descendants will remain alive,' Max said firmly.

'But you survived,' Prandus cried.

'And so will you, until you see each of your descendants die. Then you will die, like my grandfather did, knowing that you have left absolutely no progeny. It is biblical justice. Do you remember what Moses commanded the Jews to do to the children of the Midianites? kill every child.'

'But Jesus said, 'Forgive them.' '

'You should have listened to Jesus in the Ponary Woods. Now you are seeing Old Testament justice.'

'Please don't kill the rest of my family,' Prandus whimpered. 'Please, please, you are a better man than me.'

'No, I'm not. I learned evil from you. Here, let me read to you from Shakespeare.' Max opened a book to Shylock's chilling soliloquy.

If a Jew wrong a Christian, what is his humility? Revenge. If a Christian wrong a Jew, what should his sufferance be by Christian example? Why, revenge. The villainy you teach me I will execute, and it shall go hard but I will better the instruction.

'Now I am bettering your instruction.'

'No, no, I can't take this!' Prandus cried.

As Max looked up, he could see the old man was shaking all over. Prandus urinated in his pants. Max noticed and smiled.

★ ★ ★

The next evening Danielle chose to stay behind in Cambridge as Marcelus Prandus watched the murders of his six-year-old granddaughter and her father, Peter, Marcelus's younger son. They were both shot to death at close range by a young woman firing a pistol with a silencer. 'They had to be killed in quick succession, before they could go into hiding,' Max told Marcelus. 'Otherwise I would have drawn it out even further, so as to increase your suffering. Only your older son, Paul, have I not yet found.'

Max watched Marcelus Prandus writhing in pain. He had not seen such anguish in another human being since Ponary Woods. At first he imagined the death of a Prandus bringing back a Menuchen. This only plunged him into despair as he realized that nothing would ever bring back his family.

Prandus's face was a study of suffering. He was on the lowest level of Dante's Inferno and sinking even lower, his pain unimaginable to anyone other than one who had experienced the torture Max had been through. Prandus's expression reminded Max of the look in Grandpa Mordechai's face when he realized his entire family would

200

perish. For a moment Max allowed himself to feel compassion for Prandus. Then the realization hit him: Prandus had lived a full and happy life. His suffering, intense as it is, was being compressed into a few days. It would soon be over.

If Max could never take back the decades of guilt-free happiness Prandus had enjoyed, at least he would make him see that everything he had lived for had been in vain. He would die with the maudlin message of Ecclesiastes on his lips: 'All is vanity.' Max now understood what was meant when the Greek philosopher said: 'Let no man count himself content, until he is dead.' Had Prandus been lucky enough to die two days earlier, he would have died a content man. But now, when he died, he would truly wish, as Job had wished, that he had never been born. That would at least begin to make up for Prandus's happy years. Max's revenge would be short but sweet.

There was far too little revenge taken, Max thought. From the Nazis, to the Turks, to the Argentineans, to the Cambodians, to the Bosnians, most genocidal murderers had lived happy lives.

It would have been good, Max thought, for the Jews to have killed guilty Nazi murderers — the thousands who were not tried at

Nuremberg. The Jews didn't do it, despite the victims' demand for *nekama*. Although the Old Testament commanded revenge, history had shown that most Jews were uncomfortable meting it out. The survivors of the Holocaust had failed their murdered parents, children, and siblings. They were all too busy rebuilding their broken lives, establishing Israel, fighting for the rights of others.

Now that nearly all the perpetrators were dead, everyone was busy apologizing — the French, the Swiss, the Church, the banks, the Red Cross. But these apologies, unaccompanied by punishment, seemed hollow to Max. Now, Max Menuchen was getting revenge, for himself, for his family, maybe even for the Jewish people who didn't take revenge.

Max realized that he was treating his festering wounds with the powerful and dangerous medicine of revenge. He knew there was a risk that he could become like the Count of Monte Cristo, who lived for revenge, only to discover how unfulfilling its accomplishment could be.

Despite this risk, Max felt he had no choice. He was being driven to despair by his realization that the world did not care that a person who did what Marcelus Prandus had done could remain unpunished for so many years. What happened in the Ponary Woods was the work of madmen during wartime, Max understood. But what happened to Marcelus Prandus — more precisely, what *didn't* happened to Marcelus Prandus — *that* was the work of the entire civilized world over a lifetime. The world allowed — indeed helped — a mass murderer to escape justice. The message that such inaction sent was clear: the world didn't care about what happened in the Ponary Woods. *That* was what was destroying Max. That was what drove him to the vengeance in which he was now engaged.

Max recalled Danielle's parting words to him earlier that day. 'It isn't vengeance, it's justice — if it is done right.'

Max hoped they were doing it right.

27

Death

Marcelus Prandus had now seen both of his grandchildren and his younger son killed. Only his oldest son, Paul, was still alive. Max and Danielle went looking for Paul. It was only a matter of hours before they saw him enter the Salem police station, devastated by his loss. Now they were able to complete their planned revenge, professionally, without any problems. The next day, Max returned to the cabin with the last videotape. Danielle chose to remain outside the cabin, so as to allow Max to exact his revenge without distraction.

'The final solution has been accomplished,' Max said, holding the tape. 'Every genetic Prandus, except you, is dead. Soon it will be your turn, but not until you see this.'

He placed the videotape in the machine. It showed a visibly upset Paul Prandus leaving the Salem police station. As Marcelus Prandus stared hopelessly at the television screen, Max explained to him that the 'police have no idea who killed your family, because they do not know about your history in Lithuania. They are stymied. Your deception to your own son has prevented the police from protecting your family.'

Prandus uttered a grunt as the video showed Paul getting into his car, which was parked a block away from the police station. Prandus tried to turn his eyes away as he saw his son turn on the ignition. But there was no way to avoid the sound and sight of the massive explosion and fireball that instantaneously engulfed the car in flames.

Prandus screamed in rage, trying to break out of the ropes that contained him. The screams turned to whimpers as he faced the horrible reality. Suddenly he looked much older. His eyes became sunken, his skin sallow, as if the life had gone out of him.

'My revenge is complete. Now you can die at any time you wish.'

'Please, let me die now. Kill me. I can't stand being alive and knowing what happened. Please let me die. Let me end my suffering. Now.'

'That is your choice,' Max said. 'You can take these cyanide pills, if you wish.' He placed three white capsules on the table. 'It must be of your own volition, however. It must be you who decides to die. Because under your religion, only suicide precludes salvation and heaven. You must make that decision. I will not make it for you. Are you willing to endure pain here on earth to obtain a chance at salvation? Or will you choose to end the pain and assure damnation? It is your decision.'

'Please,' Prandus implored, 'don't make me choose death. I beg you to kill me. Torture me, even. But don't make me choose between committing suicide and living with my pain. Please, grant me a final wish — kill me.'

'No,' Max said harshly, pressing the rewind button on the video machine. 'You will take your own life or you will exist here with all that remains of your descendants — this tape — until you die. Having to choose is your ultimate punishment — and my ultimate revenge.'

Prandus moaned. A tortured look came over him. Then, in a voice filled with the agony of defeat, he announced his decision. 'Give me the pills. I can't endure it any longer. I want it to end. It must end. Now.'

Max placed the cyanide capsules next to Marcelus Prandus's right hand. He loosened the rope around his right arm and handed him a pen.

'First write.'

'What?'

Max dictated: ' 'I, Marcelus Prandus, in full control of my capacities, am taking my own life. I know that by committing suicide, I give up all hope of salvation. It is I who asked to die by my own hand. It is I who asked for the pills. I am ending my life in order to stop the pain caused directly by my own actions in the Ponary Woods in 1942.' '

Prandus wrote the note in big block letters and signed it. He looked at the blank screen of the television set, as if to say goodbye to his murdered children and grandchildren. Then he crossed himself and asked God for forgiveness before he reached for the pills. He quickly took the three pills in his fingers and swallowed them with a glass of water. Max watched somberly.

Immediately Prandus's face began to flush as the first of the seizures took hold of his body. His face contorted, and his tongue protruded from his mouth. He tried to speak, but only guttural sounds came forth. Then his face turned pale, and finally he was still. Silence and the smell of death filled the room.

Max walked slowly out of the shack and spoke to Danielle. 'It is over.'

Without a word, Danielle entered the

shack, untied Prandus, and watched his body fall to the floor, motionless.

She picked up the rope, wiped away the fingerprints, and retrieved the suicide note, leaving behind the dead body.

Max and Danielle walked silently out of the shack without turning back and drove away. Max's work was complete. His revenge was accomplished.

All that remained was to tell Abe Ringel what he had done and ask for his counsel.

Part Five

Apprehension

28

Finding the Body

Exactly three hours after Marcelus Prandus died, Paul Prandus and Freddy Burns burst through the door of the hunting shack. An anonymous caller had phoned Paul Prandus and told him where his father was. Paul and Freddy raced across the state.

They found Marcelus Prandus lying on the floor, his eyes wide open, his face ashen blue, his mouth contorted, his tongue bleeding.

Paul ran to his father, calling, 'Papa, Papa!' He took the old man's head in his hands and shook it. 'Wake up, Papa, wake up!' But it was obvious he was dead. Paul began to cry and then to pound the floor.

Freddy looked around for clues. At first he saw nothing. Then he noticed that the TV was on, its blue screen suggesting that a video-tape was still in the machine. Whoever had been there had not removed the tape. Freddy quickly pressed the play button. The image of young Marc skipping to school appeared on the screen.

'Paul, look at the TV,' Freddy said.

As Paul looked up from his father's corpse he saw his son being struck by a car and hurled through the air. 'Oh, no! Oh, my God, no,' Paul gasped, running toward the TV set. He watched as his son's body hit the ground and bounced. Finally, it lay motionless as the crossing guard ran toward the mangled body of the eight-year-old child. Paul became hysterical. '*Marc*, Marc . . . oh, my *God*!'

Freddy grabbed for his cell phone and dialled Paul's home number. Paul's wife answered.

'Where's Marc?'

'Freddy, is that you? Is everything okay?'

'Where's Marc? I need to know.'

'He's in school.'

'How did he get there?'

'Is everything okay? You're frightening me. He walked, like he always does.'

'What was he wearing?'

'His school uniform. Why?'

'What's the number of the school?'

'It's 555–8824. Tell me, is Marc okay? Did anything happen?'

'I'll get back to you.'

Freddy dialed the number, but Paul grabbed the cell phone from him. A nun answered, 'Sancta Maria School.'

Paul's voice shook as he spoke. 'This is Paul Prandus. Did my son make it to school today?'

'I'll check, Mr Prandus,' the nun replied.

As Paul and Freddy waited, Freddy looked back at the TV screen. He saw Paul's brother, Peter, along with Peter's daughter, being shot to death. Then he saw Paul — the very same Paul who was standing two feet away from him — being immolated in his burning car.

'Paul, look!' Freddy shouted. 'It's a fake. The whole thing is a fake.'

Paul tried to listen to the nun at the other end of the phone line. Over Freddy's yelling, the nun assured him that Marc was playing at recess and seemed fine.

Paul insisted that the nun get Marc to the phone. While Paul waited, Freddy rewound the tape to show Paul the video of his own death. Paul watched in shock as he saw himself walking out of the police station. That was real. He had been there to give them a missing persons report on his father. But the explosion never happened. The video was a fake.

'Hi, Daddy. Is everything okay? You never call me at school.' The voice at the other end of the phone was Marc's.

'Thank God, Marc, you're okay. I'll explain later. Please call Mom and tell her you're okay. Thanks.'

Paul and Freddy rewound the tape and watched it through from the beginning. Paul phoned his brother and confirmed that everyone was fine.

The perversity of what had been done to his father was beginning to sink in. Paul didn't have to imagine what his father must have been put through; he himself had just experienced it — if only for a few moments. Nothing could be worse than seeing your own son, or grandson, being killed before your very eyes, while you watch helplessly, unable to do anything. It was the worst form of torture, worse than any physical pain.

Paul had then experienced the relief of learning that his son, whom he thought dead, was actually alive. Nothing could be better. To Paul it was like a resurrection, a rebirth. In a matter of minutes he had visited hell and heaven. Now he was back on earth, looking at the body of his dead father.

Marcelus Prandus had experienced only the horror of seeing his loved ones killed. He had never learned that they were actually alive. He had not experienced the rebirth, the resurrection. He had been to hell, never to return.

'Your father died of poisoning, Paul, probably cyanide,' Freddy said as he examined the body.

Paul was hardly listening. The veins on his neck bulged. His face was red with anger. His entire body strained against his suit. He cursed — confused, broken half curses in an uncontrolled burst. Then he threatened: 'I'm gonna kill the son of a bitch who did this.'

'Paul, come here, you've got to look at this,' Freddy said, ignoring Paul's ravings and threats and holding up the right hand of the dead man.

Paul knelt next to his father's body and looked at the rigid thumb of his father's hand as Freddy touched his own forefinger to it and then tasted the powdery substance he had lifted from the dead man's thumb. 'Cyanide,' Freddy announced. 'Smell it. It smells like bitter almonds.'

'What are you telling me?' Paul demanded.

'It was self-administered. He took the cyanide himself. It was suicide, Paul. At least in form. Your father took the pill in his own fingers and swallowed it.'

'No way. Not Papa. He didn't believe in suicide. Ordered us not to turn off any machines. Papa believed in miracles. God would decide when his time had come. People who commit suicide go to hell. Not my papa. He wouldn't have,' Paul insisted, his voice rising.

'That's why I said it was suicide in form only. Whoever did this probably made him take that pill.'

'No one could have made him. What did they do — hold a gun to his head? He would have fought back, resisted. No one could have forced him to take that pill.'

'Maybe it wasn't physical force,' said Freddy. 'It may have been psychological coercion.'

'What do you mean?'

'Whoever did this is a manipulative monster. He convinced your father that he had actually killed your whole family. He made it impossible for your father to endure the suffering. The only way he could end it was — '

'That's why Papa took the poison,' Paul interrupted. 'He couldn't bear to remain alive knowing we had all been killed. I can understand that, I saw the video of Marc. What a horrible way to die.' Paul put his head in his hands. 'I'll kill whoever did this. I'll break his fucking neck.'

'If you're right, then your father was murdered. By making him believe he killed your family, he murdered your dad. You're not going to have to kill him. The state will punish him — if we can find him.'

'If they don't, I will. This bastard can't be allowed to get away with what he did.'

29

Max's Return

Max, you're back! Thank God. Rendi and I were worried sick,' Abe cried, ushering his friend into the living room. 'You look disheveled. Your shoes are full of mud. Where have you been?' he demanded. Without waiting for an answer, he continued, 'I hope you haven't done anything stupid.'

'I have done something terrible, at least in terms of the law,' Max said as he wiped his shoes and walked into Abe's home. Max was alone, having dropped Danielle at her house.

'What are you talking about? What did you do?'

'Can I talk to you as my lawyer?'

'Of course. Sit down.'

'I killed Marcelus Prandus.'

'Oh, shit, no,' Abe said, the color draining from his face. 'Why did you do such a stupid thing? He wasn't worth it. Now you're going to go to prison.'

'I had no choice,' Max replied with a stoic look. 'It was either him or me. If he had gotten away with what he did to my family, I think I would have killed myself.'

'A novel claim of self-defense, but I'm afraid it won't work,' Abe said, shifting to his lawyer's mode. 'Tell me what happened.'

'Well, actually, Prandus killed himself.'

'That's good. Go on.'

'But I fooled him into doing it.'

'What are you talking about? Stop with the riddles. Give it to me straight if you want me to help you.'

'All right, I'll start at the beginning, but I need one assurance.'

'Whatever you need. What is it?'

'Someone else helped me. I need to know that if I tell you about that person, you will not tell the authorities.'

'I can't tell the authorities anything you tell me — about yourself or anyone else — unless it involves a future crime.'

'This is about the past.'

'Fine. Then you have my assurance. Go ahead.'

'When I found out about Sarah Chava, I wanted to kill Marcelus Prandus's entire family.'

'Holy shit, Max. You didn't kill anyone else, did you?'

'No, but I wanted to.'

'Wanting to is not a crime. I've wanted

to kill about a dozen prosecutors and judges, not to mention Joe Campbell.'

'I told Danielle Grant what I wanted to do.'

'Who is Danielle Grant?'

'A colleague of mine at the divinity school.'

'Another professor! Harvard's going to have a crimson shit fit.'

'She did nothing wrong. Only I am to blame. It was my decision. She actually talked me out of killing the entire Prandus family.'

'You never could have done it. What are we talking about there? Kids?'

'I almost killed Prandus's eight-year-old grandson.'

'What do you mean, 'almost killed'? Did you do any more than just think about it?'

'I drove my car to where he was crossing the street and aimed it at him.'

'Tell me you didn't hit him,' Abe implored. 'Please?'

'It was the morning after you told me about Sarah Chava. I drove to Salem and parked near the point where I had once before rehearsed killing Marc Prandus. My actions seemed almost automatic, as if programmed by some computer. At precisely the time he had earlier appeared, Marc Prandus materialized out of the morning fog. He was alone, with his baseball glove and ball. I pressed down on the accelerator and aimed the car at the child as he was crossing the intersection.'

'Oh, my God, Max.'

'It all happened so quickly, like a dream. But it is crystal clear to me now.'

'What? What's clear to you? Tell me.'

'As the car lurched toward Marcelus Prandus's grandchild, my mind returned to the Ponary Woods. The two scenes merged. The woods of Ponary and the crossing in Salem, Massachusetts, became one as I pressed on the accelerator. In my mind's eye, I was about to kill Marcelus Prandus before Prandus could shoot my family. Then the blurred image in my mind became clearer. Suddenly it was I who was Marcelus Prandus. Little Marc Prandus was my son, Efraim. I tried to push these images out of my mind as my foot pressed the accelerator toward the floor.'

'Did the kid see the car coming toward him?'

'Yes, he did. I could see a look of panic come deep from within his eyes. The child could do nothing. I could no longer control my leg. The accelerator was on the floor. The images refused to go away. I was an instant away from becoming Marcelus

Prandus, killer of an innocent child. Prandus killed children because of who their ancestors were. I, too, was killing a child because of who his ancestor was.'

Max stopped, put his head in his hands, and began to sob. Then he looked up and continued. 'Abe, I was about to engage in what the Nazis called *Sippenhaft* — punishment of kin. A voice in my head screamed, *No!*

'I now understood — by my own standards of justice — how wrong it was to take revenge against Marcelus Prandus by murdering his grandchild. It could not be allowed to end that way.'

'So what did you do?'

'The only thing I could. I jerked the steering wheel sharply to the right, crashing my Volvo into a barrier. The air bag exploded in my face. I drove away before anyone could get my license number and somehow made it home, where I fell into a semiconscious stupor.'

'Okay. So you couldn't kill the kid. That doesn't surprise me. How did you get Prandus to kill himself? I need to know all the details.'

'The next morning Danielle Grant arrived at my house, and I told her that I was going to kill the entire Prandus family.

She told me she had a better idea. She began by explaining that the object is to punish Marcelus Prandus for killing my family without killing his family. Then she said something I will never forget.' Max paused and then continued. 'She said that the 'children must be killed, but they must not die.' '

'What the hell does that mean? It sounds like gibberish.'

'That is what I thought at first. I told her it was impossible, but she insisted that she could show me that it was possible. The next day, she took me to an exhibit by a video artist named Bill Viola at the Contemporary Art Museum. Danielle showed me a video of a man being consumed by fire. He wasn't actually being burned, but it was completely realistic. Viola did it by some kind of morphing or computer trick. I confess to not understanding it, but it looked completely realistic. Danielle then took me to her studio — she also dabbles in computer video art — and she showed me a video she herself had prepared.'

'It sounds like she was pretty deeply involved in planning whatever it is you did. Why?'

'It is complicated, Abe. She was a victim, too. She understood my need for revenge.'

'Okay. That's not important now. What is important is what you both did. Tell me what kind of a video she showed you.'

'It was like a cartoon. Very rough. She had stayed up all night putting it together. She called it a storyboard. She had drawn an old man looking out a window as a child crosses the street and is hit by a car.'

'How the hell did she find out about your accident?'

'She told me it didn't take much to figure that one out, especially after she saw my dented car.'

'What else was on her video?'

'Some people are shot or blown up until everyone lies dead in front of the old man. The old man's smile turns to a gasp as he realizes that his entire family has just been slaughtered before his eyes. The storyboard ends with the old man tearing at his hair and shrieking like a man who has just suffered the greatest loss imaginable.'

'Yeah, but that was a cartoon. Nobody but another cartoon character would be fooled by a cartoon.'

'Danielle told me that with the right video footage of the Prandus family, she could make it look like a Bill Viola finished product.'

224

'Wouldn't Prandus know that the video had been faked?'

'Prandus's generation — my generation — knows nothing about this newfangled stuff. She assured me that he would be fooled by it — if we took the next step.'

'What step is that? I don't think I'm going to like this,' Abe said, pacing around the room.

'We would have to kidnap Prandus and keep him away from phones, newspapers, and TV sets,' Max replied with the enthusiasm of an inventor.

'Why couldn't you just hold him for a while, show him the video, let him suffer, and then release him?'

'No, no, Abe. That would have been worse than doing nothing at all. If he were to learn that his family was still alive, he would die joyously, with an even greater appreciation of his family and their life. He would have defeated me — again. I could not let that happen.'

'Wouldn't Prandus realize that a man like you could never murder an entire family of innocent people?'

'No, that is the beauty of the plan. It came naturally to him to believe that I could do to his family exactly what he did to mine. He had to believe that all men were capable of doing what he did. That's how he lived with himself. Had he been a just man, he might have understood that I could never do what he did — though I actually came close to doing it. He was not just a man. He did not think like a just man.'

Abe paced around the room, deep in thought. Then he stopped and looked at Max. 'I don't know what to say, Max. The friend part of me is in absolute awe over what you managed to pull off. They say that justice must be *seen* to be done. Well, Marcelus Prandus saw it done, even though it was only virtual justice.'

'There was nothing virtual about it in Prandus's mind. It was the most real thing he ever saw,' Max said.

Abe shook his head. 'The lawyer part of me is scared out of my wits that you and that Danielle woman are going to prison for a long time. How did Danielle come up with such an incredible plan?'

'She found it in Maimonides — the twelfth-century Jewish philosopher. She called it the 'Maimonidean solution.' '

'Maimonides knew about videos?'

'No, but he knew more about the Bible than anyone in his generation. He wrote brilliant commentaries, including one of the

Book of Job. Do you remember the story of Job?'

'Only that God allows Satan to test Job by killing all of his children.'

'Right. And Maimonides argued in his commentary that God could not have actually allowed Satan to kill Job's innocent children in order to test Job. That would have been unjust.'

'The story says he did just that,' Abe interjected.

'Yes, but Maimonides interprets the story in an interesting way. He says that God only allowed Satan to make the children disappear — Satan put them in a cave — so that Job would *believe* they had been killed. They were *actually* still alive. God wanted to see how Job would react to learning that his children had died. God didn't actually allow Satan to kill them. When Job passed the test, his children reappeared.'

'Incredible.'

'It's amazing what you can find in those old books.'

'Now tell me how Marcelus Prandus died.'

As Max described Prandus's suicide in detail, Abe worried how a jury might react to the agonized death Prandus had suffered.

'I've been in this business for thirty years, but I've never heard anything like this. I've got to ask you one question before we go any farther. Where is Prandus's body?'

'I don't know.'

'What do you mean, you don't know? Where did you leave it?'

'In the cabin, but I made an anonymous call to Prandus's son and told him where the body was. I assume they have found it, and that it's in some funeral home.' Max fixed Abe with an inquiring gaze. 'What do we do now?'

'We do nothing,' Abe replied automatically. 'They may never figure this thing out. You, me, and Danielle may be the only three people in the world who ever learn of your brilliant, if diabolical, plot. I can't disclose what you told me, and if you and Danielle keep your mouths shut, maybe it will remain an unsolved crime.'

'That would be fine with me. There was only one person who had to see justice done, and he saw it with his very last vision in this world. As far as I'm concerned, justice has been achieved.'

'I doubt the Prandus family would agree,' Abe said as a worried look crossed his face.

30

Who Done It?

'May God accept the soul of this wonderful husband, father, grandfather, and friend. His years in America were truly the American dream.'

As Paul listened to the glowing eulogy, he tried desperately to control his growing rage toward the man who had killed his father. He sat in the front pew of the small Lithuanian church with fists clenched. He searched his mind for clues — anything — that would have alerted him to his father's dark past. He wondered how many others noticed that Father Grilius had not said a word about Marcelus Prandus's youth in Lithuania.

The eulogy confirmed Paul's strengthening belief that his father's death could be explained only by what he had done during the war. The videos now made even more sense. Papa had killed someone's family, and now that same some one had taken revenge by making it appear that he had killed Papa's entire family.

Paul also noticed that Father Grilius had

not mentioned the cause of Papa's death — suicide was a strong taboo among Lithuanian Catholics. Dr Michelle Burden's autopsy concluded that the cause of death was 'self-administered cyanide poisoning.' Traces of the drug had been found on his father's right thumb and forefinger. Dr Burden was certain of her conclusion, as she had told Paul after her preliminary analysis. Paul would never forget how his father looked, stretched out on the cold steel table of the morgue, naked, eyes open, mouth agape, skin blue. On the floor of the cabin he had at least looked human. On the morgue slab he had looked like a medical school cadaver about to be cut open as part of a grisly experiment. He could not get the picture of his dear father out of his mind. The vision would stay with him forever, unless he brought the killer to justice.

★ ★ ★

'I failed you. I should have been able to figure out the motive before they killed him,' Freddy said with a look of anguish as they left the church and walked toward Paul's law office.

'It's my fault,' said Paul. 'I held back.'

'You held back?!' Freddy shouted. 'This

isn't some kind of poker game. What did you hold back?'

'I held back what I suspected from the very beginning — that Papa did some bad things during the war. I couldn't face it. I was ashamed to tell you. I screwed up.'

'What do you mean, you suspected? What did he say to you?'

'It's not what he said. It's what he didn't say. There were always gaps in his stories. I never probed. I didn't want to know. We lawyers call it willful blindness.'

Freddy realized he was pushing his friend too hard, and he shifted from investigator to friend mode. 'It's only natural. He was your father.'

'And we used to be so alike. But when I enrolled in the European history course at Holy Cross, the professor lectured about Lithuania during the Holocaust. I didn't want to hear more, and I dropped the course. I had heard enough to know that I wasn't getting the straight poop from Papa. Yet I never pressed him. I did change my attitude toward him, though! I didn't want to be like him anymore. Maybe I even overreacted. I didn't want to have to deal with it.'

'It's understandable. Are you still holding anything back? Think, now, think.'

231

'I'm drawing a complete blank.'

'Think local. Think recent. Let's start with the anonymous call. Can you recall anything about the voice?'

'It sounded nervous.'

'Wouldn't you if you had just killed someone?'

'There was something else.'

'What — what?'

'A very slight accent. Not as bad as Papa's, but it was there. You know the kind that speaks English a little too well — that tries too hard to sound natural?'

'Yeah, yeah, go on. What else? Did it sound at all familiar?'

Paul thought for a minute. Then suddenly he remembered. It began as a vague shard of memory. Then it became clear.

'The old guy at the AIDS walk. Dad's friend. It was him.'

'Paul, what the hell are you blabbering about? What old guy? What AIDS walk?'

Paul told Freddy about being approached on Memorial Drive a few weeks earlier.

'You gave a stranger your father's phone number, just like that?'

'He seemed like a harmless old guy. Gave me his name.'

'Do you remember it?'

'I wrote it down,' Paul said as he leafed

through his pocket calendar. 'Yeah, here it is. Lukus Liatus.'

'That sounds more Lithuanian than Jewish. Probably a phony.'

'He couldn't have planned it. His meeting with me was pure chance.'

'How did he spot you?'

'I've seen pictures of Papa when he was my age. We looked a lot alike.'

'So he's just sitting there, contemplating his navel, when you walk by — and he sees your father.'

'Yes. That's what happened. So what do we have?'

'Let's put it together,' Freddy said in his best investigator's tone of voice. 'We've got an old Jewish man from Vilnius, who probably lives around Cambridge, had one hell of a grudge against your father, and probably knew someone named Liatus.'

'It doesn't sound like much.'

'Are you kidding? It's a gold mine. And we've got more.'

Paul stopped walking and looked at Freddy.

'This old guy couldn't have pulled this off by himself. Probably had an accomplice. Someone younger, stronger, tougher. Maybe his son — someone your age, Paul. There's something else.'

'Don't keep me in suspense.'

'Get the video.'

Paul put his copy of the video of his family's 'death' into the office machine and played it.

'Stop it there,' Freddy ordered. 'Now run it back a few seconds . . . Stop it. Right there, on the driver of the car. Was that the guy you met in Cambridge?'

'Could be. I can't really tell. It's too blurry. It could be.'

'It's a lead,' said Freddy. 'We can probably also get the make of the car.'

'You're amazing.'

'Only if I have the facts. I can't work in a vacuum. Now, fast-forward to the shootings . . . There. Look, the shooter. It's not the same person. Younger. Could be a woman. Can't tell for sure. The face isn't visible, but it looks like a woman to me. Another good lead. Now we have to turn these leads into a specific name by going to the same place the killer may have gone to try to get your father.'

'Tell me where!'

'The Office of Special Investigations in Washington. The Nazi hunters. They know who your father's victims were, and his killer probably tried to blow the whistle on your father after he met you — to get him deported. They probably told him it would take a few years.'

'And the killer figured my father would die before he would be brought to justice.'

'Right. So he decided to take the law into his own hands.'

'Get me the name of the damn whistle-blower,' said Paul, hurrying Freddy toward his office.

'You'll have to make the call. They won't talk to an investigator. But they will talk to a lawyer, especially the son of a deceased victim.'

31

Using the Nazi Hunters

'Martin Mandel here. What can I do for you?' answered the lawyer as he picked up the phone.

'My name is Paul Prandus. I'm Marcelus Prandus's son and I'm also a lawyer.'

'Are you *his* lawyer?'

'My father is dead. One of your victims killed him.'

There was silence at the other end of the phone, then a chilly, 'Let's start over, Mr Prandus. The victims were your father's, not mine.'

'You know what I mean,' Paul said curtly. 'I need to know which victims may have complained about my father.'

'You have a right to know. We opened a file on your father a couple of weeks ago, after receiving a call from a lawyer whose elderly client learned that Prandus was living in Salem. He apparently met one of his relatives on the street.'

'I'm that relative, Mr Mandel. And my chance meeting with that man may have led

236

to my father's death.'

'Wasn't your father dying of cancer? How did he die?'

'Technically, he committed suicide.'

'That's really unusual. The kinds of people we prosecute never commit suicide. Their victims do,' Mandel said with an edge.

'My father's suicide resulted from a diabolical scheme hatched by the man who blew the whistle on my father. It's a long story.'

'I've got time. Tell me.'

Paul angrily recounted the story of the kidnapping and the videotapes — as he and Freddy had pieced it together — to a startled Martin Mandel.

'I must tell you, Mr Prandus, that one part of me — the son of a Sobibor survivor — is thrilled that Professor Menuchen managed in a few weeks to do what I and the entire Department of Justice have been unable to accomplish in the decades we have been in the Nazi-hunting business — proportional justice to a Nazi criminal. Another part of me — the Justice Department lawyer, sworn to uphold the law — understands that we are in the law business, not the revenge business. As much as I personally loathe your father and what

237

he did, if what you say is true, I will be on your side.'

'If you really mean that, then catch the son of a bitch. It's your job.'

'Don't lecture me, Mr Prandus. Send me the videotape by FedEx. I'll do my job.'

32

A Time To Be Arrested

'This morning, we will be exploring the meaning of Ecclesiastes' wonderful poem about the seasons of life. The words have been set to music hundreds of times. They have been inscribed on monuments. They are, perhaps, the most recognizable pages in the entire book. 'To everything there is a season. A time to be born. A time to die . . . ' '

As Professor Menuchen recited these words to his class, three tall men with crew cuts strode into the wood-paneled classroom at the Harvard Divinity School. Approaching the lectern, the oldest announced, 'Max Menuchen, you're under arrest for murder. Everyone else stay seated until we leave.'

There were gasps from the students as their elderly teacher was handcuffed and read his rights. When the FBI agent mentioned 'right to counsel,' Max told a student in the front row, 'Please call the lawyer Abraham Ringel.'

Max knew this moment would come. He

had not known when, but he'd been certain that he would be brought to justice for what he had done.

'People like us get caught, unlike the Nazis,' he had said to Danielle.

Danielle had replied, 'And if we do, it will be your fault for making that call to his son. Without that call they wouldn't have found Prandus's body until the spring.'

'That would not have been fair to his family,' Max had answered. 'They have a right to give him a proper Christian burial, to know he is dead, to move on. They are not the guilty ones.' So Max had made the call that he knew — deep down — would probably lead to his arrest. He had also insisted that the tape be left in the machine, so that Prandus's son would know why his father had killed himself — even if that increased the likelihood that he would become a suspect.

As he was being led away, Max turned to his students and, with a wry smile, said, 'And there is a time for justice. Now is that time. I welcome this season.'

Part Six

Preparing for Justice

33

Ringel for the Defense: August 1999

'I feel like Spielberg on the first day of filming,' Abe Ringel whispered to Rendi as they walked hand in hand through the mob of reporters who seemed to follow Abe wherever he was trying a case. The opening day of a high-profile trial was always exciting to Abe. He was in charge. This was his time, his action, his element, and he loved every second of it. It was he who decided which witnesses to call, which jurors to accept, which cards to play. Despite his long experience as a criminal defense lawyer, Abe never became blasé about a new trial.

The opening of this trial carried a special excitement for Abe. For the first time in his life he was defending someone he loved, someone he cared about personally as well as professionally. Abe had always mocked his old friend and sometime rival, the late William Kunstler, who used to say he only represented people he loved. Now, as he prepared to represent his dear friend Max

243

Menuchen, Abe understood how much more satisfying it was to be an advocate on behalf of a flesh-and-blood person whom he loved than for an abstract principle in which he believed. Abe also understood how much higher the stakes were when a mistake meant not merely that a client would go to jail, but also that a dear friend might never experience freedom again.

Abe and Rendi walked halfway up the steps of the old Dedham courthouse, the same stately white building in which Sacco and Vanzetti had been tried, convicted, and sentenced to death. Although the crime for which Max had been indicted had taken place in western Massachusetts, the trial had been transferred to a venue more convenient to all the participants — and the horde of media that would be covering it live on television.

Menuchen was being prosecuted by the state of Massachusetts — which still quaintly called itself a commonwealth — even though the crime had been investigated by Justice Department lawyers on the basis of a lead provided by the Office of Special Investigations. It was, at least technically, an ordinary state crime of kidnapping and murder.

Danielle was to be tried separately as an

accessory, after Max's trial. The prosecutor wanted to call her as a witness against Max, and he could not do that at a joint trial, because of her privilege against self-incrimination. The police had learned of Danielle's expertise in video photography. They also found out that she had a weekend home near where Prandus's body had been found and that she was away from Harvard during the days Prandus was missing. Since neither defendant had been willing to speak to the police, the cases against both Max and Danielle were entirely circumstantial. The case against Max was far stronger, since his motive was so clear and the video image of the old man, though fuzzy, was a closer match to Max than the even fuzzier image of the 'shooter' was to Danielle. The prosecution believed that Abe Ringel would have to put Max on the stand to explain his actions, and if he did, Max would be forced to disclose Danielle's precise role in the crime.

As if by prearrangement, Abe stopped on the eighth step, turned, and began to speak to the rolling cameras.

'On trial today is not only Max Menuchen, a survivor of the Holocaust, whose entire family was murdered by the so-called victim of this alleged crime. It is not only the killers of the Holocaust, such as this so-called victim. It is the entire civilized world, which failed to bring so many of these killers — such as Marcelus Prandus — to justice. This trial may be one of the most important educational experiences since the end of the war. The Germans had the Nuremberg trials, the Israelis had the Eichmann trial, the French had the Barbie trial, and the Italians had the Priebke trial. The United States has never, until now, had a trial involving the Holocaust. Today that trial begins.'

'Mr Ringel, Mr Ringel!' the shouts began. Abe pointed to Mary Cooper, the *New York Times* Boston correspondent.

'Mr Ringel, it sounds as if you plan to put the victim, Marcelus Prandus, on trial. Is that fair, considering the fact that he is not here to defend himself?'

'The only person actually on trial in that courtroom' — Abe turned and pointed at the courthouse — 'is Max Menuchen. He is the only person who could end up in prison for the rest of his life if he is convicted. You will hear evidence about what Marcelus Prandus did, and the prosecutor will be his advocate — if he dares to be. And now, if you will excuse me, I must visit my client, Max Menuchen, who is in jail, having been wrongfully — in my view — denied bail.'

'Mr Ringel, Mr Ringel!' The shouts continued as Abe and Rendi entered the courtroom, went downstairs to the holding cell, and waited for Max to arrive, by locked bus, from the Charles Street jail in downtown Boston.

Within a few minutes the back door to the courthouse opened and an armed guard escorted Max into his holding cell. Abe and Rendi were allowed into Max's cell, and they embraced Max silently.

'It's absolutely remarkable,' Rendi said, trying to break the uneasy silence, 'that you can manage to look dignified even in that bright orange prison suit. I think this is the first time I've ever seen you without a tie and jacket.' Max did not answer.

Abe put his hand on Max's shoulder. 'Look, I know the cops told you that you have the right to remain silent. But that doesn't mean to your own lawyer and friend. Talk to us, Max. You're getting me nervous.'

Max sat silently, looking at the ground. Still no response.

Rendi tried again. 'You know they make you wear those things to take away whatever shred of dignity remains after they've arrested you, cuffed you, searched you, fingerprinted you, and put you in a cell with a bunch of real criminals.'

'I *am* a real criminal,' Max responded without raising his head.

'No, you're not, damn it!' Abe shouted. 'You're a law-abiding, decent person who was provoked beyond all endurance.'

'I did it, Abe, and I should plead guilty with an explanation. That is the only decent thing to do. It would have been one thing if I had not been caught. They found me, and I cannot lie. I am guilty.'

'Max, please get it into your head that you're not guilty.'

'But I did it,' Max repeated. 'I did exactly what the indictment says I did. I kidnapped him, and I caused his death. That makes me a criminal.'

'How many times do I have to tell you, 'doing it' is not a crime. For 'it' to be a crime, 'it' must have been done with a guilty mind and without a legally accepted justification or excuse.'

'I make no excuses for what I did.'

'You never would have done what you did to Marcelus Prandus if you had not been a victim of the Holocaust. As I've told you a dozen times, your alleged crime — and I emphasize 'alleged' — is the direct product of 'Holocaust survivors syndrome' — a recognized medical condition that eliminates your criminal responsibility.'

'And as I have told you a dozen times, I most certainly am responsible. If not me, who?'

'You're refusing to understand my point. No one else is responsible. It's just that you may not be legally responsible if we can prove that your crime was the product of a recognized mental condition. At least it will give the jury a legal hook on which to render a sympathy acquittal. It's our best shot.'

'It would never work. I am a responsible person.'

'It worked with Lorena Bobbit. Remember her? The woman who cut her husband's penis off?'

'She said her husband raped her.'

'Even if he did, that would not have been a defense — if her act was mere revenge. She won because her lawyer argued that she was suffering from post-traumatic stress syndrome when she did the deed, and the jury found her not guilty by reason of insanity.'

'Did they put her in a mental institution?'

'Just for observation. A couple of weeks later, they found that there was nothing wrong with her. I guess the surgery cured her.'

'She had surgery?'

'No, she *did* surgery. On her husband.'

'So you want me to say I was insane when I kidnapped Prandus and then I was cured when he died?'

'Max. It's true. You never had a decent night's sleep while he was alive. When you found out that he was still alive and was about to die a happy death, your illness got worse. Then when you found out about Sarah Chava, you snapped.'

'I cannot raise this so-called syndrome because it would be unfair to thousands of other Holocaust survivors.'

'Why?'

'Because it would make it appear as if all Holocaust survivors lack self-control.'

'There is medical literature!' Abe said. 'Some Holocaust survivors did commit crimes in the years following their liberation, and the psychiatrists who examined them concluded that their experiences instilled in them a deep-seated distrust of governments.'

'The vast majority of survivors became law-abiding citizens, despite their understandable distrust of governments.'

'Max, it's you I'm interested in. You tried to obey the law. You tried to put your faith in governments — in formal justice. They failed you, and you snapped.'

'If I were to invoke this Holocaust survivors syndrome, it would use the Holocaust as an excuse for criminality. That I cannot tolerate.'

'I can't say I agree with you, but it's your call.'

'Then it's final. I am not going to plead insanity or invoke some other kind of mental excuse. I knew exactly what I was doing. I planned it carefully. I am guilty.'

'Stop that, damn it. You're not guilty. Don't you believe that what you did was justified?'

'Morally, yes. Legally, no. What I did was just, but it was not legal. I once read that Judge Oliver Wendell Holmes scolded a law clerk for saying a judicial decision was unjust. 'We are not in the business of doing justice, young man, but rather in the business of applying the law,' he said.'

'Max, listen to yourself. You're trying to play the lawyer. You're even quoting Holmes. Did you go to law school?'

'Everyone knows that taking someone and holding him against his will is kidnapping, and if he dies, it's murder.'

'Prandus poisoned himself. It was his voluntary act. We have the note.'

'We wanted him to poison himself.'

'He could have decided not to take the poison. That gives us something to work with on the murder charge.'

'How can we get Danielle out of trouble? Can I plead guilty in exchange for her being set free?'

'I think I have a better idea. It requires that you plead not guilty and that we put up a strong defense.'

'I have no defense.'

'Yes, you do. It is called justification. We will try to convince the jury that you were both morally and legally justified in doing what you did.'

'Is this something you are allowed to argue?'

'I hope so. The judge will decide.'

'Would I get a lesser sentence if I plead?'

'The lowest sentence you could possibly get — even on a plea — is ten years. That's life imprisonment for a man of your age.'

'So if there is no difference, why bother to fight the charges?'

'Because you might win. It's unlikely that we'll get a complete acquittal on all charges, but it's possible. Remember Elie Nessler — who shot the man who had molested her son? She shot him in cold blood, with premeditation, while he was handcuffed in a courtroom. It was an open-and-shut case of murder one, but the jury convicted her of manslaughter. Your case is much more compelling. Also, by pleading not guilty, you may be forcing the prosecutor to give Danielle immunity so that she could testify against you.'

'She would never testify against me. She would go to jail first.'

'Not if she knows, but the prosecution doesn't, that her testimony won't hurt you one bit.'

'Now, I'm totally confused.'

'Good. Let's hope the prosecution is equally confused.'

'I don't like the fact that you are treating my trial as a game.'

'I don't like it, either, but that's what trials have become. We're gonna play by the rules. And we're going to try to win. Now it's time for you to dress up in your professor's suit so the jury will be fooled into believing you were granted bail.'

As Max changed out of his jumpsuit, he continued to complain. 'I hate this charade. Can't we just tell the truth?'

'Which truth, Max? Our truth, or their truth?' Abe patted his arm. 'See you in the courtroom. Look somber, but confident.'

'I hate this.'

34

Tactics

'It's a bad tactic, Daddy,' Emma insisted as the Ringel family discussed Max's case over a dinner of pasta and pesto sauce — the Ringel version of fast food. 'It could alienate some women jurors and backfire against Max. Tell him I'm right, Rendi.'

'I'm not so sure you're right this time,' Rendi replied, gulping her tomato juice. 'Why is Abe's defense of justification for Max so different from 'battered women's syndrome'?'

'C'mon. It's so obvious. A battered woman is in actual fear when she kills her batterer. It's classic self-defense. Max killed for revenge. And I'm personally glad he did. Face it, Daddy, his victim posed no current danger to him or anyone else.'

'Yes, he did,' Abe joined in. 'If Max had not done something to Prandus, Max would have done something to himself. It was Max or Prandus. Classic self-defense.'

'I can't believe that Max would ever have killed himself. He survived the Nazis. He's strong. And in any event, it's not self-defense when the person killed isn't in the process of assaulting the person who kills him.'

'Score one for the almost second-year law student,' Rendi said, patting her stepdaughter on the back. 'I think she's got you there, Abe.'

'Pretty good. Who did you take criminal law from, Justice Scalia?' Abe smiled.

'Can't you ever stop joking, Daddy? This is serious. Max's life is on the line. My professor taught us that the theory of justification doesn't apply to killings that are not done in self-defense.'

'That's because she doesn't teach the old case of the sailors who ate the cabin boy. You can tell your professor that not all cases are decided on theory. If I can get the judge to charge the jury with a justification defense, the sympathy factor may click in. Then it's anybody's guess.'

'You'll never get a judge to give a justification instruction in a case where the person killed didn't pose a current threat.'

'Maybe. There is a case in New Jersey where a woman had been abused repeatedly by her first husband, then her second husband threatened her and she killed him. The judge told the jury they could consider the abuse by the first husband in assessing her state of mind when she killed the second husband. You have to admit, there's an analogy there, sweetie.'

'We didn't study that case, either. Where did you find it?'

'On *Geraldo*.'

The debate between Abe and Emma about the tactic to be employed in Max's defense continued for an hour without resolution. Emma advocated a reasonable doubt defense: keep Max off the stand and argue that the circumstantial evidence didn't prove beyond a reasonable doubt that Max had kidnapped and killed Prandus.

'We'll just wait and see,' Abe concluded. 'After the prosecution puts on its case, we'll have a better idea if we need to put Max on the stand. Max would make a great witness. One of the few who would tell the truth. The problem is that the truth could kill him in the minds of some jurors. In the meantime, Emma, I have a job for you. I really need you to do this.'

'That's the first time you've ever said you *needed* me to do something. It must be big.'

'It is, sweetie. I need you to speak to Max in a way that I can't. He loves talking to you. I need more information. Things he won't tell me. Maybe he'll open up to you. Talk to him, please.'

'I'll try, Daddy, but I don't know whether it will help. He's a stubborn old man.'

'No one can resist your charm, sweetie.'

35

Dori's Story

'Uncle Max, Daddy believes that if you hadn't done what you did to Marcelus Prandus, you would have killed yourself. Is he right?'

'And hello to you, too, Emma. That is some way to start a conversation with a friend you have not seen in weeks. No 'Hello.' No 'How has jail been treating you?' No white lies about how good I look even in this prison uniform.'

'I'm sorry. I've never been good at chitchat. I guess I have a lot to learn about bedside — or in this case jail cell — manners. How are you doing?' Emma asked, looking around the dreary surroundings of the jailhouse.

'I am fine, considering the circumstances. And I understand how eager you are to do your job. So let us dispense with the, how do you call it, 'chitchat' and get right to your question. It is impossible to know what I would have done if Marcelus Prandus had died in his bed, surrounded by his adoring children and grandchildren. I would have been devastated, but I cannot speculate as to what I might or might not have done.'

'I don't think you would have hurt yourself. You're strong. You survived the Nazis. You fought the Arabs. You're a survivor, and survivors like you don't kill themselves,' Emma emphasized in the tone of one giving a pep talk.

As Emma said these words, she noticed Max looking off in the distance, as if he were thinking about something else. Suddenly tears filled his eyes.

'I'm thinking of my friend Dori,' said Max.

'You started to tell us about Dori at the seder. I wanted so much to ask you about him, but it was so late, and you were drained.'

Max moved closer to Emma.

'Please tell me about Dori. Maybe that will help answer Dad's question.'

'It is a sad and difficult story.'

'I want to hear it.'

'Dori became the replacement for my family. I found him in the displaced persons camp to which I had been sent, on the outskirts of Munich.'

'What do you mean, you found him?' Emma asked.

'He had been a neighbor in Vilna. I didn't

know him well, since his family was not religious. I recognized him. We immediately became inseparable.'

'What did he look like?' Emma asked.

'You would have liked him. He was handsome and strong. He looked like a poster for Zionism. Tan complexion, black curly hair, muscular — even after what he had been through. And tough! You've never met anyone as determined as Dori. Also very opinionated. He would have given you a run for your money, Emma. His family had been Zionists. They were among the first to be killed. Dori had joined the partisans very early on — before the Nazis took away his family.'

'Did he know your sister?'

'Only to say hello. I showed him the picture. He looked at it and said, 'I remember her. She was very beautiful.' '

'Was Dori part of the group that wanted to take revenge?' Emma asked.

'Not in the beginning. He was devoted to Zionism, and he argued that revenge would distract the Jews from their primary task of creating a new state. 'Channel your anger against the British and the Arabs,' he would tell me. 'Forget about the Nazis. They were in our past.'

'He believed that the Nazis who had

murdered our families were stupid, small people who would live guilt-ridden, miserable, obscure lives. They were not worth risking our lives over. He urged me not to allow revenge to stand in the way, because it would destroy us like it did Michael Kohlhaas.'

'Michael who?'

'It is a Prussian story about revenge which begins with a man who mistreated a pair of Kohlhaas's horses and ends with Kohlhaas's burning down several towns, killing the residents. It is a sad story of the destructive effect of revenge, which became an important symbol for both of us. Dori saw that I was in danger of becoming Michael Kohlhaas, since I could get joy only from seeing my enemies suffer.'

'That doesn't sound at all like you,' said Emma.

'I remember one day as I was working on the camp newspaper, Dori walked in and saw me smiling. He said, 'Aha, I caught you smiling.' I explained that I was working on the article about the mass suicide of Joseph Goebbels's entire family in the last days of the war.'

'That made you happy? Why?' Emma interrupted.

'Because that monster had to kill his own children — all six of them — before killing himself and his wife.'

'Why his children?'

'Because he believed that Jewish survivors would take revenge against his children and torture them.'

'They never did,' Emma said.

'The point is that he believed we would take revenge, and that drove him to killing his own children.'

'And that made you happy?' Emma asked incredulously.

'Yes, Emma, it did. It was appropriate revenge, because many Jewish parents felt it necessary to kill their own children in order to spare them the torture of the Nazis. Well, Joseph Goebbels must have felt at least some of the pain of these parents.'

'Didn't you get any satisfaction from the Nuremberg trials?' Emma asked.

'I obtained no pleasure from seeing a few Nazis hanged, or even from Hitler and Göring killing themselves. These people were not human. They were abstract figures in some distant drama. They had completed their mission of destroying European Jewry, but they had failed to Nazify the world, and for this failure they had to die — either by their own hand or by the hand of those who had conquered them. It had nothing to do with justice. It was some perverse form of destiny. I wanted to see Marcelus Prandus suffer.'

'My dad tells a joke about people so obsessed with revenge that they would rather see their enemies suffer than themselves be rewarded,' said Emma. 'I'm afraid you may be offended.'

'Since I have been in jail, it is difficult to offend me.'

'Okay. It's about these two Jewish neighbors from Riga who had a long-standing feud. Moishe finds an old lamp out of which comes a genie who grants him three wishes, but with the condition that everything the genie gives Moishe, he will give double to his enemy Yakov.'

'I think I see where this is going.'

'Moishe asks for one hundred rubles. It materializes, but Yakov soon appears holding two hundred rubles. Moishe then asks for a beautiful woman. One materializes. Next morning, Yakov is bragging that two beautiful women appeared in his bedroom. Finally, in exasperation, Moishe asks the genie, 'Would it hurt me very much if you removed one of my testicles?' '

'That's not very funny.'

'It's not funny to you because *you* would have willingly given up one of your testicles in exchange for Prandus losing both of his.'

'You're wrong. I would have given up *both* of my testicles in exchange for Prandus losing only one of his. That is how frustrated I was over not being able to secure any justice for my family. Dori made me understand that my own father would have wanted me to go to Palestine rather than to chase his killers.'

'So did you go to Palestine?' Emma asked.

'Yes, on a rickety old boat that almost didn't make it. We had to evade the British blockade.'

'Sounds scary,' Emma replied.

'It was, but the trip was wonderful. It was full of survivors going to a new place for a new life.'

'What happened to Dori?' Emma asked.

'We served in the same army unit. Dori became the commander, and he distinguished himself as a ferocious fighter willing to risk his life by leading the most dangerous assaults. His battle cry was '*Acharai!*' — the Hebrew word for 'after me.'

'After the war, Dori became a completely different person. His energy seemed to wane. The determined look on his face disappeared. He was living his dream, but it was not satisfying to him. Even his complexion began to turn pale. I worried about him. But I was so busy building my career that I did not listen to him. Then came the trip to

Germany in 1956. By that time I was an established scholar teaching at Hebrew University.'

'You followed in your father's footsteps,' Emma noted.

'Yes, and I was invited to Cologne for a conference on the Christian and Jewish interpretations of Ecclesiastes. Dori wanted to come with me to show the Germans they had failed.

'When we arrived in Cologne, Dori looked around in amazement at its obvious affluence. The Marshal plan had turned Cologne — along with much of the rest of West Germany — into an economic boom-town.

'When we arrived at our hotel, Dori could not control his anger. 'They won the fucking war!' he screamed.

'I tried to calm him down, but he continued on like a madman. 'Did you see what Cologne looks like? It's a paradise populated by genocidal murderers. I can't believe it. It's so damn unjust to see killers rewarded.' '

'As we walked the streets, we passed hundreds of men in their thirties, forties, and fifties. Most of them must have served in the war, some of them in the SS and the Gestapo. We saw the faces of killers, and they were smiling.

'Dori could not stand the thought that these murderers were walking free, with their wives, children, and parents.

'He was inconsolable. I saw him cry for the first time since the war. We held each other until Dori suddenly broke away and, with a wild look on his face, exclaimed: 'We must find a Nazi — just one Nazi murderer — and kill him.'

'He insisted that it would send a powerful message: that no Nazi killer can live without watching his back at all times — that somewhere out there is an avenging angel who can strike at any time. Then he quoted Ivan Kamarzov: 'I must have retribution, or I will destroy myself.' '

'What happened? Did Dori attack any former Nazis?'

'He tried to pick fights with several German men, but they were invariably polite and friendly. Whenever he said he was an Israeli the response was always the same: 'I have the greatest respect for the Isreali people.'

'I could see Dori's frustration turning to depression. Away from Israel, he lost his bearings. He felt adrift. Revenge is often a function of powerlessness and hopelessness, and Dori felt utterly impotent walking among the new Germans.

'Then there was his guilt. Like so many

other young men who survived, Dori had abandoned his parents, his younger brother and sister, and his grandparents. He was convincing himself that if he had remained in the ghetto, maybe he could have helped his family to escape. I tried to persuade him that it would have been impossible to save the very young and the very old, but Dori was not thinking rationally. Frustration, guilt, depression, loneliness, and a sense of purposelessness are a dangerous combination, especially in an alien place far from home.'

Max stopped, sighed deeply, and continued. 'While I was presenting a paper at the conference, Dori walked up the several hundred steps to the top of the Dom Church, sat on a bench, and wrote me a note.'

'Oh, no,' Emma whispered.

'It was a short note, and I remember every bitter word,' Max replied with tears in his eyes.

Dear Max,

Hitler promised the German people that if they killed the Jews, Germany would be better off. They killed the Jews, and Germany is better off. I cannot live in a world in which genocide is rewarded. Nor can I do what Michael Kohlhaas did. I am a Jew. I cannot kill the innocent, though every fiber in my body cries out for revenge. Were I to remain alive, and were my frustrations to mount, I could become a Kohlhaas. That must not happen, for the sake of my family name, for the sake of the Jewish people, and for the sake of my own soul. I know only one way to make sure it does not happen.

I love you, and I know that you will figure out a better way.

Shalom,

Dori

'You lost Dori, too,' Emma said, sobbing.

'Yes. And his loss was in some ways the worst. Dori's suicide was the last thing I expected. If I had been told that Dori was under arrest for killing a German, I would not have been shocked. But this! Why? Why is it the victims who suffer, while the killers go on with their lives?

'The next days were among the worst in my life. I could not leave Germany without Dori's body, but the German authorities insisted on conducting an autopsy. I would not go back to the conference. I did not want to see anybody, or be consoled by anybody, especially by Germans. I sought out the synagogue and found a young Lubavitch rabbi from America who took care of the ritual preparations of the body. 'He fell,' the rabbi insisted, not wanting to confront the difficult religious response to suicide.'

'He didn't fall. He jumped. Didn't he?' Emma asked.

'Of course he jumped. Yet who was I to make the rabbi's job more difficult? So Dori, the man who survived the Nazis and the Arabs, fell to his death by accident. That is what the death certificate said. It spared the Germans the need to acknowledge their responsibility for yet another Jewish death.'

'Did you get any comfort from the Jewish survivors in Cologne?'

'No, for them suicide was an all too common phenomenon.'

'That's so sad. What did you do?'

'I made a vow to myself. I would never allow Hitler to determine any decision in my life. Hitler was dead. I was alive. Up until now, Hitler made all the important decisions for me and my family — decisions about life and death. And it was Hitler who made the decision for Dori. During my visits to the Cologne synagogue, several congregants had told me that they were staying in Germany 'to show Hitler that he failed in his goal of ridding Germany of all the Jews.' Others had told me that they were planning to leave

Germany because Hitler did not deserve to have Jews contribute to the building of the new Germany. Hitler was still making the decision for these survivors from his grave. Not for me, no more!'

'Where was Dori buried?'

'Dori's body was buried with full military honors at a Jerusalem cemetery for veterans of the War of Independence. The rabbi in Israel acknowledged that the cause of death was suicide, but declared Dori a victim of the Holocaust. Jews who took their own lives during the Holocaust were not considered as having committed suicide, but rather as having been killed by the Nazis. Sometimes it just took a bit longer.'

'Did Dori's suicide increase your need for revenge?'

'No. It convinced me that I had to get on with my life, if I was to avoid the despair that drove Dori to his death. I knew that I could never eliminate my need for revenge, but I believed that time cools passions and if I could postpone my need for revenge long enough, perhaps it would abate.'

'Did it?'

'Yes. Until the seder and finding Prandus. Then I felt like Dori. I had to do something. If I did nothing, knowing that Prandus was so close, I would become Dori.'

'I was wrong, Uncle Max. I'm so sorry,' Emma said softly. 'Thank you for telling me about Dori.'

Max paused and then placed his hand on Emma's arm. 'I must thank you for listening to me. It has helped me greatly. I wish I had listened to Dori.'

36

Cox for the Prosecution

Erskine Cox pushed his wheelchair past the receptionist through the district attorney's office. Even before it came to a stop in front of the large oak desk with the nameplate 'Georgina Droney, District Attorney,' Cox was shouting: 'I think I know why you picked me to prosecute this case, Mrs Droney. And if I'm right, it stinks. I don't want any part of it.'

'Calm down, Erskine, and tell me why you think I picked you.'

'Because I'm a cripple, and it takes a cripple to prosecute a cripple. I'm a physical cripple, and Menuchen is going to claim he's an emotional cripple.'

'Please take that giant chip off your shoulder, Erskine, and face the facts.'

'What facts? That I need a wheelchair?'

'No — that you're my goddamned best prosecutor. When is the last time you lost?'

'I've only been in the office two years.'

'And you haven't lost one yet.'

'So far you've given me the easy ones.'

'They were only easy because you prosecuted them. You're good, damn it, but this case will determine how good. You're prosecuting a victim, and that's always tough.'

'I don't believe that victims have a license to break the law — to kill.'

'I read your article in the *Harvard Law Review.*'

Cox had written a brilliant attack on the recent use of victimization as a defense, focusing on cases such as the Menendez brothers, Lorena Bobbit, and battered women's syndrome. It was entitled 'One Victim's Wrongs Do Not Make It Right.'

'Is that why you picked me?'

'It was a plus.'

'And was this a plus, too?' Cox asked, pointing to his wheelchair.

'Look, Erskine. Face reality. You're a great prosecutor. Great prosecutors use every advantage they have to beat sleazy defense lawyers who use every trick in the book.'

'So we should be just like them?'

'There's one difference.'

'Yeah, I know. We have the truth on our side. We prosecute only people we believe are guilty. They defend anyone who can pay a fee.'

'That, and the fact that we play by a different set of rules.'

273

'That's my point, Mrs Droney. I don't feel comfortable using my wheelchair as a prop.'

'I wish it were a prop, Erskine,' Mrs Droney said softly.

Cox had been a star athlete at Harvard — crew, squash, and diving. During an Olympic diving tryout, he had broken his back in a freak accident and would never walk again.

'I can't tolerate anyone feeling sorry for me, Mrs Droney, and I'm not going to try to generate any sympathy for myself.'

'I know that. I've watched you in court.'

'Then what advantage do you think I will bring to the case with my wheelchair?'

'Precisely what you just told me.'

'What do you mean?'

'You just told me that you refuse to generate sympathy for yourself on the basis of what you experienced.'

'So?'

'That's the message I want your wheelchair to send. It will contrast sharply with the message I expect Ringel to try to send: namely, that the jury should show sympathy to this killer because of what he experienced.'

'I can live with that,' Cox said as he wheeled himself out of his boss's office.

37

Judge Tree and the Jury — For Justice:
August 1999

'There will be no disruptions or demonstrations
in my courtroom,' Judge Jackson Tree
bellowed in his deep baritone voice. 'This
is one of the most serious and difficult cases
I have ever tried, and it will be tried by the
judge and jury — not by the crowds, not
by the media, and not by any grandstanding
lawyers. Do I make myself clear?'

'Yes, Your Honor,' Abe Ringel and
Erskine Cox responded like schoolchildren
in unison.

'Now you in the back,' Judge Tree
said, pointing to a group of six men
who wore swastika armbands on brown
shirts emblazoned with 'The Aryan Sons of
Justice.' Three of them had demonstrated on
the courthouse steps while the others saved
seats for them in the courtroom.

'You do have the right to demonstrate,
but you will leave your signs outside of my
courtroom.'

'Thank you, Judge. They were scaring me,'

said an old woman garbed in a concentration camp uniform.

Judge Tree scowled at her and said, 'Now, look, ma'am, in this courtroom you are no better than they are. Everyone is equal here, regardless of his or her views. I don't want to hear a word from you, either.'

Then, turning to Abe Ringel, he said, 'I will not tolerate any plants, props, choreographed demonstrations, or the like. I just want to make that clear before we pick a jury. I don't want a mistrial. And I want everyone in this courtroom to know who is in charge here.'

Judge Jackson Tree was a take-charge person, an experienced former prosecutor known for his no-nonsense approach to trials.

Jackson Tree was six feet four inches tall, thus giving rise to his inevitable nickname, 'Oak.' He had played basketball for Harvard in the 1970s and had been a magna cum laude graduate of 'the' law school, as he always called it. He was two years behind Abe Ringel, whom he had come to know during his years as a prosecutor. They were not friends, though they respected each other professionally.

The prosecutor, Erskine Cox, was a Harvard classmate of Jackson Tree. They had belonged to the same moot court team, but they were not personal friends.

'Okay, let's pick a fair jury — a jury that neither side is completely happy with,' Judge Tree announced as the bailiff brought in the first panel of potential jurors.

'All right, ladies and gentlemen of the jury venire. Is there anyone who believes they cannot serve on this jury, which will run about a week?'

Judge Tree obviously enjoyed this part of the process. Massachusetts had just adopted a universal jury service system, under which no one was automatically excluded because of who they were or how important they thought their job was. Judge Tree had been instrumental in pushing for this system and was proud of it.

A man in his early forties rose. 'I run a small business — ten employees. I'm indispensable to its operation.'

Judge Tree looked the businessman directly in the eye and said, 'The cemeteries are full of indispensable people. If you were sick for a week, would your business go under?'

The businessman hesitated, and before he could answer, Judge Tree continued. 'Remember, you're under oath, and this is a public record. If you answer in the affirmative, I intend to send your answer to your bank. We'll see how they consider the fact that your business would go under if you were gone for a week. Let's see what that does to your credit rating.'

'I guess my business could survive without me for a week,' the businessman said sheepishly as he sat down.

'And I bet it will make more money in your absence,' the judge said, unable to resist getting the last word. 'All right, any more indispensable people in this jury pool?'

One brave soul, a woman in her thirties, rose.

'Your Honor, I'm a lawyer, and I have a civil trial scheduled, starting on Friday.'

'I have news for you, young lady. They probably don't teach you this in law school, but jurors are more essential to our justice system than lawyers — or even judges. Get your priorities straight. I'll talk to the judge and get your trial postponed, or another lawyer will take over.'

'But Your Honor, I've been preparing for this trial — '

The judge cut her off. 'Does the name Justice Breyer mean anything to you?'

'Yes, sir, he's on the United States Supreme Court.'

'Pretty important job, right?'

'Right.'

'More important than yours?'

'Of course.'

'Well, guess what happened when Justice Breyer was called to serve on one of my juries?'

'He served?'

'Damn right he did. He didn't try to get out of it — unlike you. He served.'

'Yes, sir.'

'And do you know what I would have said if he had tried to get out of it?'

'I think I can guess, Your Honor.'

'Can you guess what I'm going to say to you, young lady?'

'I think I can, and I withdraw my request to be excused.'

'That's the attitude I like to hear. Any more excuses?' Judge Tree asked rhetorically. Without pausing even a beat, he continued. 'Okay, let's see if any of the potential jurors are biased against either side.'

Abe Ringel loved jury selection. 'All we need is one,' he said to Henry Pullman, the jury expert. 'Who do we love? Who do we hate?'

Pullman had drawn up his usual list of desirable and undesirable characteristics. Leading the list of undesirable characteristics was 'belief that the system always works.'

'I don't want any bankers, or other people from the top of the food chain.'

Pullman showed Abe a cartoon he always carried around with him. It showed three fish. The biggest fish was eating the medium-size and saying, 'Life is always just.' The medium-size fish was eating the tiny fish and saying, 'Life is sometimes just.' The tiny fish was eating nothing and saying, 'Life is never just.'

'I want a jury of twelve tiny fish who believe that life is always unjust,' Pullman barked.

The first potential juror to be questioned was a man in his early fifties named Jim Hamilton who had worked in the front office of the Boston Celtics organization for twenty years, until Rick Pitino — the new Celtics coach — had cleaned house.

'When you were with the Celtics, how did you respond when players made excuses for playing poorly?'

'Red never tolerated excuses,' the man said, referring to the legendary Red Auerbach.

'What about you?'

'I agree with Red.'

Abe's questions were designed to give the prosecutor enough faith in Hamilton so that he would not use one of his six peremptory challenges on this potential juror, whom Pullman had rated a nine on his scale of ten.

'I have no objections to this juror,' Abe declared.

'Nor do I,' said a satisfied Erskine Cox.

The next potential juror was a man named Larry Kane who had served in the military during the Vietnam War and was now an insurance salesman.

'I rank him in the middle — a four or five,' Pullman whispered.

'Have you ever felt a desire to take revenge on someone?' Abe asked Kane.

'Sure, hasn't everybody?'

'Have you ever acted on it?'

'I guess. In small ways.'

'Such as?'

'Let me think . . . I've screwed some competitors out of commissions, after they did that to me.'

'Anything worse?'

'Not that I can think of.'

'On the basis of your experience as a military policeman, do you believe that most criminal defendants did what they are charged with?'

'I don't believe it. I know it.'

'If at the end of this case, after hearing all the evidence, you conclude that the defendant is probably guilty, how will you vote?'

'Guilty.'

'Your Honor, I move to challenge this juror for cause.'

'On what ground?' barked Judge Tree.

'On the ground that he would vote for conviction on the basis of a conclusion that the defendant is *probably* guilty.'

'That was a trick question, Mr Ringel. He will apply the correct standard after I instruct him on what it is. Denied.'

'Okay. I use my first peremptory challenge on Mr Kane.' Abe Ringel had a policy of using a peremptory on a juror he challenged unsuccessfully for cause. No reason to have a resentful juror sitting around waiting to get even with the lawyer for trying to get rid of him.

The next potential juror was a twenty-eight-year-old woman named Marsha Goldberg, who worked as an advertising executive at a local TV station. Pullman ranked her a six. Abe asked her a few routine questions and accepted her.

Erskine Cox began his questions:

'Have you studied the Holocaust in school?'

'Just touched on it.'

'Were any of your relatives victims?'

'Not that I know of.'

'Where does your family come from originally?'

'Pittsburgh.'

'No. I mean before they came to America.'

'I don't know. Somewhere in Eastern Europe. Poland. Russia.'

'Peremptory.'

So Ms Goldberg was dismissed.

After two more jurors — both young women — were accepted, Cox used another peremptory challenge on a middle-aged man named Carl Cohen.

The instant Cox said the word *peremptory*, Judge Tree rose to his full height, banged his gavel, and said, 'Chambers — now.'

As soon as the lawyers entered the chambers, Judge Tree was all over Cox.

'Don't make me embarrass you in front of the jurors, Mr Cox. I see what you're trying to do. Have you read the *Bumpers* case recently?'

'Yes, Your Honor. It says that peremptory challenges may not be used racially.'

'Well, you appear to be using them religiously, and I won't tolerate it.'

'Your Honor, the victims of the Holocaust were Jews, and Jews have a particular reason for hating the victim in the case, Marcelus Prandus.'

'And blacks hate racism, and women hate sexism, but they can all be fair jurors. So can Jews. I'll give you this one. But if you use another peremptory against a Jewish juror, I will see a pattern. Do you understand?'

Abe remained silent. He could have tried to save Juror Cohen, but Pullman had ranked him a three. Abe himself was ambivalent about Jewish jurors, worried that they might lean over backward to show that they would never resort to vengeance.

Everyone loved the next juror, a woman named Sandy Kelley. She seemed fair, friendly, and eager to please.

Several other jurors quickly passed muster as well.

Near the end of the day, eleven jurors had been seated. Each side had used five of their six peremptories. The next potential juror — perhaps the final one — was a seventy-six-year-old woman named Patricia McGinnity, who had been a housewife and now — since her husband had died several years ago — spent her days helping out around the church. Pullman had ranked her a three. 'Too religious, too conservative, too set in her ways.' Cox appeared to like her.

'Use your last peremptory, Abe. She's the Virgin Mary. We don't need her.'

'Who knows what we get if we bump her. We could get Adolf Hitler as our next juror — without any peremptories left.'

'Hitler you could challenge for cause. Even

Tree would give you that one,' Pullman whispered.

'I have a good feeling about this old lady,' Abe said. 'Let me ask her a few questions.'

'You're nuts,' Pullman replied.

'Mrs McGinnity, you don't approve of suicide, do you?'

'No, I don't. People shouldn't play God.'

'Do you believe it's ever right to take the law into one's own hands?'

'Objection, Your Honor,' Cox said. 'What she believes is irrelevant. The law doesn't believe in it, and if she is to serve on the jury, she must obey the law.'

'Nice speech, Mr Cox,' Judge Tree said with a smile. 'I'm sure Mrs McGinnity got the message. Overruled. You may answer.'

'If governments deny us basic rights, such as practicing our religion, we have the natural right to resist. We may have to pay a price for it, at least here on earth.'

'Strike her. Strike her,' Pullman whispered furiously.

Abe looked at Judge Tree and said, 'We have no problem with Mrs McGinnity.' Neither did Cox. The jury was seated. The trial was ready to begin.

Court TV made a motion to televise the trial, and both sides agreed. Max wanted the trial to serve as an educational vehicle about the Holocaust. The prosecution wanted it to serve as an educational vehicle about the dangers of taking the law into one's own hands. And Judge Tree, who was on the Massachusetts State Judicial Commission, which was evaluating the impact of televising trials on the criminal justice system, saw this case as a perfect experiment. He would prove that a high-profile and emotional trial could be televised without becoming a circus. The entire nation would be watching *Commonwealth of Massachusetts* versus *Max Menuchen.*

Part Seven

Justice on Trial

38

The Prosecution's Case

'Mr Cox. Try your case,' announced Judge Tree.

'Ladies and gentlemen of the jury,' Cox began, moving in his wheelchair closer to the jury box, 'this is a classic case of felony murder. We will prove that the defendant, Max Menuchen, with the help of an accomplice, hatched a plan to kidnap an old man and torture him psychologically. As a result of this torture, the old man took his own life, while in a distraught state deliberately induced by the defendant.'

Cox moved his wheelchair around the courtroom as if he was pacing. Then he brought it to rest directly in front of Patricia McGinnity, the old woman who had been selected as the last juror. Cox looked directly into her eyes, eliciting a warm smile from her pale lips. He continued to talk — to Mrs McGinnity.

'This case is analogous to one decided nearly seventy-five years ago. In that case, the defendant broke into the third-story bedroom of a sixteen-year-old girl, intending to rape her. The girl jumped out the window and was killed in the fall. In that case, the judge charged the jury that if the act of jumping was directly caused by the attempted rape, the defendant was guilty of felony murder, even if he never intended for the girl to die.'

'Objection, Your Honor.' Abe was on his feet, arguing, 'That was an underage girl. This was a mature man. That was three-quarters of a century ago, when sexual mores were different. A rape victim was considered to be 'damaged goods.' Today — '

'Overruled. The jury can figure out the differences. Proceed, Mr Cox.'

'In this case, we will prove that this defendant intended for his victim to die. Indeed, the entire plan would have failed if the victim did not die before learning the truth. It was a cruel and bizarre plan, and tragically, it worked exactly as intended.'

Mrs McGinnity shook her head up and down, signaling apparent agreement with Cox's analogy — or was it merely politeness? 'We shudda used our last peremptory,' Pullman whispered.

Abe responded reassuringly, 'I bet she smiles at me, too.'

Cox continued, positioning his wheelchair

in front of the poker-faced Muriel Baker.

'No crime is ever committed without a motive. The defense may try to suggest a good motive for these bad and criminal acts. But the judge will tell you that good motive — and we by no means concede that the motive here was good — is not an excuse or a defense for crime. Your job is not to figure out *why* the defendant did what he is accused of doing, but only to decide *whether* he did what he is accused of doing. We will prove that beyond any reasonable doubt. When all the evidence is in, we will ask you to convict the defendant of kidnapping and felony murder.'

'Mr Ringel, do you have an opening statement at this time?' asked Judge Tree.

'Beyond reminding the jury to keep an open mind until all the evidence is in — which I know you will tell them to do — I reserve my opening statement until after the prosecution has presented its case.'

'Fine. I do remind the members of the jury to keep an open mind, to adhere to the presumption of innocence, and to listen to all the evidence before deciding anything. Now we are ready for the first witness.'

'The prosecution calls Danielle Grant.'

From the back of the courtroom, Justin Aldrich — who was representing Danielle

291

Grant — shouted, 'Objection, objection!'

'Chambers,' said Judge Tree, pounding the gavel.

When they reached the judge's chambers, Ringel, Aldrich, and Cox were already arguing.

'Talk to me,' Judge Tree demanded, 'not to each other and not at each other. What's the basis for your objection, Mr Aldrich?'

'My client is a co-defendant, Your Honor,' Aldrich insisted. 'The prosecution can't call her. She has a privilege against self-incrimination, and she's darn well going to exercise it.'

At the mention of privilege, Cox pulled a document out of his pocket and put it in front of Judge Tree.

'Use immunity, Your Honor. It trumps the privilege. She has to testify, and we can't use her answers against her at her trial.'

'They can't do that, Your Honor,' Aldrich said imploringly. 'How can we ever be sure they won't use her answers?'

'Because the prosecutor in her case won't find out what she said in this trial,' Cox said.

'You're going to put him behind a Chinese wall?' Judge Tree asked, invoking the metaphor used by lawyers.

'Exactly.'

'But you can't build a Chinese wall around a high-profile case like this one. Everyone in America will be watching it on TV and reading about it,' Aldrich insisted.

'Precisely,' Cox said smugly.

'Wipe that smile off your face, Mr Cox, and tell us why you're so pleased with yourself. Aldrich here seems to have a point.'

'We agree, Your Honor, that everyone in America will know what Ms Grant testified to. That's why we sent her prosecutor to China — literally. He's investigating a drug import case in northern China, and he's literally behind the Chinese Wall.'

'Pretty good reason for being smug, Cox. Now it's your turn, Aldrich. What's the problem if the next prosecutor is ten thousand miles away?'

'The jury impaneled in the Grant case will know about her testimony,' Aldrich sputtered.

Judge Tree shook his head in disagreement. 'We will see to it that you strike any such juror, Mr Aldrich. You know as well as I do that we can always find twelve jurors that read only the sports pages.'

'But we can never be sure that some of my client's compelled testimony won't leak through the wall,' Aldrich complained.

'The burden will be on the prosecution,

and it is a heavy one,' Judge Tree said, looking directly at Cox.

'We understand our burden,' Cox replied. 'And we realize that we may get 'Northed.' '

'Northed' referred to the Oliver North case, in which the court of appeals reversed Colonel North's conviction on the ground that some of the testimony he had given to Congress under a grant of use immunity might have seeped through the Chinese wall erected in that case; North could not be retried because of this possibility, and he went free.

'As long as you understand the risks and are willing to incur them, I rule that Danielle Grant may be compelled to testify against the defendant, Max Menuchen,' the judge said. 'Let's get back to the courtroom and get Ms Grant on the stand.'

Danielle Grant walked slowly to the witness stand, inspected the Bible she was handed, raised her right hand, and swore to tell the truth.

'Ms Grant, what did you do on the early evening of May twenty-ninth, this past year?'

Danielle looked Cox straight in the eye and responded, 'I helped Professor Max Menuchen kidnap Marcelus Prandus. We did it together, as part of a plan that I designed.'

As soon as Cox heard this answer, he knew he had fallen into a trap.

'I move to declare Ms Grant a hostile witness, Your Honor,' Cox demanded.

'On what ground, Mr Cox?' said Judge Tree.

'She's taking an immunity bath.' Her lawyer had told her to answer Cox's questions in the most self-incriminating manner, so as to broaden the scope of her immunity.

'That may be true, but she's helping you *in this case*, Mr Cox. You made your bed, now you have to lie in it. Denied.'

Cox continued to question Danielle, trying to ask narrow questions.

'Where did you take Marcelus Prandus?'

'We took him to an abandoned hunting shack in the Berkshires.'

'What did you do to Prandus when you got him to the shack?'

'We tied him to a chair and made him watch videos.'

'What did the videotapes show?'

'They showed each of Marcelus Prandus's children and grandchildren being killed.'

Several jurors gasped.

'As far as you could tell, did Marcelus Prandus believe that all of his children and grandchildren had, in fact, been killed?'

As he asked the question, Cox looked to

295

see whether Ringel would object. There were several bases on which an objection could have been raised. Ringel remained silent. This gave Cox a clue to his likely strategy and defense. It suggested that the defense might not be an 'I didn't do it,' factual claim.

Danielle responded forthrightly, 'I was there when Max played the first video. It was apparent from his actions that Marcelus Prandus believed his grandson, Marc, had been murdered. He screamed and cried uncontrollably. Nobody could have faked those feelings.'

'Where were you when the other videos were played?'

'I chose not to be there so that Max could face Prandus alone.'

'Was it Max Menuchen's plan that Marcelus Prandus would believe that his children and grandchildren had been murdered?'

'Yes, that was our plan.'

'Was it also your plan that he would continue to believe that they had been murdered until he died?'

'Yes, if he suspected that they were not dead at any time before his own death, the plan would have backfired.'

'To your knowledge, did he ever suspect that his children and grandchildren had not actually been killed at any time before his death?'

'No, he did not.'

'Was it part of your plan for Marcelus Prandus to die during the kidnapping?'

'Yes, it was.'

'Did you plan to kill him?'

'I was prepared to kill him if he did not die from his cancer or kill himself, but I don't believe Max Menuchen would have killed him.'

This answer caught Cox off guard. 'Objection, Your Honor,' Cox said, his voice rising with frustration.

Abe smiled and stood up. 'He can't object to the truthful answer given by his witness to his question.'

'Denied,' ruled the judge.

Now Cox had to improvise, but he was not too worried, because legally it really did not matter whether Max intended to kill Prandus, as long as Prandus died as a result of the kidnapping and while that felony was still in process.

'Did you have to kill him?' Cox continued.

'No.'

'Why not?'

'Because he killed himself.'

'If you know, why did he kill himself?'

Again Cox waited for the anticipated objection

from Ringel. Again Ringel remained silent.

'He killed himself because he believed that we had killed his entire family and that we did it in revenge for what he had done to Max's family fifty years earlier. It's right in the note you subpoenaed from us.'

'And it was you and Max Menuchen who caused him to believe that you killed his family, was it not?'

Again no objection.

'Yes, that was our plan.'

'And the plan worked?'

'Yes.'

'And as a result of the plan, Prandus took his own life, believing that his entire family had been killed and that he was somehow responsible for their deaths?'

'Yes.'

'Now, I'm going to ask you a question, and in order to avoid you giving hearsay testimony, I would like you to try to answer yes or no, without any elaboration, if you can.'

'Okay.'

'When you previously testified that Mr Prandus believed that his family had been murdered in revenge for what he had done to Mr Menuchen's family fifty years earlier, were you referring to Mr Prandus's service as an auxiliary policeman in Lithuania during the Nazi occupation?'

'Yes, I was.'

'Just one more question, Ms Grant. Were you given use immunity if you testified truthfully?'

'Yes, I was.'

'Have you testified truthfully?'

'To the best of my ability, yes.'

'I have no further questions of this witness. Mr Ringel may cross-examine.'

The jurors sat straight up in their chairs as Abe Ringel walked toward the witness. Abe realized that jurors expected cross-examination to be dramatic — especially when the witness was an accomplice who has been given immunity. Abe noticed Jim Hamilton, the ex-Celtics employee, leaning forward in anticipation of the fireworks. Abe looked Danielle Grant straight in the eye and asked her one question: 'I know you want to tell the whole truth, Ms Grant. Is there anything that happened which was not brought out by Mr Cox's questions to you?'

'Sidebar, Your Honor,' Cox steamed, pushing his wheelchair to the bench. 'Can't you see what he's doing, Your Honor? This is a fix. He's helping her avoid prosecution by trying to give her an immunity shower on top of her bath. It's wrong. It's sneaky. And it stinks.'

'Look, Mr Cox, I'm not going to tell Mr Ringel how to try his case, any more than I'm telling you how to try yours. His question to Ms Grant is proper — albeit unusual — cross-examination. I don't care if he's giving her an immunity shower or even a Jacuzzi. That's your problem — and the problem of your pal over in China. Objection denied. Ms Grant, you may answer Mr Ringel's question.'

Danielle used the opportunity to describe in detail the visit to the museum, the way she had taped and edited the video, and the role she had played in the kidnapping. After she completed her ten-minute answer, Abe announced, 'I have no further questions for this witness.'

Cox called Dr Albert Stone as his next witness. He put the psychiatrist through the usual process of establishing his credentials as an expert in grief-induced suicide. He asked him whether he had listened to Danielle Grant's testimony and read the autopsy and forensic reports, and then he continued.

'On the basis of what you have heard and read about the cause of Marcelus Prandus's death, do you have an opinion as to the cause of death?'

'Yes, I do, Mr Cox.'

'And what is your opinion?'

'I am absolutely certain that Mr Prandus took his own life.'

'On what is that opinion based?'

'On two kinds of evidence, the first forensic, the second psychiatric.'

'Please explain.'

'The autopsy showed that the cause of death was cyanide poisoning. There was cyanide residue on his fingers. The note said it was suicide. That conclusion is corroborated by the psychiatric evidence of grief and motive to commit suicide. It was suicide induced by grief.'

'In what way did the grief induce the suicide?'

'Mr Prandus believed that his entire family had been murdered and that his own actions, many years earlier, were the cause of his family's death. He could not bear that responsibility and so he ended his life.'

'Have you reached that expert opinion with a high degree of medical certainty?'

'Yes, I have.'

'No further questions.'

Abe stood up and said to the judge, 'Now, this witness I do wish to cross-examine.'

'Go ahead, Mr Ringel.'

'Dr Stone, have you examined other

situations in which people took their lives because they felt responsible for the death of loved ones?'

'Yes, several such situations.'

'Would you please describe them.'

'Last year, a lawyer from Connecticut took his own life after his three-year-old child, whom he was supposed to be watching, drowned in a pool. In another case, a minister killed himself after he had caused an automobile accident killing his two children. He was drunk when the accident took place. In a third situation, a mechanic took his own life after he beat his wife to death. In yet another case, a young mother killed herself after she had shaken her baby and caused him to end up on a respirator, brain dead.'

'Is it fair to say that in each of the cases you described, the person who committed suicide was actually responsible for the deaths or injuries which precipitated the suicide?'

'I think that is fair, though it is not always the case.'

'When is it not the case?'

'Sometimes a mentally disturbed person will blame himself for something that he had little or nothing to do with.'

'But that kind of fantasy blaming is not characteristic of people without a prior history of mental illness who end up killing themselves, is it?'

'Not generally.'

'Do you know of any cases, within your experience where a previously mentally healthy person fantasizes responsibility for something he did not do and kills himself because of that fantasy?'

'No, I do not.'

'Do you know anything about Marcelus Prandus that would suggest a preexisting mental illness?'

'No, there was nothing in his medical records or history to suspect mental illness.'

'Is it fair to conclude, therefore, that if Marcelus Prandus believed that what he did to the Menuchen family fifty years earlier was horrible enough to provoke the revenge killing of his entire family, he was not fantasizing?'

'This is outrageous, Your Honor!' Cox shouted, nearly rising from his wheelchair. 'This witness has no idea what Mr Prandus may or may not have believed or done. I move to strike.'

'He opened the door, Your Honor, by asking Dr Stone about the cause of Prandus's suicide. I should be allowed to probe his answer.'

Judge Tree fixed Abe with a stern look.

'Very clever, Mr Ringel. I see where you are going, but I'm not going to let you go there, certainly not with this witness. He doesn't know enough about what happened fifty years ago to help you on that. Objection sustained. Question is to be disregarded. Now on to your next question.'

'I have no further questions, Your Honor,' Abe said, satisfied that he had planted a seed of curiosity in the minds of the jurors as well as the judge.

'Who else are they going to call?' Max asked Abe in a whisper.

'Well, they can't call you, and there are no other eyewitnesses. Maybe Paul Prandus — to generate some sympathy for his father.'

'Can they do that? It doesn't sound fair. He doesn't know what his father did.'

'They can, and they probably will.'

'I call Paul Prandus as my next witness,' Cox announced.

'Objection, Your Honor,' Abe said, knowing it would be denied.

'What's the matter, Mr Ringel, are you afraid of the truth coming out?' the judge replied with an edge. It was Judge Tree's patented way of discouraging frivolous objections. Abe got the point and quickly sat down.

Paul Prandus looked directly into Max's

eyes as he took the oath. His hatred was palpable.

As Cox began his examination, Paul Prandus took a deep breath, clearly struggling to maintain control. His jaw clenched. He was a lawyer, and he knew what he had to say in order to see his father's killer convicted. And Paul Prandus wanted Max Menuchen convicted and sentenced to spend the rest of his life in prison.

'When was the last time you saw your father alive?'

'At his birthday party, with his children and grandchildren. He was very happy.'

'When did you next see him?'

'I never saw him. Only his dead body on the floor of the shack where Freddy Burns and I found him. Then I saw him on the table in the morgue,' Paul said, holding back tears.

'Mr Prandus, the official cause of death was suicide. Do you believe that?'

'Objection, Your Honor,' said Abe. 'He is not an expert on cause of death. Let them call another expert if they want to dispute her findings.'

'I'll allow his opinion as a son who knew his father. You may answer.'

'My father loved life. He would never have killed himself. That man,' Paul said, pointing to Max, 'killed him by taking away the most important reasons he had for living — his family.'

Judge Tree called a recess as Paul continued to glare at Max.

39

Freddy Burns

'You've put on a couple of pounds, Freddy, my man. You're beginning to look like my accountant,' Abe said, patting the private investigator on his expanding spare tire as they left the courtroom for the morning recess.

'Shows you how far I'm willing to go for my clients. Nobody's gonna suspect I'm a PI with this pot. It's a great cover,' Freddy laughed.

'It's been, what, ten years since you took the bullet?'

'More like fifteen. Time flies when you have to limp through life.'

'Looks like it hasn't slowed you down much. You still get the interesting cases.'

'Any case you're on the other side of is interesting, Abe. Hey, why don't you ever hire me so we can be on the same side for a change?'

'My wife's a PI. We keep it in the family. And now my daughter is going to law school. I'll be ready to retire soon.'

'Abe Ringel playing golf? No way. You'll die in court. Me? I'll die in some dark alley looking through binoculars at some married guy shtupping his secretary.'

'You guys did a nice job tracking my client — professionally speaking.'

'We got a little bit of unexpected help from the Office of Special Investigations. I'll bet it's the first time those guys blew the whistle on a Jewish victim. But they did the right thing. Your client had no right to do what he did.'

'The jury will decide that,' said Abe. 'Did your guy have any idea what kind of a shit his father was?'

'No way. I knew the old man. Seemed harmless enough to me. It really destroyed Paul just to learn what his old man had done, and then to find him dead . . . '

'Does your guy know that it was my guy who called to tell him where the body was?'

'Didn't take Perry Mason to figure that one out.'

'My guy really felt bad that the family would be hurt. His only grievance was against the old man. He didn't want to cause any unnecessary pain.'

'Maybe he just wanted to rub it in. Wanted Paul to see the tape and think his own kid had taken a hit.'

'No way. The tape was left behind so that Paul would understand why his father had killed himself. Max knew he was taking a risk by leaving the tape. Maybe a part of him wanted to get caught and stand trial. If he hadn't dropped a dime, your guy wouldn't have found the body for months.'

'It sure was isolated out there. I'll give you that. I don't think you guys are gonna walk on this one, Abe. It seems open and shut on the law.'

'All I need is one sympathetic juror.'

'But if that's all you get, we'll just try it again. My guy is pretty pissed, and Cox is with him all the way.'

'Yeah. But are you with him all the way? I remember when you were lying on the gurney waiting to have your bullet removed and they took the shooter first. Remember what you said to me?'

'I was in pain and under medication.'

'You said it again a week later.'

'I was still in pain.'

'Don't you think my guy was in pain when he did what he did?'

'I didn't actually kill the guy who shot me. I just said I wanted to. Big difference, Counselor.'

'Still, I'm betting there's a small part of you that understands what my guy did.'

'Hey, I'm not on the jury. Direct your advocacy at the one juror you think you can get. Leave me out of this. I'm just a working stiff trying to make an honest buck.'

As the recess ended and Abe walked back into the courtroom, he was thinking about which 'one juror' would be most important to his client. He thought he knew.

Cox resumed his examination of Paul Prandus. 'What was the reaction of your children to their grandfather's disappearance?'

'My son, Marc, was devastated. He was very close to Grandpa Chelli and visited him nearly every day. He couldn't imagine why anyone would want to hurt him. He still can't.' Paul's voice was rising. 'That man destroyed my father and tried to kill my son.'

'What about the rest of the family?'

'They were all very upset,' Paul said in an agitated voice. 'The adults all knew that our father was dying. The children had been told that he was very sick. At first we thought maybe he had been taken to the hospital, but we checked. We were all quite distraught. It was awful.'

'Did you eventually find him?'

'No,' Paul replied with an edge to his voice. 'I never found him. I found his body. I'm only glad my son was not with us when

310

we found Papa's body.'

'I have no further questions.'

Abe rose slowly, looking deeply into Paul Prandus's blue eyes. He was not certain what tack to take with this witness. Ordinarily he did not cross-examine children of a victim, for fear of creating more sympathy. Abe had sensed something in Paul Prandus. He had not been able to test his instincts by talking to Paul directly before the trial, since Paul was a government witness and the prosecutor might make noise about trying to influence a prosecution witness. Nor had Abe wanted to conduct a full-fledged investigation of Paul Prandus. His brief conversation with Freddy Burns had given Abe some insights into the younger Prandus. He had also gotten Rendi to poke around just a little into Paul's background — public record information and the like. Most important, Abe had observed Paul Prandus at every opportunity.

An interesting picture was beginning to emerge. The picture was of a tightly wound man who could be made either to break or to bend on cross-examination. Abe had a tough decision to make. He decided to go with his instincts and ignore the rule of cross-examination he had learned in law school that cautioned against asking any question to which he did not already know the answer. Abe had learned, through painful experience, that general principles always had exceptions, and he sensed the opportunity for an exception here.

'Mr Prandus, please tell us about your family.' It was an open-ended question — a softball that Paul Prandus could hit out of the ballpark.

'Before my father's death, we had a wonderful family life. We all lived within a mile of each other. My brother and his wife, his daughter, my wife and son. It all ended with Papa's death.'

Unperturbed, Abe pitched him yet another softball. 'Did your father have a good marriage?'

'He and Mama were deeply in love.'

'Did he treat his children well?'

'He could be a bit old-fashioned and stern, but he loved us very much and we loved him.'

Max was growing visibly upset at the line of questioning and Paul's answers. He passed Abe a note that read: 'You are creating sympathy for Marcelus Prandus, why?'

Abe glanced at the note, asked the judge for a moment to confer with his client, and whispered to Max, 'Trust me, it's a set up. You'll see the payoff when we put on our case. I know what I'm doing.'

'I certainly hope so, because the jury is falling in love with the Prandus family.'

'Then my plan is working,' Abe said, resuming his gentle questioning of Paul Prandus.

'Since the time you can remember, did your father live a generally happy life?'

'My father was full of life, laughing, lots of friends, surrounded by family. He had his unhappy moments — when Mama died. When one of his grandchildren was hospitalized with a high fever. When he learned he had cancer. But in general, his life in America was very happy.'

Abe moved on to another subject, pausing for a moment for the previous testimony to sink in.

'What were your feelings toward Max Menuchen when you first learned that it was he who had kidnapped your father?' Abe asked.

'Rage, anger, fury. He had killed my father in cold blood. Those are still my feelings, but unlike your client, I have been able to control them,' Paul said, straining against the witness chair.

'When you learned who killed your father, what did you do?'

'We called the authorities.'

'Did they come?'

'Yes, of course.'

'You say, 'Of course.' Can you imagine the police not coming in response to your call?'

'No, of course not. My father had been kidnapped and killed. It was a case for the police.'

'What if the police refused to come?'

'They couldn't refuse.'

'Please, just imagine the situation where you called the police to report a kidnapping and killing, and they said they were too busy.'

'Objection, Your Honor,' Cox said. 'It's speculative and hypothetical. This man is not an expert witness. He's the victim's orphaned son. He shouldn't be asked ridiculous hypothetical questions.'

'Please give me some latitude on cross, Your Honor. The prosecution asked this witness about his state of mind, and I should be able to test his answers with hypotheticals.'

'All right, Mr Ringel. I'll give you some latitude, but don't abuse it. Get to the point quickly.'

'Thank you, Your Honor. Now, Mr Prandus, please tell the jury, to the best of your ability, what you would have thought if the police had refused to respond to your call.'

'My anger would have increased.'

'What if the man who you believed killed your father was simply walking away as a free man and returning to his normal life?'

'Objection, Your Honor, he's making his closing argument through this witness. It's not fair. Stop him.'

'You are beginning to get a bit far afield, Mr Ringel. Rein it in. Bring it home,' the judge admonished. 'But you can answer, Mr Prandus.'

'I would have become enraged.'

'To the point of trying to stop him from leaving?'

'Yes, probably.'

'Even if it were against the law?'

'Well, I would have tried to call the police — to invoke the law — but you asked me to imagine that they refused to come.'

'That's right. Now I want you to imagine something even more extreme.'

Silence.

'Imagine the police saying to you, 'We won't come because your family is Lithuanian. We don't respond to the crimes committed against Lithuanians.' '

'Objection. This is becoming absurd. He's playing the ethnic card. You've got to control him, Your Honor. This is all irrelevant.'

'No, Mr Cox. It's becoming interesting

and relevant,' Judge Tree replied. 'Now I know what Mr Ringel is getting at. You may continue, but just for a few more questions.'

'Thank you, Your Honor. Now, Mr Prandus, is it not fair to say that your rage would have increased if the police refused to help you because you are Lithuanian?'

Paul was seething with rage. He could see exactly what Abe was doing, but he was determined to keep his composure. 'I cannot imagine that happening, but yes, if it did, it would increase my rage.'

'You say you can't 'imagine that happening.' Have you studied what happened in Lithuania during the Second World War?'

'Yes, I have.'

'Did the police come to help the Jews during that period?'

'No. They did not.'

'Did the police help to kill the Jews?'

'I don't know, maybe some did.'

'Was your father a member of the militia?'

'Yes, he was.'

'Did he help the Jewish citizens of Lithuania?'

'I don't know.'

'Did he participate in the killing of innocent Jewish citizens of Lithuania?'

'Objection, Your Honor. This witness is not on trial, and neither is his late father.'

'Overruled. He may answer, if he knows.'

'I don't know,' Paul Prandus said angrily.

'I have one final set of questions,' Abe said, pointing to the videocassettes on the prosecutor's table. 'Have you watched the videotapes that were shown to your father?'

'Yes, I have.'

'It must have been very painful for you to watch pictures of your child being killed.'

'It was torture. Your client is a very cruel and sadistic man.'

'Can you imagine anything worse than having to watch those videos?'

'Yes!' Paul shouted. 'Having to watch them believing they were true — the way your client made my father watch them, and the way I watched them before learning they were fake.'

'What if the videos had been actually true?' Abe said in a soft voice.

'They were true to my father,' Paul replied, his voice rising in pitch, 'and they were true to me for a few painful minutes.'

'What if they actually turned out to be true?'

'But they didn't, thank God,' Paul said, crossing himself.

'If they had been real — if my client had

actually murdered your son — could you have taken his life?'

'Yes, I could have,' Paul Prandus said, looking directly into Abe's eyes. Paul stopped himself from saying, 'What makes you think I still won't?'

'One final question. If you were to come to believe that your father actively participated in the killing of innocent Jews and that he was never brought to justice for his crime, would you understand the rage that was felt by a surviving family member of his victims?'

'Objection.'

'Sustained.'

'I could understand it, but I still could never have done what that man did,' Paul said, ignoring the judge's ruling and pointing to Max.

'I have no further questions.'

'Just one redirect, Your Honor,' Cox said, moving his wheelchair near Paul Prandus. 'Can you ever imagine yourself killing a helpless old man who is tied to a chair?'

'No, I don't think I could.'

'One recross.'

'Go ahead.'

Abe walked to within a few feet of the witness box and looked into Paul's blue eyes. 'Even if you had just learned that the old man in the chair had killed your son?'

Paul paused, then he responded, looking at Max, not Abe.

'Maybe I could have killed him.'

'Even if he were tied to a chair?'

'Even if he were tied to a chair.'

'Does either side plan to recall this witness?' Judge Tree inquired as Paul Prandus began to rise from the witness chair. Normally Abe would keep his options open with an adverse witness and respond by saying that he might recall the witness. This would result in the witness being excluded from the remainder of the trial in order to prevent him from hearing the other witnesses and tailoring his testimony to fit neatly into the prosecution's case. But Abe had a hunch about Paul Prandus, and he wanted him to hear the remaining witnesses. From now on, Abe would treat Paul Prandus as if he were the 'one juror' he had to win over.

'No, Your Honor. We have no objection to the witness remaining in the courtroom during the remainder of the trial.'

Paul Prandus took a seat in the front row of the spectator section, next to Freddy Burns and directly behind Erskine Cox.

Cox ended his case by playing for the jury the videotapes made by Danielle. The jurors gasped audibly as they watched each of

Marcelus Prandus's descendants being killed. From these chillingly realistic videotapes, it was easy to understand how Marcelus Prandus had come to believe that his family had been killed. It was a dramatic ending to what appeared to be an open-and-shut case for the prosecution, especially in light of the lack of cross-examination by Abe Ringel. The defense seemed to be conceding the essential elements of the crimes charged.

That night on Court TV and radio talk shows around America, Abe Ringel was being pilloried for his lackadaisical defense to what appeared to be a strong prosecution presentation. Joseph Genevese, a former prosecutor, accused Ringel of deliberately throwing Max's case in order to prevent Danielle from being tried. Lori Levenberg, the CBS legal consultant, predicted that it would only get worse the following day, when Abe began his defense.

40

The Defense Case

Although he had done this a thousand times, Abe was always nervous at the beginning of the defense case. He knew that under the law he didn't have to prove anything. The entire burden was on the prosecution. Early in his career he had learned that while the prosecution had the burden in theory, the defense carried a heavy burden in practice. Most jurors assumed — perhaps only in the back of their minds — that defendants were guilty. Why else would they be on trial? And they were right, as a matter of common sense. The vast majority of criminal defendants were, in fact, guilty. That was the reality, and Abe knew it. In his lectures he would say, 'Thank God most defendants are guilty in this country. Would anyone want to live in a country where the majority of people charged with crimes were innocent? That may be true in Iraq or Iran or China, but not in the U.S. — and in order to keep it that way, we need zealous defense attorneys who are prepared to defend the guilty along with the innocent.'

Now that Abe was defending mostly innocent people, he realized how much more of a burden that placed on his shoulders. Losing for a guilty defendant was not difficult — it was the defendant's fault. Losing for an innocent defendant was the lawyer's fault. Losing for an old friend was intolerable. And Abe knew that the chances of losing for his friend Max were considerable, especially since he had to begin his opening statement by essentially conceding that Max had committed the acts necessary to establish the crimes of kidnapping and felony murder.

'Ladies and gentlemen of the jury, I did not challenge the prosecution's evidence in this case because it is true — at least as far as it went. But you will hear the whole truth in our presentation. I will also present two interesting and compelling questions about causation. The first is: Can a defendant be said to cause the death of a victim when it is the victim himself — by his own act of free will — who takes his life? But that is not all this case is about. It is about causation of a different kind. What could have caused a law-abiding seventy-five-year-old Bible scholar — a man of peace, not violence; a man of the mind, not the sword — to have devised the diabolical plan that my client, Max Menuchen, stands charged of devising and implementing?

'The prosecution deliberately avoided asking that question because they were afraid of the answer — of the *whole* truth, which is supposed to come out at a trial. We will present the whole truth — not only *what* happened, but also *why* it happened. Max Menuchen will not shrink from admitting exactly what he did, but when you hear why he did it — and when you hear what he considered, but refrained from doing — you will ask yourselves, what would I have done if I had been in his shoes? As you listen to the defense case, I implore you each to ask yourselves what you would have done if you had experienced what Max Menuchen experienced.

'The judge will instruct you on the law you must apply. He will tell you that no act alone is ever a crime. There must be an evil intent and a lack of justification. It will be your responsibility to apply the law, as the judge gives it to you, to the facts as you find them — and then to decide whether the acts committed by Max Menuchen were criminal, rather than justified or excusable.'

Even before Abe sat down, Cox was objecting.

'Your Honor, the law doesn't allow a justification defense in this kind of situation. If it did, anyone could simply decide to take the law into his own hands if he was dissatisfied with what the courts did. I know of no case supporting Mr Ringel's proposed defense, and I object.'

Judge Tree nodded his head in apparent agreement. 'Do you have any precedent, Mr Ringel? If you do, show it to me — in chambers.'

'I do, Your Honor,' Abe said, rustling through some papers and winking at his daughter, Emma, who was seated in the front row of the spectator section. It was Emma who had remembered this precedent from a history course she had taken at Barnard entitled American Radicalism in the 1960s, 1970s, and 1980s. She had researched the case and brought Abe the results that he was now using on Max's behalf.

As soon as Abe entered the chambers, he began speaking. 'The precedent is President Carter's daughter, Amy, right here in Massachusetts,' he said. 'Amy Carter, along with several other protesters, including the late Abbie Hoffman, was charged with trespass and disorderly conduct for occupying a University of Massachusetts building in which a CIA recruiter was interviewing applicants. They claimed that it was 'necessary' for them to commit this crime in order to prevent the greater injustice of CIA actions. The judge allowed the jury to consider the necessity defense under Massachusetts's law, and the jury acquitted the defendants. Here, I have the judge's instructions in that case.' Abe handed Judge Tree and Erskine Cox a ten-page photocopy. 'This case is far more compelling than the Amy Carter case, and in that case the jury acquitted the defendants.'

'This is ridiculous, Your Honor,' Cox said, his voice rising. 'That was Judge Browning from Tanglewood. He was a hippie. That was a crazy time. This is no precedent for the 1990s. If you let Ringel use the Abbie Hoffman defense, you're going to turn this trial into another 'Chicago Seven' case.'

'No, I won't, Mr Cox. I'll maintain order in my courtroom, and I'm going to let Mr Ringel try his case. There is some precedent. We can't have one law for a president's daughter and another for the rest of us. You can argue your case to the jury, Mr Cox, but I'm not going to keep the jury from hearing the defendant's side, whatever my own personal feelings might be.'

When they returned to the courtroom, the judge indicated the defense could proceed.

'I call as my first witness Max Menuchen.'

Max walked slowly to the witness stand, looking older than his seventy-five years. His gentle smile was gone. His face was even paler than usual. He felt uncomfortable in the courtroom, especially as he approached the witness chair. As a teacher he was accustomed to asking the questions, not answering them. He didn't like the games both sides seemed to be playing, and he was not sure what was expected of him. All he knew was that his liberty — and, equally important, his integrity — was at stake. Abe had told him to relax and tell the truth — 'our truth.' Max affirmed rather than swore on the Bible. He sat in the witness chair and sipped a glass of water as Abe asked him to describe his educational background. After about ten minutes Max had completed the answer. Abe continued.

'Professor Menuchen, please tell the jury where and when you were born.'

'In Vilna, Lithuania, in the year 1924.'

'Would you please describe to the jury what happened on April second, 1942.'

Abe waited for a possible objection from Cox, but Cox was happy to allow Menuchen to provide the motive for his criminal acts. It would corroborate the only relevant issue: that he, in fact, did commit them.

Max looked each juror straight in the eye

as he recounted the events of that day, beginning with the Passover seder and ending with the murder of his entire family. He spoke quietly, trying to control his emotions. The jury listened attentively, some sobbing, others with a shocked expression. Judge Tree, too, was spellbound.

In the front row, behind the prosecutors, Paul Prandus — the victim's only family member in the courtroom — appeared stunned by Max's testimony. It was one thing to hear a sanitized version from his father's old friend. It was quite another thing to hear from a surviving victim an unvarnished account of what his father had done. Paul put his head in his hands. He sensed the eyes of the courtroom on him, asking him silently how he could tolerate being the son of a monster. Part of him wanted to tell everyone in the courtroom that his father had never told him about these terrible things. Another part of him wanted to defend his father. His hatred of Max grew more intense for putting him in this position.

As Max completed his account of the murders in Ponary Woods, a man stood up in the back of the courtroom and shouted, 'Liar! There was no Holocaust. Death to the Jew killer and his Jew lawyer!' As the courtroom marshals pounced on the neo-Nazis, one of them shouted, 'We want the Jew lawyer to defend our freedom of speech!' Then he laughed and gave Abe the finger.

At the rear of the courtroom, Marcelus Prandus's two old friends from the Lithuanian — American Social Club, Peter Vovus and the man in the wheelchair, smiled.

Judge Tree banged his gavel and shouted, 'Recess!' as everyone in the courtroom tried to regain their composure. Paul sat silently as those around him left the courtroom.

During the recess Max grabbed Abe by the shoulder and said, 'I must ask you a question. You would not actually defend the right of those neo-Nazis to say what they said, would you?'

'Not in a courtroom, Max, but on a street corner, yes, I would.'

'It is wrong. So wrong what they are saying. They have no right to say there was no Holocaust.'

'That's the most important right of all, Max — the right to be wrong.'

'I do not agree with you, Abe, but I do love you.'

After the recess Abe continued his questioning by focusing first on the war years, the time in the displaced persons camp, the period Max spent in Israel, Dori's suicide, and his eventual move to the United States.

Then he asked, 'Professor Menuchen, please tell the jury, as best you can, what thoughts you had about Marcelus Prandus during all these years.'

'I thought about him every day of my life, from the time in Ponary Woods until the day he died. Then I stopped thinking about him.'

'What did you think about him?'

'How he was never brought to justice. How so few of them were ever brought to justice.'

'Objection!' Cox shouted. 'It is not relevant what happened to other people. Make him stick to Marcelus Prandus.'

'Sustained,' agreed the judge. 'Stick to the specific victim here.'

'Fine,' Abe replied, directing his statement as much to Max as to the Court.

'Focusing exclusively on Marcelus Prandus, when did you first think about revenge?'

'Probably while I was lying in the grave — and ever since. For many years I was able to control my obsession with revenge, first because I did not know where he was and second because I always had some hope that Prandus would be subjected to justice.'

'When did you lose that hope?'

'It was gradual. It came to a head when I learned that my sister had died, and that Marcelus Prandus could not even be deported and that he would die surrounded by his family.'

'What did you then decide to do?'

'I decided to kill his oldest grandchild.'

There were gasps from several jurors. Although the prosecutor had learned of the aborted plan to run over Marc, they had decided not to charge Max with that crime, since Max himself had aborted the plan. Now it was the defendant who was telling the jury what he had almost done.

Abe then had Max describe how he had planned to run over Marc on his way to school and how he had crashed his car into the barrier.

'Was that crash an accident?'

'No. I told people it was, but it was the only way I could avoid hitting the boy. I just could not go through with it.'

'What did you then decide?'

'I actually considered killing the entire Prandus family. I thought it might be easier to throw a bomb at a group of people than to run over one young child. I don't know whether I could have done it. Then we came up with a perfect plan for a just punishment that was directed exclusively at the man who

330

had killed my family and that was in some way proportionate to what he had done.'

'Objection,' Cox said. 'I move to strike the word *just* from the previous answer.'

'Sustained.'

Abe continued. 'And what would such a punishment be?'

Max described how it would have to equal the agony his family had suffered before dying yet could not cause undue pain to innocent Prandus descendants. He related how he had asked Danielle Grant to help him think of something, and she had devised a plan after reading the commentary by Maimonides on the Book of Job. 'It was my decision to turn the abstract plan into concrete action,' Max said.

'Professor Menuchen, would it have been your preference to see justice done by some government?'

'Objection, Your Honor. His preference is not on trial. What he actually did is on trial.'

'I'll let him put what he did in context. Overruled. You may answer.'

'Yes, absolutely. That is what I hoped for all the time.'

'Why did you finally decide that you had to take the law into your own hands?'

Cox nearly bolted out of his wheelchair.

'Objection, objection! He didn't 'have to' do anything. He decided to seek private revenge.'

'No, Your Honor,' Abe replied. 'It's our position that he had no choice — that he had to take revenge. Let him testify.'

'Please rephrase the question, Mr Ringel.'

'Fine. Why did you finally decide to give up on the law, Professor Menuchen?'

'It was a gradual process. I finally gave up on the law when I learned that Prandus was dying of cancer and could not be deported. The time for justice had run out. Then I learned what Prandus did to my sister. That resolved any doubts in my mind.'

'What did you learn about your sister's fate?'

'I learned that Marcelus Prandus had kidnapped my sixteen-year-old sister and raped her, then gave her as a present to a Nazi general who also abused her. When the general was finished with her, he sent her to Auschwitz.'

Max began to sob and shake as he completed his answer. From the spectator section, Paul stood up and screamed, 'My father was not a rapist!' Judge Tree banged the gavel and told Paul to sit down and be quiet. Abe saw this as a perfect

opportunity to turn his client over to
the prosecutor for cross-examination, so he
sat down, barely whispering, 'No further
questions.' The judge recessed the trial for
the day.

41

Marc and Emma

'Why did that man kill Grandpa Chelli, Daddy? And why did he try to run me over?' Marc Prandus was looking directly at Max Menuchen as he and his father, Paul, took their seats behind the prosecutor's table in the courtroom.

Paul was expecting these questions from his son now that he had decided to bring him to the trial. In the beginning he'd thought he could protect his inquisitive child from the ugly truth surrounding his grandfather's death, but the trial had become headline news, and the TV reporters were referring to the late Marcelus Prandus as a 'Nazi mass murderer,' a 'killer of children,' and a 'rapist.' It was the talk of Marc's classmates, and the principal had called to alert Marc's parents to the problem. It was time to have a talk with Marc — to put his grandfather's actions in some understandable context.

Marc had asked to come to court early in the trial. Paul had not wanted him to hear Max Menuchen's gruesome testimony. He was certainly glad he had not brought him yesterday. Today, however, Menuchen was being cross-examined by Cox. It was the right day to bring Marc. Spending a day in court talking about Grandpa Chelli might provide a useful opportunity for a father-son discussion.

Paul decided to arrive at court a few minutes early so that he could explain what was happening and why Max Menuchen had done the terrible acts of which he stood accused. Paul knew it would not be an easy job to strike the appropriate balance: he could not defend what Marc's grandfather had done, yet he could not permit his son to think of his late grandfather as a monster.

'Your grandfather was a good man. He loved you. He loved all of us. But he did some bad things, many, many years before you were born, even before I was born.' Paul had his arm around Marc and was whispering to him as the courtroom began to fill with journalists, lawyers, and assorted court watchers. Emma Ringel and Rendi took their seats in the front row behind the defense table, across the aisle from Marc and Paul Prandus.

'I loved Grandpa so much, Daddy. I don't care what he did a million years ago. Why did that old man have to kill him?' Marc

335

whispered back, tears in his eyes.

'He was wrong. It's a complicated story. I'm not sure I can explain.'

'I understand more than you think. My friends in school talk about it.'

'What do they say?'

'Dennis told me that the old man was a Jew who needed to get revenge for something Grandpa did. He said Jews are taught not to forgive.'

'Well, that's not the way I want to put it. Let me put it a little differently. Do you know what it means to be a patriot?'

'Sure. The flag and all that.'

'Grandpa was a Lithuanian patriot.'

'I know,' Marc said. 'He always told me how beautiful Vilnius was. He even took me to the Lithuanian club once. He told me not to tell you.'

'Just imagine how terrible it must have been for him when Hitler conquered it.'

'Did Grandpa work for Hitler?'

'Everyone in Lithuania worked for Hitler.'

'What did Hitler make Grandpa do?'

'Some terrible things — like hurting Jews.'

'Did Grandpa want to hurt the Jews?'

'This is the part you may not understand.'

'Yes, I will.'

'What do your teachers tell you about Jews, Marc?'

'They tell us that Jesus was a Jew and that Judaism is the older brother of Christianity.'

'That's not what Grandpa's teachers told him. They told him that the Jews killed Jesus.'

'That's not true. The Romans killed Jesus. The Jews were his disciples.'

'You're right. That's not what Grandpa's teachers, priests, and even parents taught him, though. They taught him not to like Jews. And then something happened to Grandpa's father that made it even worse.' Paul related to Marc the story of his great-grandfather's death in the bar and how everyone had blamed it on the Jews.

'Grandpa thought that by hurting Jews, he was avenging his father's death. That's the way people thought in those days. When Hitler told him to arrest the Jews, Grandpa agreed with Hitler.'

'The kids in school said that Grandpa didn't just arrest Jews, Daddy. He helped to kill some of them.'

'Grandpa believed he was doing the right thing.'

'Then it wasn't right for that old man to kill Grandpa, was it?'

'No, it wasn't.'

'And it certainly wasn't right for him to try to run me over. What did he have against me? I wasn't even born when Hitler was around.'

'He knew how much Grandpa loved you, and he figured that if he hurt you, it would hurt Grandpa.'

'That isn't fair. He's a terrible person, that old man.'

'Yes, he is, and I hope he goes to prison.'

'I hope he dies,' Marc said contemptuously. 'Will the court make him die for killing Grandpa?'

'No. We don't have the death penalty in Massachusetts. He'll probably go to prison, but it's possible he could go free.'

'He can't go free. He killed Grandpa. He almost killed me. He can't go free. That wouldn't be fair,' Marc said, raising his voice.

Emma and Rendi could now hear what the child was saying as they pretended to continue their conversation about Cox's upcoming cross-examination.

'That man is a lawyer, like me,' Paul said, pointing to Abe, who had just walked into the courtroom. 'He's trying to persuade the jury that the old man did nothing wrong.'

'That's gross. The lawyer knows it was wrong for the old man to kill Grandpa.'

'He's just doing his job.'

'You mean like Grandpa?'

'I guess,' Paul replied without thinking much about his answer.

Emma could not pretend she did not hear the last exchange. She bolted out of her seat and confronted Paul Prandus. 'How dare you tell your son that what his grandfather did to Max's family is anything like what my father is doing in this courtroom.'

'I intended no such comparison, young lady. And what I tell my son is our business. Now, please leave us alone.'

'It becomes my business when you mention your father and my father in the same breath.'

'Please let's not have this discussion in front of my son.'

'Why, what are you afraid of — that he'll learn the truth about his grandfather — that he was a murderer?' Emma said pointedly. As Rendi pulled her away, Emma turned to Marc Prandus and whispered, 'Your grandfather wasn't just doing his job. He was killing innocent people.'

'Quiet!' Paul shouted. 'He's only a child. I'm just trying to give him some frame of reference for what his grandfather did. He loved his grandfather.'

'Max loved his baby son, too. Did you tell your son what his grandfather did to Max's baby son and his pregnant wife? Did you?

I didn't see him in the courtroom yesterday for that testimony.'

'*Shut up!*' Paul shouted, the veins becoming visible on his neck.

'Calm down,' Rendi said, forcing herself between Paul and Emma.

'Mind your own business,' Prandus snapped at Rendi, whispering, 'Bitch,' under his breath.

'Nice word coming from the son of a man who raped young girls,' Emma hissed.

'Let's get out of here,' Paul said as he pulled his frightened son out of his seat and hustled him out the door. As they were leaving, Marc turned to his father and asked, 'What if they win?'

'There's nothing we can do.'

'Yes, there is, Daddy.' Marc clung to his father with a determined look on his face. 'We can kill him.'

42

Paul's Decision

Paul couldn't sleep that night. What kind of a man am I? He thought to himself. He was furious at Abe Ringel for the way he had used him during the cross-examination. He was enraged at Emma and Rendi for humiliating him in front of his son. But most of all Paul was angry with himself for remaining so passive in the face of such a concerted attack on his family.

His rage bubbled up from within. He felt like screaming, like pounding someone. He longed for the days of his youth, when he could deal with frustration by acting out. He cursed his adulthood, his responsibility, his need to control himself. At a rational level, he knew that his childish ways were inappropriate. Still, he fantasized about hurting Max.

Paul thought about his dead father — a man's man. He would have known what to do. He would have acted like the godfather of a wronged family, not some wimpy lawyer.

Suddenly it all became clear to Paul. He

knew what he had to do. A plan began to form in his mind. A satisfied smile curved his lips as he finally drifted off to sleep.

The next morning at seven A.M., Paul and Freddy were in the ring of the local gym, boxing a few rounds. Paul loved boxing. It was such an unlawyerly sport. His sparring partners were cops, mechanics, and factory workers — men who worked with their hands and sweated, as his father had. Freddy used to be a good boxer before his injury. Now he just stood, flat-footed, as Paul danced around him, landing an occasional jab on his gloves. It was a good exercise, and it gave the two friends a chance to talk man to man.

'Marc says I should kill him if he gets off,' Paul said, landing a left hook on Freddy's glove. 'I've got to do something. My son thinks I'm a wimp.'

'Don't even talk like that. It's ridiculous. Did Marc actually say that?'

'Yeah, he did. He was angry at what happened in court yesterday.'

'It was just kid talk, Paul. Forget about it.'

'I can't forget about it. Maybe Marc is right.'

'Cut that out. Do you want to spend the rest of your life in prison for proving you're a tough guy?'

'What makes you think I'd be convicted? If he gets off for killing *my* father on the ground that my father killed *his* family, I'll use his defense. If he can do it, why can't I?'

''Cause that's not the way the world works, Paul. You know that. You're not thinking like a lawyer, you're thinking like a son. Just put it out of your head. He's not gonna get off, and if he does, you'll get on with the rest of your life. You're young, you've got Marc, your wife, a future — everything Max Menuchen doesn't have.'

'He killed my father.'

'Because your father killed his father. It has to end somewhere. You just can't keep killing each other. Your families will become the Hatfields and McCoys.'

'It can't end with him just walking away, Freddy. It just can't end like that. If he gets off, I've got to do something. What would you do?'

'Well, I'd think of something that wouldn't get me into trouble. I don't want to spend my weekends visiting you in some godforsaken prison.'

The men finished their boxing, and Paul Prandus changed back into his 'lawyer's costume,' as he called it. But as Paul Prandus left the gym, Freddy sensed that he was still not thinking like a lawyer.

43

Cross-Examining Max

Erskine Cox maneuvered his wheelchair so that it was between the jury and the witness. He swiveled it toward the witness and asked him sharply, 'Did you actually see Marcelus Prandus shoot anyone other than your wife and child?'

'No, of course not. He shot me right after that. I was unconscious.'

'How do you know whether he shot anyone else?'

'I saw the graves. I found my grandmother's body.'

'How do you know that they were not shot by another person?'

'What is the difference who shot them? Prandus was in charge.'

'It's for the jury to decide whether that makes a difference. Are you certain it was Prandus who shot you?'

'I will never forget his shooting my pregnant wife and baby. Then he shot me.'

'You say the bullet struck you in the head and rendered you unconscious.'

'It did.'

'Have you ever heard of retrograde amnesia?'

'Yes. It is when someone is traumatized and does not remember what happened immediately prior to the trauma.'

'Do you believe it sometimes occurs?'

'I have no reason to disbelieve what experienced doctors say.'

Cox then lifted himself out of his chair and asked, 'Would you disbelieve me if I told you that I have no recollection of what happened in the hours before the diving accident, which knocked me unconscious and left me unable to walk?'

'Objection, Your Honor,' Abe interjected. 'He's testifying, not asking a question.'

'Sustained. Stick to what happened to Professor Menuchen.'

'Are you aware of the medical term *confabulation*?'

'Vaguely.'

'Do you know what it means?'

'I think it is when a person with memory loss fills in the blanks by making up events.'

'Is it not possible, then, that you believe that you actually remember seeing Marcelus Prandus shoot your wife and child, whereas the truth is that you are confabulating these events?'

345

'That is not possible. I do remember,' Max said, raising his voice.

'Maybe you are remembering your confabulation.'

'Objection. That is not a question.'

'Sustained. Put it as a question, Mr Cox.'

'I think I've made my point. I'll move on to something that the witness clearly does remember.

'You do remember kidnapping Marcelus Prandus, do you not?'

Max wiped his eyes and replied firmly, 'I do.'

Cox continued in a staccato tempo. 'You do remember transporting him to an isolated cabin, do you not?'

'I do.'

'You do remember tying him to a chair, do you not?'

'I do.'

'You do remember making him watch videos that appeared to show his family being killed, do you not?'

'I do.'

'You did intend for him to die without ever learning that his family was alive, did you not?'

'I did.'

'He did take his own life after being shown the videos and while he was under your control, did he not?'

'He did.'

'No further questions.'

'Only a couple of questions on redirect, Your Honor,' said Abe, rising.

'Had Marcelus Prandus been punished by some government for what he did to your family, would you have kidnapped him?'

'Objection. Calls for speculation.'

'I'll let him answer,' Judge Tree ruled.

'No, I would not have. I am not a violent person.'

'One more question,' Abe said, looking in the direction of Paul Prandus. 'After you secured your revenge, how did it make you feel?'

'Objection. This is not *The Oprah Winfrey Show*. Who cares how he felt?'

'Overruled. Remorse is always relevant. You may answer, briefly.'

'I did not feel remorse for what I had done to Prandus, only to the other members of his family. Neither did I feel pleasure from Prandus's suffering. It was not completely satisfying. It left a bitter taste.'

'I have no further questions of this witness,' Abe said, and Max stood up.

'Fine. We'll take up motions and legal arguments the rest of today, and we'll resume testimony tomorrow at nine A.M. sharp,'

Judge Tree announced.

That night the pundits continued to pound Abe Ringel for raising the Abbie Hoffman defense. 'It will never work in the 1990s,' legal commentator Joe Genevese predicted confidently.

44

Emma's Trip

'I told you it would backfire,' Emma said as she and Abe watched *Larry King Live*.

'The jury's watching *Friends*. They don't care what Genevese says,' Abe replied, somewhat defensively.

'They may be thinking the same thing. And some of them may be wondering whether Max was — what was that word?'

'Confabulating.'

'Cox planted a seed there — that bastard. It wasn't fair what he did, especially testifying about his own injury.'

'The judge stopped him,' said Abe.

'Not until after he made his point. Did you see the jury?' Emma asked rhetorically.

'Sure. They're always interested in the human side.'

'You've got to win, Daddy. I can't bear the thought of Max dying in prison after what he went through.'

'I don't know, sweetie . . . There's something missing from our case. It doesn't have a sense of completeness. I'm worried.'

'Is there anything I can do?'

'Not that I can think of. It's in the hands of fate — and my closing argument.'

'Then you can do without me for the long weekend? I promised Jacob I would go to Amsterdam with him to meet his family. It's his father's seventieth birthday. He wants to introduce me to everybody. We were supposed to go a few months ago, but we put it off to do your research. This is our last chance before school begins.'

'Go, sweetie. I'll make do without you.'

'I'll only be gone five days. I'll be back before closing arguments.'

'Good. I'll try mine out on you. Can I drive you to the airport?'

'Jacob is coming by. We'll go together. Go back to your preparation. You need the time.'

'Thanks for the vote of confidence.'

45

In the Cell

'Well, how did we do? Will I be spending the rest of my life in these clothes?' Max asked as he ate a porridge of indeterminate flavor.

'I have to be honest, Max. We're losing. I can see it in the jurors' eyes. Pullman says the same thing. There's something missing.'

'We have told the truth. That is all we can do,' Max replied.

'We may not have told the jury the whole truth — because you may not know the whole truth. That's certainly what the prosecutor is going to try to prove. He just told me he is calling one brief rebuttal witness this morning, a doctor named Woolfram Gutheil.'

'I don't know any such doctor.'

'He's a shrink. They're probably going to ask him about confabulation.'

'I did not make up what happened at Ponary Woods. How dare the prosecutor suggest I did! He reminds me of those terrible people who say there was no Holocaust.'

'You mean the ones I said I would defend?'

351

'What a world we live in. It's getting a bit too complex for this tired old brain,' Max said, shaking his head.

'Let's get back to confabulation, Max. You've got to put this in context. Cox is no Holocaust denier. He's just a lawyer doing his job. Confabulation is a fact of life. I've used it myself in cross-examining witnesses. The beauty of it, from the lawyer's point of view, is that no matter how honest the witness is and how certain he is that he remembers, it is always possible that the memory is an unconscious confabulation. There is always a doubt.'

'Unless there is an eyewitness.'

'That's right. Now don't tell me you know about an eyewitness to Ponary Woods.'

'I only wish there were one. The only other witnesses were Sarah Chava and the killers,' Max said sadly.

'I'm sorry. I shouldn't have said that,' Abe said as he finished his breakfast and straightened his tie for court. 'Let's see what Dr Gutheil has to offer.'

'Abe, I trust you. I just don't understand you.'

'Hardly anyone does,' he said, flashing a quick smile. 'Ask Rendi and Emma.'

'Thank you, Abe, regardless of how this ends up. Thank you for being a friend.'

46

Confabulation

The short, balding man with the white goatee took the witness stand and swore to tell the truth in his distinctive Viennese accent.

'Are you an expert in memory loss?'

'Yes. I have studied that subject for forty years.'

'I am aware of Dr Gutheil's expertise, having used him as a witness on several occasions myself. I will stipulate to his expertise,' Abe said.

'Have you studied Holocaust survivors?'

'I have. I, too, am a survivor. Terezen,' Dr Gutheil said, rolling up his jacket to show a number tattooed above his wrist.

'Have you made a particular study of the memory of Holocaust survivors who were traumatized?'

'Yes, I have.'

'Would you tell the jury about your conclusions?'

'I studied several different groups. The first consisted of survivors who did things of which they may later have been ashamed — for example, those who served as *capos* or who served the Nazis in other ways. And those who took food from weaker inmates or who abandoned their families. After they were liberated, some of these people honestly forgot what they had done and adopted the stories of others who had done praiseworthy things.'

'Objection. There is no suggestion that Max Menuchen did anything of which he was ashamed. This testimony is irrelevant.'

'I'll tie it together, Your Honor. Give me a minute,' said Cox.

'Fine. Tie it to this defendant or drop it.'

'Is it true that most survivors felt shame just for surviving, while their family members perished — even if they did nothing shameful?'

'Yes. Many believed they could have done more — that they survived because of selfishness.'

'Even if that wasn't true?'

'Correct.'

'Did you also study survivors who were seriously injured, such as by shooting?'

'Yes. Many of them had retrograde amnesia with confabulation.'

'Explain.'

'They lost their actual memories for what

354

occurred prior to their injury, and then reconstructed the events circumstantially.'

'What do you mean?'

'They filled in the blanks by assuming that certain events had occurred.'

'Let me ask you a hypothetical question: assume that an eighteen-year-old was shot in the head and rendered unconscious by the bullet. He then wakes up and sees members of his family dead. Is it likely that he would have retrograde amnesia for the events immediately preceding his injury?'

'Quite likely.'

'Is it likely that he would then confabulate what must have occurred?'

'Yes.'

'Would he realize that he was confabulating?'

'Probably not. That is the tricky part of confabulation. Even when the patient honestly believes that he is actually remembering this real event, he may be remembering the confabulation. We can never know, without external evidence.'

'So in my hypothetical, even if the patient 'remembers' that a particular individual shot him and his family, it is entirely possible that another individual may actually have done the shooting.'

'That is entirely possible. Without another witness — an independent person who saw the same event and remembers it the same way — it is impossible to know.'

'No further questions, Your Honor. Dr Gutheil, if a person honestly believes that he saw a particular person murder his pregnant wife and baby, would his passion for justice be just as great regardless of whether it was an actual memory or a confabulation?'

'I don't know. I have never studied that question. It is an interesting one, but I'm afraid I can't help you.'

'Why don't you try? Let's consider this logically. In the mind of the victim, the person is the killer. Doesn't it follow that his passion for justice would be identical?'

'Logically, perhaps, if the mind were always logical. Passion is as much a function of the unconscious as of the conscious. If the unconscious 'knows' that the memory is confabulated, maybe the passion will not be as great.'

'That is speculation, isn't it?'

'Yes, but so is its opposite.'

'No further questions.'

'The prosecution rests.'

'Does the defense have any surrebuttal?'

'May I have until Tuesday morning to decide, Your Honor? Dr Gutheil was a surprise witness. I want to assess the impact of his testimony before I decide whether to

356

rest or call a surprise of my own.'

'Okay. Tell me Tuesday by nine A.M. Have a happy Labor Day, everybody.'

Abe was bluffing. He had no surprise witness in mind, and he wanted to spend the long weekend thinking about whether to try to find one.

47

The Surprise Witness

The bus transporting prisoners was late on Tuesday morning. One of the prisoners had experienced a seizure on the way from the jail to the courthouse, and the bus had to take him to the prison hospital. The jurors were seated, and everyone was waiting for the defendant to arrive.

There was no time for Abe to tell Max that he had no other witness to call. The case would go to the jury with Abe feeling a sense of incompleteness and with the prosecution having planted the seed of confabulation. Pullman was predicting a conviction on both counts.

As soon as Max was brought into the courtroom, Judge Tree barked, 'Call your next witness, Mr Ringel, if you have one. The jury has been waiting long enough.'

Abe remained uncharacteristically silent.

'Do you have a surrebuttal expert, Mr Ringel? Or are you going to rest?'

Abe looked at Judge Tree in frustration. He had decided against another expert witness after conferring with several neuro-psychologists and psychiatrists. No reputable expert would disagree with Dr Gutheil. Abe could, of course, argue in his summation that it didn't really matter whether Marcelus Prandus actually pulled the trigger as long as Max believed he had. Yet he was worried that some of the jurors might feel differently about what had been done if they weren't certain that Prandus had actually pulled the trigger.

How could he close this loop? As Abe was pondering this question, his daughter, Emma, burst through the courtroom door and ran up to Abe. She was huffing and puffing as she blurted out, 'Recess, Daddy, ask for a recess.'

'What ground?'

'Make one up. It's important. We've gotta talk. Don't rest. I found someone.'

'Your Honor, my daughter here tells me I need to request a recess before I decide whether to rest. And I have learned never to disagree with my daughter. May I ask the indulgence of the Court for a few moments?'

'I have a daughter, too, Mr Ringel. You have two minutes to confer with her and make up your mind whether to rest or call a witness. Two minutes.'

Abe and Emma scurried over to a corner of the courtroom. 'This had better be good,' Abe whispered. 'What do you have? An eyewitness?'

'Next best thing, Daddy. We found a letter that Sarah Chava wrote just before she died. She describes everything she saw in Ponary Woods. It matches what Max remembers. He wasn't confabulating. He was right on. The letter proves it.'

'How did you find the letter, sweetie? More important for now, how can we authenticate the fact that she wrote the letter? Judge Tree is not going to just take our word for it.'

'We have a live witness. He's outside with Jacob. I ran ahead. We found him late last night and flew him in. This morning. I tried to call you this morning, but I couldn't reach you. I reached the clerk's office. They told me the trial was resuming. I rushed over. You've got to call. I've prepped him. Here are my notes.'

As Emma handed her father the airline stationery on which she had scribbled her notes, Judge Tree banged his gavel. 'Time's up, Mr Ringel. Call your witness or rest.'

Abe announced, 'I have one final witness,' and then turned to see a tall, blond man walk through the door at the rear of the courtroom. As he strode down the aisle, every eye focused on his face — his deep blue eyes, his high cheekbones, his wavy blond hair, his pale complexion. The surprise witness reached the front row of spectators and turned to his right. His eyes locked on the man who had spent the entire trial sitting in the row behind the prosecutor's table. The two men stared at each other in shock. Everyone else in the courtroom began to murmur and whisper as the recognition set in that the man being called to the witness stand was no stranger. Peter Vovus was engaged in heated conversation with the old Lithuanian man in the wheelchair, who was gesturing wildly at the man being seated in the witness chair.

Max Menuchen's heart skipped a beat: to Max, the man's features resembled those of the Lithuanian killers who had filled his nightmares, yet there was something about his eyes that was closer to home. Who was this man who stirred such a confusion of emotions in him?

In a strong voice, Abe spoke: 'I call as my final witness, Max Menuchen.' A shudder went through the courtroom, broken only by the prosecutor's shrill objection. 'That is not Max Menuchen!' Cox bellowed. 'He's making a mockery of this proceeding.'

'Everything will become clear in a moment,'

361

Abe assured the judge. 'With the court's permission, I would like to begin questioning the witness. My daughter tells me that he does not need a translator.'

'Proceed,' ordered Judge Tree, as eager to solve the mystery as everyone else in the courtroom.

'What is your name?' Abe asked the tall stranger.

'My name is Max Menuchen,' the man replied with a thick Eastern European accent.

'How did you get the name Max Menuchen?'

'My mother gave me that name at my birth.'

'Who was your mother?'

'My mother was Sarah Chava Menuchen.'

Even before the witness could complete his answer, the elder Max bolted out of his chair and ran toward the witness box, followed by a bailiff. 'You are Sarah Chava's son? Oh, *gottenyu*. Is she alive? Please tell me,' he implored.

As Judge Tree banged his gavel and shouted for order, the witness replied in a said voice, 'No, my mother has been dead for more than fifty years. I was a child when she was killed.'

'I think it's time for a recess,' Judge Tree announced. 'We're not going to get anywhere until there is a brief reunion. Quarter of an hour, and then we reconvene.'

48

Rebirth

The two Max Menuchens were escorted into the adjoining counsel room that had been reserved for Abe's legal team and for interviewing defense witnesses.

'You are really Sarah Chava's son — my nephew?' the older man asked awkwardly, tears flowing from his eyes.

'I am Sarah Chava Menuchen's son. She wrote in her letter that her brother, Max, had been killed at Ponary Woods, along with the rest of her family. I have always believed — until last night — that I was the only living member of the Menuchen family.'

'Your mother saw me shot at Ponary Woods. She had every reason to believe I had died along with the rest of the family. I managed to survive. I had no idea that Sarah Chava had lived long enough to have a child. Thank God. Thank God,' the older man exclaimed, moving toward his nephew. They embraced silently for a moment until the younger man began to cry.

Max asked his nephew, 'Do you have children?'

'No, I do not,' the younger man answered.

Abe, Emma, and Rendi stood back and watched as the two men looked deeply into each other's eyes.

The younger man finally broke the silence. 'My mother named me after you. She loved you more than anything. She wrote in her letter that she wanted to keep your memory alive by naming me after you. I am honored.'

'And I am honored to share my name with you,' the older Max said.

'I'm afraid that we're all going to have to learn the rest of the story from the witness stand,' Abe said. 'Bailiff says we've got to get back into the courtroom.'

The two men named Max Menuchen walked side by side back to the courtroom as the older man reminisced to his nephew about his beloved sister. He took the old photograph of Sarah Chava out of his pocket and showed it to her son. He had never seen a picture of her. He had only imagined how she looked. 'She was even more beautiful than in my dreams,' the younger man said, gripping the photograph.

Abe walked with Emma. 'How did you find him?'

'Some good investigative work and some

great luck,' Emma said, smiling.

'You told me you were going to Amsterdam to meet Jacob's parents.'

'That's where we went. We were having Shabbat dinner with Jacob's parents, and I was talking about how Max had searched all over for Sarah Chava with no trace. Jacob's mother asked me whether Max had looked in the convents around Auschwitz, since one of her friends had been saved from Auschwitz by the Carmelite nuns. Who would have ever thought to look there? Max was looking in all the wrong places: Vilna, Israel, the displaced persons camp. So we decided to look in the belly of the beast — in the convents surrounding Auschwitz itself. I have a college classmate — Donny, remember him, Daddy? — he's been helping to build a Jewish center in Auschwitz. I called him — asked him to go to some of the local convents and ask some questions.'

'And he found Max?'

'Not right away. In the third convent he looked, they told him about a young girl who had been rescued from Auschwitz by the nuns and hidden in the convent until the liberation. She was pregnant. The Nazis would kill the women as soon as they became pregnant, since they didn't want Jewish babies. The nuns sneaked her out in a coffin. She had to lie next to a nun who had died of typhus. She decided to stay in the convent. She had nowhere else to go. She was sixteen years old. The nuns helped deliver the baby. In gratitude she served the nuns. Cleaned for them. Cooked. Anything they wanted. When the war was over, she decided to leave the convent and try to make a life outside. She moved to a city not too far away from Auschwitz and stayed in touch with the nuns. After she died, the nuns took Max back, a little orphan. They took care of him until he was old enough to leave. He, too, kept in touch. The nuns knew where he lived in Krakow, and Donny found him last night. Donny pulled some strings, and early this morning Max got on a plane from Warsaw. Jacob and I flew in from Amsterdam. We met an hour ago at Logan. I interviewed him briefly in the cab from the airport and jotted down some notes. That's the skinny. I'm sure you'll get the fat from the witness.'

'You're great, sweetie. I can't believe you actually pulled this off. Next time, *please* give me a little heads-up,' Abe said, giving his daughter a hug.

'I didn't want to tell you until I was sure he could be here,' Emma said apologetically.

'No problem, as long as you prepped the witness.'

'I did the best I could, Daddy.'

★ ★ ★

'May I continue to question the witness, Your Honor?' Abe asked Judge Tree.

'Yes, but no more outbursts. The last one was understandable. The next one will be punished. This is still a trial. Do you understand?'

'Yes, Your Honor, we understand,' Abe said, looking at the defendant. Then he turned to the witness and resumed his questioning.

'How old were you when your mother died?'

'Three years old.'

'Do you remember her death?'

'No. However, she wrote about the events leading up to her death in a letter to me.'

'How did you get the letter?'

'She pinned it to my jacket.'

'I move the admission of the letter into evidence,' Abe said.

'Objection, Your Honor,' Cox replied.

'On what grounds?'

'Two grounds, Your Honor. First, it's hearsay. Second, it hasn't been authenticated.'

'Mr Ringel. The floor is yours.'

'First, as to the hearsay objection. Although we acknowledge that it is hearsay, we will show that it was written in contemplation of death, and deathbed letters are an exception to the hearsay rule, because they carry indicia of truthfulness. People don't lie on their deathbeds.'

'He's right, Mr Cox,' Judge Tree said with a smile. 'There is such an exception. We all learned about it in law school. This is the first time I've actually seen a deathbed letter. I will admit it, provided you can authenticate it.'

'We can, Your Honor. The defendant recognizes his sister's handwriting. Moreover, he has a picture with his sister's handwriting on it,' Abe said, displaying the back of the old photograph. 'We can show that the handwritings match.'

'I will accept Mr Ringel's representations and withdraw my objections, Your Honor.'

'Very generous of you, Mr Cox. I was going to rule against you anyway. The letter is admitted. What language is it in?'

'It's in Yiddish. I will have the witness translate its contents.'

'Any objection?'

'None, Your Honor.'

'You may proceed.'

'Have you read the letter?'

'Many hundreds of times. It was my only real connection to my mother — until today.' As the younger Max said these words, he looked at his uncle nervously.

'Do you have that letter with you?'

'I carry it with me all the time.'

'Could you please read and translate the letter for the Court and the jury?'

'Yes,' Max said, retrieving the letter from a leather case in his pocket.

My dearest son Max,

I will soon die and I must write this letter so that you understand who you are and how much I love you. I was sixteen when tragedy struck. Out of that tragedy you were born and my three years with you have been wonderful. I am so sorry that I am leaving you alone, without my family, the way I was left alone. I hope and pray that the nuns who were so kind to me will take you in — as I have begged them to. You are a strong and smart boy and I know that you will make something of yourself.

Your name is Max Menuchen. It is a great name. You are named after my brother, who was murdered in Ponary Woods. His murderer was Marcelus

Prandus, who made me watch as he shot everyone else in my family. Everyone. He told me that he wanted the honor of personally carrying out the Führer's orders.

As the younger Max read these words, Abe could see several jurors shaking their heads. This was the corroboration of the defendant's account. Max continued to translate the letter.

I have also asked the nuns not to show you this letter until you reach the age of thirteen. I must tell you the truth, painful as it may be to you. I was spared the fate of my family in the Ponary Woods only because I was a young girl. Marcelus Prandus raped me and then gave me to a Gestapo general. When he was finished with me, I was put on a train to Auschwitz to service the German guards. A nun was assigned to examine me for disease and found me to be pregnant. She managed to sneak me out of Auschwitz to the Carmelite convent, where I gave birth to you. As soon as I saw you, I knew that Marcelus Prandus had to be your father. As you grew older, the resemblance grew even clearer. There could be no doubt that the very man who killed the entire Menuchen family, except for me, had fathered the last Menuchen. Every time I look at you, I am reminded of the man who killed my family. Yet every time I look at you, I love you more and more.

As he read these words, the witness's eyes locked on those of his half-brother, Paul Prandus. Emma had briefed the younger Max about his half-brother and where he always sat in the courtroom. Paul turned away almost reflexively. Then he turned back and looked directly at the man who was half Prandus and half Menuchen — the son of a murderer and his victim.

As alike as the half-brothers appeared in superficial physical features, they seemed to have little else in common. Paul Prandus was inscrutable; his body was controlled, tight, rigid — hiding all emotion. The younger Max, in stark contrast, gazed openly at Paul, his curiosity obvious. When he spoke — even when he read and translated his mother's letter — he gestured with his entire body, his face becoming a symphony of expressiveness. Every so often he flashed an ironic smile that reminded Abe of the older Max.

Abe asked Max to complete his translation of the letter as the silent ballet of communication continued among the witness, his half-brother, and his uncle — joined together not only by a terrible history, but also by a common genetic bond.

I worry that you will try to take revenge against your own biological father. I do not care about him, but I care deeply about you. I know that if you were to kill the man who gave you life, it would destroy you. Seek justice by becoming a Menuchen and by keeping the Menuchen seed alive. Your very life teaches renewal and forgiveness. I can face my death only by believing that you will live a long and good life, my darling son. Keep this letter with you as a reminder of the mother who loves you so dearly and who longs to remain next to you.

With all my love forever, Mother.

Every eye in the courtroom was damp as Abe questioned the witness about matters not covered in the letter.

'Tell us what happened when your mother left the convent,' Abe asked gently.

'My mother heard that some Jewish survivors had moved to a town called Kielce, not too far north of Auschwitz. We moved there. The nuns told me that she was relatively happy in Kielce, though she met no one she knew. She did not want to go back to Vilna, because the memories were so bad.'

Although Cox could have objected to this testimony as hearsay, he allowed Max to answer, realizing that the jury would resent any interference with their learning the remainder of Sarah Chava's tragic story.

'How long did you and your mother live in Kielce?'

'From March 1945 until July 1946.'

'What happened in July 1946?'

'The Kielce massacre,' Max said sharply.

'What was the Kielce massacre?'

'A large group of Polish nationalists, who resented the Jews returning to their homes in Kielce, went on a rampage.'

'Against whom?'

'Against the hundred or so Jews who had managed to survive the Nazis. There had been twenty-five thousand Jews living in Kielce before the war. Some of the survivors moved back, with others, such as my mother, moving into homes other Jews had owned.'

'So what happened?'

'The Polish nationalists arranged for the police to confiscate the few weapons the Jews had gathered to defend themselves, and the next day an armed crowd murdered forty-two

Jewish survivors and wounded dozens more. Many were women and children. This was after the Nazis had left,' Max said, shaking his head. 'Now the Poles started to kill Jews.'

'What happened to your mother?'

'She took me, and we hid in a basement. That night,' Max continued in an agitated voice, 'a group of teenage boys with knives found us and stabbed us both. My wound was not serious, but my mother was stabbed in the stomach.'

'How long did she live?'

'They took us to a makeshift hospital in the synagogue, where my mother remained alive for four days.' Tears formed in Max's eyes as he went on. 'Then her stomach became infected, and there were no medicines.'

'Did she know she was going to die?'

'Yes, she did. She wrote the letter so that I should always know my history — my family's history. She pinned it to my jacket, along with a letter to the nuns at the convent.'

'Why the nuns?'

'All the Jews of Kielce were either dead or dying or had run away. My mother believed that all the surviving Jews, few as they were, would be killed by the Poles. The nuns were the only people she knew and trusted. She was nineteen when she died, without family or friends. She had only the nuns, who took me in until I turned thirteen.'

'Then what happened?'

'I moved to Krakow and got a job as an apprentice electrician. I also enrolled in English classes. In 1985, I joined Solidarity and became a local representative. I was sent to prison twice by the Communists for political activities. When Solidarity took over the government, I ran for a seat in the legislature. I lost after my opponent spray-painted Stars of David on my election posters. I never tried to hide the fact that I was Jewish, but my opponent made it sound as if I were hiding some terrible secret about my background.'

'What did you do after you lost the election?'

'I went back to being an electrician. I began to study Hebrew.'

'Did you ever marry?'

'No.'

'Why?'

'I do not want to have children.'

'Why not?'

'Because of all the cruelty, and who my father was. I do not want to bring more Pranduses into this world.' As he spoke these words, the younger Max looked at Paul

Prandus. Paul squirmed in his seat but gave no other reaction. The older Max looked at his nephew with both disappointment and understanding.

Abe could see tears in the eyes of several jurors as he completed his examination of the witness with the usual, 'I have no further questions. The defense is prepared to rest.'

'Any cross-examination?' Judge Tree asked, knowing the answer.

'No, Your Honor,' Cox replied. 'The prosecution rests as well.'

49

Emma's Idea

'What a day, Daddy. How can we top this?'
Emma said proudly as she walked her father
out of the courtroom.

'We're going to have to, sweetie. Surprise
witnesses like Max junior make the headlines,
but I'm going to have to tie it all together for
the jury in my closing argument. Bottom line
is still that Max senior did what he did to
Marcelus Prandus, and it wasn't exactly by
the law books.'

'I don't care about the law books. What
Uncle Max did may technically be a crime,
but it was morally just. We've got to win.
Uncle Max can't be allowed to die in prison.
I couldn't bear that.'

Abe couldn't resist tweaking his daughter.
'An interesting distinction coming from the
same law student who made me promise
never to represent anyone who was guilty.'

'Stop acting like a law professor who just
caught his student in an inconsistency. Okay,
you have my permission to represent any
defendant who's morally innocent, even if

he's legally guilty. Contract amended. Are you satisfied?'

'You see, sweetie, it's a bit more complex than my not representing guilty defendants. There is often a moral continuum. We both agree that Max is at the good end of that continuum. There are a lot of defendants somewhere in the middle.'

'That's bull, and you know it. Joe Campbell wasn't even on your goddamned continuum. Yet you jumped through hoops to defend him until he almost killed your own daughter.'

'Sweetie,' Abe said gently, reaching for his daughter's hand, 'you know that I thought Campbell might be innocent when I first took his case. You can't just drop a client in the middle of a case when you begin to suspect he might be guilty.'

'That's why I could never defend anyone who might be guilty. I couldn't deal with getting a guilty defendant off.'

'Except, of course, if he were morally innocent in your unbiased opinion — like Max.'

'Yeah, like Max. How can anybody care about what happened to that monster Prandus after what he did to the Menuchen family and especially to Sarah Chava?'

'Cox seems to care. The judge seems to

care. The jurors seem to care. The law is supposed to care about even the most despicable victim.'

'That's why the law is an ass. How can the law convict some poor African American drug dealer when mass murderers like Marcelus Prandus were never even prosecuted? If I were a black juror, I don't know if I could vote to convict a black drug dealer.'

'That would be racist, Emma.'

'Well, what do you think it was that led to an all-white jury in Alabama acquitting Thomas Coleman thirty years ago — even though he admitted killing a civil rights worker in cold blood? We studied that case in legal history.'

'Why do you think they call it history, sweetie? That was a long time ago.'

'Our professor showed us Coleman's recent obituary from the *Times*. He lived to be eighty-six years old, he played dominoes at the courthouse every day with his friends, and died surrounded by his family. Some justice!'

'I am afraid that perfect injustice is a lot more common than perfect justice.' Abe sighed.

'I'd gladly settle for imperfect justice, Daddy. But I don't even see that. It's so damn hypocritical for people to posture about 'law and order' and 'making the punishment fit the crime' when thousands of the world's worst criminals remain free. Justice is a joke, Daddy, and not a very funny one.'

'It's not a joke if you're the victim, sweetie. Haskell once gave me a book that described Nazi murderers — the killers of his family and others like them who were leading guilt-free and respected lives. Haskell went through two phases in dealing with this troubling issue. At first he worked hard to defend even the most vicious criminals, feeling that no matter how horrendous their crimes, they did not compare with what others had gotten away with. Then he turned his passion to seeing that all Nazi criminals — even old ones — were punished.'

'I can imagine myself prosecuting Nazis, but I can't imagine myself working to put some common criminal in jail while so many Nazi killers remain free.'

'Remember how you felt when Joe Campbell went off to jail?'

'That was different. He tried to kill me.'

'Some people might think, what's the difference if one Joe Campbell gets away with it, when so many Nazi killers remain free? We can't let the Nazi make a joke out of our legal system.'

'I guess you're right.' Emma sighed. 'It's so damn frustrating, watching Max suffer in jail because he did what the legal system couldn't do. The legal system broke its contract with Max. It didn't protect his family, and it didn't punish those who killed them. Now it's demanding its pound of flesh. It isn't fair.'

'Aha,' Abe said.

'Did I give you an 'aha,' Daddy?'

Aha had become a code word in the Ringel family for the style Abe had developed over the years of asking lots of rhetorical questions during his argument. It got the jurors to interact with him. He strongly believed that the most effective advocacy occurred not when the lawyer shoved an argument down the throat of a juror, but rather when the lawyer allowed the juror to come up with the argument — or at least think he had. It gave the juror a greater stake in the argument. Abe called this the 'aha theory of advocacy,' after the joke Haskell had once told him about the Jewish man who had ordered chicken soup in the same restaurant every night for years. This time the waiter noticed the customer wasn't eating it, so he asked him, 'Is it too hot?' No answer. 'Too cold?' No answer. 'Is there a fly in it?' No answer. Finally, in frustration, the waiter said, 'I'm gonna taste

381

it myself and see what's wrong.' The waiter comes over to taste it, but there is no spoon. The customer looks at the waiter and says, 'Aha!'

Abe believed that jurors were like the waiter. They had to discover for themselves what was missing, and then you could say, 'Aha!'

'What's the 'aha' in what I said, Daddy?' Emma asked.

'You're just gonna to have to listen to my argument,' Abe replied. 'You'll see.'

50

Closing Argument: The Prosecution

It was now time for closing arguments — when lawyers strut their stuff and orate. This was it — the final words the jury would hear from the lawyers before they deliberated.

Cox wheeled his chair so it faced the jury.

Again he picked out one juror — this time it was Sandy Kelley, who never lost her smile, even when the testimony was gruesome.

'Ladies and gentlemen of the jury, you have heard a lot of emotional testimony. There was a surprise witness. Even I had to hold back tears when the defendant's nephew testified. Do not allow emotions to get in the way of your responsibility, which is to apply the cold law to the hard facts. Cutting through all the emotions, this case is open and shut. You could ignore everything presented by the prosecution and just focus on the testimony presented by the defense — indeed, by the defendant himself — and it would still be an open-and-shut case. Max Menuchen confessed to you. He admitted that he kidnapped the victim, tied him to a chair, and made him watch videos of his entire family being killed. He then assisted the victim in taking his own life. All the elements of the crime of kidnapping and felony murder are admitted by the defendant himself. Believe him. He is telling the truth. If you do believe him, you have no choice but to convict him. The law demands no less. You may understand why the defendant committed these crimes — I think I do after listening to him and his nephew — but to understand is not to forgive. If you were to find the defendant's criminal acts to be justified, you would be sending a terrible message of lawlessness — an invitation to every aggrieved citizen to take the law into his or her own hands.'

Cox watched Sandy Kelley's reaction to his words. She continued to smile, but she also seemed to be shaking her head in agreement. Cox turned to Faith Gramaldi and continued, 'If you were to acquit this guilty killer, you would also be encouraging one of the worst abuses of the legal system — putting the dead victim on trial. Marcelus Prandus cannot defend himself. I certainly will not defend what he may have done fifty years ago. Nor will I dispute the defendant's recollection, after hearing it corroborated by his late sister's letter. Whatever he did does not justify this defendant in becoming his judge, jury, and executioner.'

As Paul Prandus listened to the prosecutor refusing to defend his father, he wondered why his murdered father was as much on trial as the defendant. Why didn't he have anyone speaking up for him? His father had told him that unless you were there, you could never understand. How could these jurors even begin to understand?

Cox continued, 'No society can tolerate the kind of personal revenge outside of the law that this defendant took.'

Cox then went down his checklist of admission, in staccato style, which came from Max's answers to his cross-examination questions. Then he implored the jury to apply the law, as the judge would instruct them to do, without emotion or favor. He sat down after only fifteen minutes, again declaring that this was 'an open-and-shut case under the law. And nothing Mr Ringel will say can change that.'

51

Closing Argument: The Defense

Now it was Abe's turn. Abe had no checklist. He had few facts, and he had precious little law. He thought about the old legal saw, 'When you have the facts on your side, hammer the facts. When you have the law on your side, hammer the law. When you have neither, hammer the table.' Abe was not a table banger. He was part surgeon, part psychologist, and part rabbi. His job was to make the jurors put themselves in Max's situation. He needed a proper balance of both emotion and logic in order to persuade the jurors that what Max did should be found justifiable in law. At the very least, he needed one or two jurors to feel in their guts that they could not cast the first stone against Max's desperate actions — to feel 'There but for the grace of God go I.' Abe began slowly — almost academically.

'Members of the jury, why do we have law? We have law because individuals have made a social contract. Under that contract, each individual gives up his or her inherent right to protect themselves and their families and to secure personal justice in exchange for a promise of governmental protection and governmental justice.' As he said the word *contract*, Abe looked at Emma and smiled in appreciation as he continued his argument.

'A great French philosopher named Rousseau coined the term *social contract*, and a great American jurist named Oliver Wendell Holmes explained it in commonsense terms: 'People would gratify the passion for revenge outside the law, if the law did not help them.' We all know how powerful is the need to see justice done. The law recognizes that need in a variety of ways. That is why we have a number of defenses that recognize the possibility that the law will not always be able to keep its side of the bargain — its side of the social contract.'

Abe saw that his abstract, philosophical arguments were beginning to lose some of the jurors. Joe Parola suppressed a yawn. Sandy Kelley fidgeted in her seat. It was time to get more specific.

'Self-defense,' Abe said in a tone of familiarity. 'You've all heard of self-defense, right?' Parola and Kelley nodded. He had gotten them back — at least for the moment.

'Once Max Menuchen learned that the murderer of his family was living not far from him, it became a matter of life or death: if Max Menuchen did not bring Marcelus Prandus to justice, he would have killed himself. Either the mass murderer had to die or his victim had to die. Given that tragic choice, don't you agree that it would have been a far greater injustice if Max Menuchen had killed himself than that Marcelus Prandus killed himself? Remember the sixteen-year-old girl who threw herself out of the window rather than submit to rape? Mr Cox told you about her in his opening argument.'

A number of jurors nodded. 'I bet Mr Cox wishes he had never mentioned that case in light of what happened to Max Menuchen's sixteen-year-old sister. Wouldn't it have been better if that sixteen-year-old had killed the man rather than killing herself? And isn't it better that Marcelus Prandus died a few months early, than that his only surviving victim take his own life?'

Paul listened intently to Abe's argument, growing angrier by the minute. 'He's playing God,' Paul whispered to Freddy. 'How does he know whose life was more valuable — a father and grandfather who was loved and needed by his family, or a bitter, childless old man with no family and few friends?'

Abe continued, 'Lest you think that I am merely speculating about the possibility that Max Menuchen would have killed himself, remember how many Holocaust survivors did just that: some famous, such as Primo Levi, Jerzy Kosinski, and Bruno Bettelheim, Tadeusz Borowsky, and Paul Celan; others obscure, like Max's best friend, Dori Bloom.'

Abe paused to let the reference to Dori Bloom sink in. Then he moved on to another part of his argument.

'The law says that the defense of justification must 'be considered by the jury standing in the shoes of the defendant.' I ask you now to try on those painful shoes.' As he said these words, Abe subtly slipped off one loafer and worked his foot back into it. 'Imagine yourself as the young Max Menuchen, watching his family gunned down, being shot himself, and miraculously surviving. Then imagine yourself as the old Max Menuchen, learning that the killer of your family was living as a free and honored citizen, surrounded by loving family, never having been brought to justice for his horrible crimes against your family. Finally,' Abe said, lowering his voice, 'imagine yourself learning that your sixteen-year-old sister was raped before being sent to a death camp, which — unbeknownst to you — she miraculously survived, only to be murdered four years later, after giving birth to her rapist's child. Would you believe that the government had lived up to its part of the social contract?'

Abe paused a full thirty seconds to let the jurors answer that question themselves. Aha, he thought as he watched several jurors shake their heads in apparent agreement. Then he continued, turning toward Patricia McGinnity, the older woman.

'You have all heard of cases in which a woman is repeatedly battered by her husband or boyfriend. She calls 911. The police do nothing. He continues to batter her. She continues to seek help from within the system. The system fails her. Finally, realizing that she can get no justice, she kills her batterer when he is sleeping.' Abe noticed Emma frowning as he made the analogy. He hoped none of the jurors noticed. Then he moved to the 'aha' part of the argument. 'Self-defense? No. Not according to what Mr Cox told you, because she could have kept trying to call the police. She knew the police would not help her. So she helped herself. She saved her own life, because no one else would help her. Is she wrong? Is she a criminal? Juries all over the country have refused to convict such women, and when they have, governors have pardoned them or commuted their sentences. Why? Because they understand that in the absence of legal justice, personal justice becomes inevitable.'

'Objection, Your Honor,' Cox said loudly. 'I hate to interrupt my brother during closing argument, but he is asking the jury to disobey the law — to engage in jury nullification. That's wrong.'

'He has a point, Mr Ringel. Stick to the law.'

'Okay. Let's talk about the law of kidnapping. The object of the defendant's actions was not to kidnap Marcelus Prandus. There was no ransom. The object was to make Marcelus Prandus experience what he had made Max Menuchen's family experience. No more, no less. No innocent people were harmed. No unnecessary violence was committed.'

Abe thought he observed a slight nod from Sandy Kelley.

Had Abe been watching Paul Prandus, he might have noted a tightening of his chin and an angry look in his eyes, as Paul remembered how he — an innocent Prandus — had been made to suffer by watching the video and believing, even only for a few minutes, that his son was dead.

'If you place yourselves in the shoes of

391

Max Menuchen, you will not be able to convict him of murder. Marcelus Prandus took his own life. His actions were his own. No one forced him to kill himself. He did it because he knew he was responsible for what he believed had happened to his family.'

Abe paced in front of the jury for several seconds as he constructed an argument in his mind.

'Marcelus Prandus deserved to be punished. He did not deserve to live out his life with no retribution for his evil deeds. Yes, it would have been better if society could have punished Marcelus Prandus, but that was not to be. When governments do not do justice, the social contract is broken and the citizen is returned to the state of nature, where natural law prevails.'

State of nature, Paul thought to himself. Isn't that where I will be if this jury were to acquit my father's killer? If he had the right to exact revenge if the law didn't do its job, why don't I have the same right?

Abe stood directly in front of Patricia McGinnity as he explained natural law. 'Natural law demands that the murderers of one's family be brought to justice. As a well-known American judge recently put it: 'When law is inoperative, private revenge becomes an inescapable duty.' '

Paul once again took note, as Abe continued. 'I ask you, was law operative for Max Menuchen? No! And so it became his inescapable duty to exact private justice. Would you have done anything less?'

Can I do anything less? Paul thought.

Again Abe paused for silent answers. Then he continued.

'The eminent Harvard philosopher Robert Nozick draws an important distinction between retribution and revenge. Retribution is directed against a criminal act and satisfies society's needs. Revenge is entirely personal and can be directed at slights or insults. Retribution is done without personal pleasure. Revenge brings about pleasure at one's enemy's pain.

'I ask you, did Max Menuchen get any pleasure from what he did to Marcelus Prandus? No, he did not. He told you that. And Mr Cox asked you to believe him. He tasted vengeance, and as its after-flavor was bitter. Indeed, that's how you tell a good person from a bad one: a bad one enjoys revenge; a good one engages in retaliation, though it brings him no pleasure.

'I implore you to end the chain of violence and to do justice — finally — to Max Menuchen and his family by finding the defendant not guilty.'

As Abe walked toward his chair, his eyes never left the jury box. He was looking for some reaction to his final words. All he got was the ever-present smile on Sandy Kelley's face.

52

Closing Argument: Rebuttal

Now it was time for Erskine Cox to get the final word — the rebuttal summation, thought by many lawyers to be the most important single argument in the case, because it cannot be answered by the other side. For this short argument, Cox exchanged his wheelchair for a pair of crutches and stood, grimacing, in front of the jury box, so that the jurors could see that he offered no excuses and would ask for no special consideration because of what had befallen him. Abe had no choice but to quietly admire Cox's unspoken advocacy as he began his final argument.

'There is only one way to end the chain of violence — only one way to do justice — apply the rule of law to all alike,' Cox began. 'Not the way Marcelus Prandus did, and not the way Max Menuchen did.' Cox pointed at the defendant. 'Private revenge may be understandable, but it is simply not acceptable under the rule of law. Indeed, it is the function of the law — as Mr

Ringel correctly argued — to replace private revenge. If the law fails, improve it, but do not replace it with private vengeance, else you give every citizen the power to decide when to kill.'

Cox walked haltingly away from the jury box in the direction of the defense table. It took him a full minute to maneuver himself in front of the defendant as he continued. 'Not everyone who suffered as Max Menuchen did felt it necessary to take revenge by killing those who killed their family members. Elie Wiesel wrote books — great books. Simon Wiesenthal brought Nazis to justice — legal justice. They did not kill, and they did not commit suicide. In life, we have choices. Some choose to obsess about the past, while others take the hand they've been dealt and do their best.'

As he said these words, Cox took a labored step. Then he turned to the defendant and continued, 'And not everyone is a Max Menuchen. Some violence-prone individuals will see an acquittal in this case as an invitation to respond to every perceived slight with an escalated response. Just think of what is happening on our highways. One car cuts off another; the other driver responds by making an obscene gesture; guns are drawn; shots are fired; someone lies dead. In the name of what? Revenge? The philosopher Robert Nozick may understand the subtle difference between revenge and retaliation,' Cox said in a mocking tone. 'Will the drunken driver with his loaded revolver? No.'

Cox noticed nods of recognition from several jurors.

'No wonder Francis Bacon called revenge 'a kind of wild justice.' And what he said about it should govern your decision: 'The more man's nature runs to revenge, the more ought law to weed it out.' That is your job, ladies and gentlemen of the jury: to weed out revenge by convicting this vigilante killer and kidnapper. It is your duty to apply the law. Do not shrink from it.'

With that the morning session was over, and Judge Tree recessed the trial until after lunch. As Abe left the courtroom, he approached Freddy Burns and struck up a conversation. 'Paul's a mystery to me. I can't get a reading on him. You hang around with him a lot, right? So at least I know he's a poor judge of character,' Abe teased.

'Who should he be hanging around with? You? He hates your guts. I told him you weren't so bad — for a lawyer. But you know how it is. He thinks you set up that whole confrontation with your daughter to make him lose his cool. He believes you manipulated the shtick with your surprise witness — the younger Max Menuchen. He's really upset that he learned about his half-brother from the witness stand. I don't think he can handle it.'

'Yeah, I can imagine. Want to grab a bite?'

'Sorry. I can't be seen eating with the enemy. Some other time, when the case is over.'

'Okay. See you back in court.'

As Abe walked away he noticed Paul Prandus walking toward Freddy. Paul said something to Freddy, and the latter responded by grabbing Paul and saying, 'You just can't do that.' An animated conversation followed — with lots of gestures. Abe couldn't hear the words. Suddenly, Paul stormed away. Something was up, Abe thought, staring after the retreating figure.

53

The Judge Instructs

Now it was Judge Tree's turn. He would be instructing the jury on the law. Unlike most of his colleagues, who read the standard, often incomprehensible definitions of the charged crimes and applicable rules, Judge Tree prided himself on talking to the jurors in language they could understand.

'Let me tell you a story,' the judge began, sitting on the railing of the jury box like an old friend shooting the breeze.

'There was once an old king who ruled his country as a tyrant. His subjects demanded laws, so that they could know what they were allowed to do and what they were not allowed to do. The king wanted to keep the laws secret, so that he could enforce them according to his whim. So he hired a bunch of lawyers to write the laws so that nobody but other lawyers could understand them. That, ladies and gentlemen, was the beginning of 'legalese' — the most incomprehensible of languages.' A few of the jurors and spectators chuckled.

'I will not speak to you in that language. I will try English — ordinary *street* talk — because I want you to understand the law. And if I say anything you don't understand, stop me and I'll try to explain. Okay?'

A chorus of okays came back.

'Let's start with murder. There are two kinds of murder involved in this case. The first is premeditated murder: a Mafia hit man kills a rival.

'The second is more complicated. It's called felony murder, and its name suggests, it is a killing that takes place during a felony — in this case a kidnapping. If you decide beyond a reasonable doubt — and I'll explain what that means in a minute — that the defendant held Marcelus Prandus against his will for a considerable period of time, that is kidnapping. It doesn't need to be for ransom. Holding him against his will is enough. Now, if Prandus died as a result of a kidnapping, then the kidnapper is guilty of felony murder, even if the kidnapper didn't want him to die. If he did want him to die, it's even easier. Now, here is the question in this case. What if Prandus killed himself? It's for you to decide whether the kidnapping caused him to kill himself. That's your judgment call. Just remember, you can't say yes unless you're convinced

400

beyond a reasonable doubt. Any questions so far?'

No hands went up.

'Okay, now to reasonable doubt. That's a hard one. No one really knows what it means, and the Supreme Court won't tell us. I'll try to give you some guidance. Normally, in life, you make decisions on the basis of what is more likely. You have two ways of getting home from the courthouse. One is slightly shorter, safer, and more scenic. So you pick that way. This is different. Here, if you conclude that it is more likely than not that the defendant is guilty, you're supposed to find him not guilty. That's because not guilty doesn't mean innocent.

'A finding of not guilty means only that the prosecution didn't prove its case beyond a reasonable doubt. It left you with an uneasy feeling that the defendant might not be guilty. If, on the other hand, you do conclude beyond any reasonable doubt that the defendant is guilty under the law, you should convict him and not let your emotions get in the way.

'Any questions?' Again no hands.

Paul Prandus wished he were a juror so that he could raise his hand and ask the obvious question: how could there be any kind of doubt? Didn't Max Menuchen admit

401

that he had kidnapped and murdered his father? If the jury acquitted, it could be only out of sympathy, not justice.

'Okay, I have one remaining item of business with the lawyers before I wrap up the instructions. Sidebar, gentlemen.

'I'm still up in the air about your final suggested instruction, Mr Ringel. You've asked me to tell the jury that they are the conscience of the community, whose job it is to find the facts. But then you want me to say that in applying the law to the facts, they should be guided by their own sense of justice. I'm disinclined to say that, but I'm willing to hear from you briefly.'

'Thanks, Judge. The jury *is* the conscience of the community. That was the message of the famous John Peter Zenger case, even before we became a nation. In that case, the jury refused to convict a New York publisher of defamation, even though the colonial law required his conviction. In the centuries since that case, juries have continued to serve as the conscience of the community. There is no reason why they should not be told what their job is.'

'Mr Cox, I'm certain you disagree.'

'I don't disagree with Mr Ringel's description of what juries have done — for better or worse. Southern juries acquitted whites who murdered black civil rights workers, and other juries have refused to convict some who deserved to be acquitted. My quarrel is with the appropriateness of Your Honor explicitly telling the jury that they may engage in jury nullification. You should not be inviting them to break the law.'

'It's a close call,' Judge Tree said. 'There are cases on both sides. I don't like the instruction for the reasons so ably argued by Mr Cox, especially in a case like this one, in which there was so much emotional testimony. But I do think that doubts about instructions of this sort should be resolved in favor of the defendant. I'm going to give it, not exactly as Mr Ringel drafted it, but in substance. I will tell the jury that they should be guided by their sense of justice.'

'Objection, Your Honor,' Cox said, with no hope of prevailing.

'Duly noted, Mr Cox.'

Judge Tree then completed his instructions, and the jury began its deliberations.

It would be a long wait for Max Menuchen, for Paul Prandus, for Abe Ringel — and for an anxious public, which continued to debate the pros and cons of Max Menuchen's unusual means of achieving justice.

That night the TV talk shows asked

the inevitable question: 'Do you think the defendant Max Menuchen did the right thing?' The experts nearly all said no. The laypeople who called in to the shows were split down the middle.

Part Eight

Justice?

54

The Jury Deliberates

Abe watched as the jurors disappeared from view. What he wouldn't have given to be a fly on the wall of their deliberations. He understood the reasons jurors must be free to consider the evidence behind closed doors. Still, he wished he could learn whether his arguments — his ahas — had worked.

★ ★ ★

The twelve jurors entered the windowless jury room and moved uneasily around the large table. They did not know where to sit or how to begin their deliberations. They didn't even know how to go about selecting a foreperson.

Sandy Kelley was a short, feisty, warm Irishwoman in her late forties whom everyone got along with. Jim Hamilton said out loud what the other jurors were thinking: 'Why don't we make Sandy foreperson?' The others nodded in agreement.

'Okay, so let's start with kidnapping. They

snatched him, tied him up, and made him watch those horrible videos. If that's not kidnapping, what is?'

'There was no ransom,' observed Janet Gold.

'Judge said there didn't have to be,' snapped Sandy.

'Maybe, but he also told us to use our common sense — our sense of justice, I think was how he put it,' said Joe Parola, stretching his large arms.

'What about murder?' Sandy asked.

'I can't vote to convict for murder,' said Joe Parola. 'The bastard killed himself, and he got what was coming.'

'That's ridiculous,' interjected Faith Gramaldi. 'Prandus would never have killed himself if the professor hadn't made him watch the videos.'

'The professor would never have made him watch the videos if Prandus hadn't killed his whole family,' said Gold.

'The bastard got what was coming to him,' repeated Parola.

'No one has the right to play God,' said John Dolan.

'What do you think we're being asked to do?' replied Gold.

Parola stood up, getting more agitated. 'How many of you can look me in the eye and tell me you wouldn't have done worse if that bastard killed your family?'

'Would you please stop calling him a bastard,' Muriel Baker said. 'He's dead, and it makes me uncomfortable.'

'Okay, but he who is without sin, let him cast the first stone.'

'I'll cast the first stone,' said Charles Duncan. 'I know that I could never kill a man who was strapped into a chair.'

'You mean, like an electric chair?' Parola interrupted.

'You know that's not the same,' Duncan shot back.

The oldest, Patricia McGinnity, had not yet spoken. Sandy pointed to her after she raised her hand politely.

'I'm seventy-six years old, and I've lived a bit longer than the rest of you. That doesn't make me any smarter, but it also doesn't make me any dumber.

'I used to think God would straighten all this out. My nephew, who is a Jesuit priest, told me something I want to share with you. He said there are two times in life you should behave like an atheist — when you should act as if there were no God. The first is when you are asked for charity. Give as if God were not there to help. The second is when you are serving on a jury. Decide the case as if there were no God and no hereafter. I'm not going to play God. I'm going to be old Patricia McGinnity, a God-fearing, churchgoing woman, who is going to decide this case as if there were no God and no hereafter.'

There was a momentary silence, and then the discussion continued.

While the jurors continued to deliberate, Max was allowed to remain in the courtroom. Judge Tree was extremely lenient with visitation, and he kept the courtroom open until eight o'clock at night, in the event the jury needed guidance. The only people in the courtroom were the older Max and the younger Max. Occasionally, Abe would drop by, sometimes with Rendi. Emma and Jacob had begun their classes. Danielle was told to stay away, in the event that she was brought to trial.

These days in the empty courtroom helped Max to establish a connection with his newfound nephew. The two of them would sit for hours, talking. Max was pessimistic about the outcome of the case, especially after several days passed with no verdict. Abe had told him that a quick verdict generally meant acquittal and that a slow verdict could mean trouble. But Max also felt that regardless of the outcome, he had

410

won. Prandus's death seemed to be helping Max to put the past behind him and had brought to light a new Menuchen. The younger Max paced. The TV pundits all predicted conviction on both counts.

55

Verdict

On the third day of deliberations, the shouting inside the jury room became so intense that reporters were actually able to hear some of the jurors' words. The bailiffs told Judge Tree, who called the jury back in.

'Time for the 'Ex-Lax charge,'' Judge Tree whispered to the lawyers. That was the name given to a jury instruction designed to unblock an apparently deadlocked jury. Judge Tree turned toward the jurors, none of whom were now smiling, and said, 'I would like you to go back and try to reach a verdict. Whoever is holding out should listen carefully to the others. If they convince you, change your mind. If they don't, stick to your guns.'

'What does that mean?' Max asked Abe.

'It means the judge doesn't want a hung jury, because a hung jury means starting all over again.'

'We would have to go through the entire trial from the very beginning? Isn't that

412

double jeopardy?' Max asked despondently.

'No. A hung jury doesn't count as a trial. It's like a 'hindoo' in sports. A do-over. We start all over again with a brand-new jury. Judges hate a hung jury. It's a sign of failure. It makes it seem that the first trial was a waste of time and money.'

'What about lawyers? What would you think of a hung jury in this case?'

'It's like kissing your cousin. It's a tie, though it's a hell of a lot better than a conviction.'

'Do you think there will be a conviction, Abe?'

'I don't know. It's possible. The Ex-Lax charge has a way of coercing holdout jurors to go along with the majority. If they come back soon, it may be a bad sign.'

As Abe was finishing his thought, the bailiff announced, 'The jury has completed its deliberations.'

'Uh-oh,' Abe said, putting an arm around Max.

The jury filed back to their seats in the courtroom. There were looks of anger on some of their faces.

'Have you reached a verdict on either or both counts, Madame Forelady?' Judge Tree inquired.

There was utter silence in the courtroom.

'We are hopelessly deadlocked on both counts,' Sandy Kelley said, throwing up her hands in exasperation. 'No one will budge. We give up.'

There was a collective groan from the spectators as both lawyers lowered their heads dejectedly.

'Well, I guess we'll just have to start all over again with a new jury,' the judge announced, shaking his head in frustration.

Paul sat in shocked silence as the significance of a hung jury registered. He'd known what he was going to do in the event of a conviction. He'd known what he had dreamed of doing if the jury had acquitted. But this — a hung jury. It didn't resolve anything. The jury had not done its job. The legal system had failed him and his father.

As Paul listened halfheartedly to the judge and lawyers doing their increasingly irrelevant legal business, he strained to control himself.

Judge Tree announced that he would schedule a retrial within two weeks.

Paul watched Abe rise to respond. He saw Max whispering in his lawyer's ear. Everything seemed to be in slow motion with the sound turned off. Paul's brain was pounding with conflicting emotions. The Prandus within him was demanding revenge.

Paul looked into the eyes of Abe Ringel, as the lawyer sought bail for his client. He felt nothing but hatred for his fellow lawyer. It was Ringel's fault — this hung jury. The cop-out, the injustice of uncertainty. The need to undergo the emotions and humiliation of a trial once again.

Then Paul looked at the man who had driven his father to suicide. He felt even greater hatred. After all, this was the man who had considered murdering his innocent eight-year-old son. This was the man who had tortured his father — and him — by creating that diabolical video. He remembered the face of his father laid out on the steel table of the morgue — the father he loved, but whose evil deeds he could not comprehend, the father whose death cried out for revenge. He remembered his own son's demand for justice. Now he, Paul, must do something to balance the ledger.

Suddenly, Paul's conflicting thoughts coalesced into action. He reached under the bench and opened up the large litigation briefcase he had brought into the courtroom. As a lawyer well-known to the security guards, he had been waved around the metal detector. He was part of the system of justice, sworn to nonviolent resolution of conflicts. The irony was not lost on Paul as he reached slowly into the briefcase. His hand found a box about the size of a milk container. Quickly he pulled it out and cradled it in his arms. Then he stood up and quickly bolted through the low swinging doors that separated spectators from participants. He had been a spectator to justice for too long. Now he was becoming a participant. He ran toward the defense table as Freddy shouted, 'Don't do it, Paul! Think of your son.'

An overweight bailiff grabbed Paul, but the athletic younger man easily broke loose, knocking the startled bailiff to the ground. In an instant, Paul was standing face-to-face with Max, looking into his eyes. It was all happening so fast.

Max did not say a word. His expression did not ask for pity. He was, after all, looking into the eyes of a Prandus — a different Prandus, but a Prandus nonetheless. Max remembered the steel-blue eyes of the man who had shot him. They looked the same.

In one quick motion Paul opened the box, removed a strangely shaped metallic object, and thrust it toward Max.

★ ★ ★

At the very moment Paul was reaching into his litigation bag, something else was

416

happening at the rear of the courtroom. The old Lithuanian man in the wheelchair, who had been to court every day, reached behind him and opened the compartment that housed the chair's motor. Quickly he pulled out the thirty-eight-caliber pistol he had secreted there that morning. The old man did not see Paul dashing through the low swinging doors as he raised his arm and took careful aim at Max Menuchen, the man who had killed his best friend. As the old man squeezed the trigger, he shouted, '*Ker[br]stas!*' the Lithuanian word for 'revenge.'

The old man got off one round before Peter Vovus pounced on him, knocking the gun away and cursing at him in Lithuanian.

The lethal bullet was aimed directly at Max's heart. An instant earlier it would have shattered Max's vital organs. Instead, the bullet smacked against the metal object that Paul had just thrust in Max's direction. It made an eerie clanging sound and ricocheted into the wall. Max was knocked to the floor. For a moment he thought he had been attacked by Paul Prandus. Then he realized that the metal object that had saved his life was the Marrano chalice, the same chalice that Marcelus Prandus had stolen from his family, along with their lives.

There was pandemonium in the courtroom as bailiffs removed the old man in the wheelchair. Abe helped Max to his feet as the shaken judge gaveled for order. Two bailiffs were holding Paul Prandus.

'The chalice belongs to your family, not to mine,' Paul said.

Then he announced, 'I do not want a retrial. No jury will convict this man, and this hung jury is better than an acquittal. No more trials. We have had enough.'

'This man' — Cox pointed at Max — 'don't you want him brought to justice?'

Judge Tree interrupted. 'I want to know, and I want to know *now*,' he shouted at the court guards, 'how a gun found its way past security today.'

A sheepish guard tried to explain. 'We don't search wheelchairs, Your Honor.'

'From now on even the pope gets searched, and I don't care if he's in a wheelchair. Now back to the business at hand. Mr Prandus, we'll deal with your behavior later. Now, complete what you were saying.'

'If the jury had acquitted this man, I don't know what I would have — ' Paul broke off his statement, stood up tall, looked directly at Max, and spoke in a whisper:

'The cycle of revenge must stop before it consumes even my son. We don't need any more lawyers, judges, and jurors to sit in judgment over this case. It's too complex for the law. It has to be resolved outside of the courtroom. I want revenge, not justice, and my religion tells me I am not entitled to revenge. The charges against Max Menuchen and Danielle Grant should be dropped.'

The two Maxes stood speechless as they watched Paul Prandus walk away. For the first time since Ponary Woods, the older Max Menuchen understood that justice was possible even from someone whose father was capable of unmitigated evil. For the first time since he'd learned who his biological father was, the younger Max was not afraid of being part Prandus. For the first time since she was raped by her grandfather, Danielle Grant — who was sitting in the rear of the courtroom to hear the verdict delivered — saw powerful evidence that evil and goodness were personal and not inherited.

Max was in a daze as events moved quickly around him. Erskine Cox announced that he would accede to Paul's wishes and drop the charges. Judge Tree ordered the indictments dismissed and announced that Max and Danielle were 'free to go.' Max thanked Abe and turned quickly in the direction of his nephew. Abe walked over to Freddy

Burns and whispered, 'Thanks for whatever you did.'

Freddy smiled and said, 'I had no idea what he was going to do. Frankly, I was scared shitless he was going to try to hurt Max — or you. Instead, he saved Max's life from that idiot in the wheelchair.'

'By accident,' Abe interjected.

'If you believe in accidents,' Freddy added, looking upward. 'Paul's a conflicted man,' he continued. 'His good side won out, thanks to you and a little help from upstairs.'

'Why thanks to me? He hates me.'

'Yes, he does. But I think your arguments eventually got to him — on some level. That was your plan all along, wasn't it? Paul was the one juror you had to convince. That's why you allowed him to remain in the courtroom after he finished testifying. Right?'

'Guilty as charged,' Abe acknowledged with a wry smile.

The two Maxes embraced tightly, tears flowing from their eyes. As the younger Max took his mother's letter out of the letter case and kissed it, Abe Ringel thought of the talmudic saying that Haskell Levine had always kept on his office desk: 'He who kills even one human being, it is as if he killed the whole world. He who saves even a single human being, it is as if he saved the whole world.' To that Abe silently added, 'He or she who achieves perfect justice in relationship to even one human being, it is as if they had achieved perfect justice for the whole world.' Abe was thinking as much of Paul Prandus as Max Menuchen.

Epilogue

'This seder is a lot better than last year's,'
Max said, lifting his wineglass. 'To Abe
Ringel, the greatest lawyer since the original
Abraham.'

'Cut it out, Max. Clients like you make
my job a pleasure, though I must admit there
were some nail-biting days.'

It was a grand seder, reminding Max of
the Menuchen tradition in the old country.
In addition to Abe, Rendi, Emma, and Max
— all of whom had been at last year's
eventful seder — there were the younger
Max and his new wife, Rachel. Rachel was
the granddaughter of a survivor who had
remained in Warsaw after the war. She had
been a longtime friend of the younger Max,
but the friendship had quickly blossomed
into a romance and then marriage when
Max returned to Poland after the trial.
Now she was pregnant and expecting a
baby. They were deciding whether to make

422

their home in the United States or in Israel.

The older Max, too, was considering a return to Israel after he retired from Harvard at the end of the semester. He had accepted a one-year position as visiting scholar at Hebrew University.

Only Emma was alone, having broken up with Jacob shortly after the trial. Although Abe was upset at the breakup, Max was pleased that Emma was opening herself to new relationships.

'Come visit me in Israel for the summer,' Max suggested. 'There are lots of audacious young men there who will make you forget Jacob.'

'No way,' Abe answered, not giving Emma a chance. 'I want her here in Cambridge. Why don't you come work for me this summer?' he implored her. 'I'll assign you only innocent defendants.'

'No way, Daddy. I've had it with criminal law. It's too gruesome. There's too much pain all around and too little justice.'

'Didn't your father's advocacy in Max's case restore some of your faith in the practice of criminal law?'

'Maybe, but I'm still turned off of criminal law. I need something that makes me feel good every day.'

'What's Angie doing this summer?' Rendi asked.

'I was afraid you might ask that,' Emma said sheepishly.

'I knew it,' Abe shot back. 'She's working for Cravath. Wall Street. I knew it.'

'Worse. She's going to Hollywood. An entertainment law firm. They represent Leonardo DiCaprio, Michael Jackson, John Grisham — all the hot stars. She's really psyched. Wants to produce films. I got an offer from the same firm. I was tempted. It's not real enough for me.'

'So, what other offers do you have?' Rendi asked.

'Women's Basketball League. Lawyer, not player, unfortunately. Also, not real enough. And it would remind me of Joe Campbell.'

'Come on, work with me, sweetie,' Abe pleaded. 'I'll give up my criminal practice and become a civil lawyer, just for you.'

'You're sounding desperate, Daddy. Bad advocacy.'

'So what are you thinking about doing this summer?' Rendi asked.

'I have an offer to work with Professor Stith as a research assistant. She wants to recommend me to the Supreme Court Justice she clerked for. She told me she thought I would make a great law clerk.'

'You would make a great anything, sweetie. What would you be working on with Professor Stith?'

'I'll be writing an article entitled 'A Disloyal Daughter Reveals All the Dirty Little Secrets of Her Defense Lawyer Father.' '

'You wouldn't,' Abe shot back.

'Just kidding, Daddy. Your secrets are always safe with me,' Emma replied, hugging her father. 'As long as you stick to defending the good guys like Uncle Max.'

The seder reunion continued with the older Max telling stories, the younger Max drinking a few too many toasts, and Abe continuing to banter with Emma about her future. Although the seder was more reunion than religion, Abe insisted on covering the important rituals.

'It's time to welcome Elijah. You're on, Emma.'

As Emma rose from the seder table to open the door, she cast a worried look in Max's direction, wondering how he would react. Max smiled and said, 'Go ahead, Emma. The ghosts are all gone. Only Elijah is out there now.'

Emma opened the door to the cold night air.

A tall blond man wearing a raincoat was standing in the light drizzle. Emma, startled, jumped back. Max saw the face of the man and moved quickly toward Emma.

The man at the door was Paul Prandus. He spoke: 'I was waiting outside until your celebration was over. I thought you would all be together tonight. I did not want to intrude, but I must speak to all of you.' Paul looked at Max, who was standing between him and Emma.

'You saved my life. You are not an intruder,' the old man said coldly, motioning Paul into the house.

'I want to forgive you for what you did to my father,' Paul said in a near whisper. 'And I want to ask you to forgive me for what I thought about doing to you if the jury had found you not guilty.'

'What did you think of doing?' Max asked.

'I was prepared to kill you,' Paul said flatly. 'In my heart, I was guilty of murder. Then, after the jury deadlocked, I experienced a hung jury in my own mind. That's when I understood that a hung jury was exactly the right verdict. No one could be of one mind about what happened. The law is a blunt instrument. It is not refined enough for a case like this one.'

Max nodded. 'I, too, came to realize that a hung jury was the correct verdict. I did not deserve to be found innocent. Nor did I deserve to be found guilty. I was legally guilty, but I do not believe I was morally guilty.'

Paul shook his head in agreement as Max looked deeply into his eyes and said, 'You are not Marcelus Prandus. You I can forgive.'

'Thank you,' Paul said, lowering his head. 'Your forgiveness is important to me.

'I hope I can also be forgiven for what I said and thought about you,' Paul said, looking first in the direction of Abe and then Emma. They each nodded their heads.

'I must ask you one question, if I may,' Max said. 'If you were prepared to kill me, why did you bring the Marrano chalice into the courtroom?'

'Because it belonged to your family, not mine. No matter what I might want to do to you, I could not keep it. It would always remind me of what my father had done to your family.'

Standing awkwardly, Paul remained silent as everyone looked at him, each thinking private thoughts. Then, as the older Max walked in the direction of the door to open it for Paul to leave, Paul walked over to the younger Max and said, 'I want to know my brother.'

There was an awkward silence in the room.

Then the younger Max stood up and took Paul's hand in both of his. Quietly he said, 'My brother.'

The older Max lifted the Marrano chalice and handed it to the younger Max. 'I want you to have this. It is a Menuchen family heirloom, and you are the future of the Menuchen family. Pass it on to your child, and to your grandchildren. But first,' the older Max said, 'let us drink to the future, without ever forgetting the past.'

He filled the wine goblet and passed it around. Paul Prandus took the last sip.